CW00933132

MURDER AT MILL PONDS HOUSE

MICHELLE SALTER

Boldwood

First published in Great Britain in 2025 by Boldwood Books Ltd.

Copyright © Michelle Salter, 2025

Cover Design by Rachel Lawston

Cover Illustration: Rachel Lawston

The moral right of Michelle Salter to be identified as the author of this work has been asserted in accordance with the Copyright, Designs and Patents Act 1988.

All rights reserved. No part of this book may be reproduced in any form or by any electronic or mechanical means, including information storage and retrieval systems, without written permission from the author, except for the use of brief quotations in a book review. This book is a work of fiction and, except in the case of historical fact, any resemblance to actual persons, living or dead, is purely coincidental.

Every effort has been made to obtain the necessary permissions with reference to copyright material, both illustrative and quoted. We apologise for any omissions in this respect and will be pleased to make the appropriate acknowledgements in any future edition.

A CIP catalogue record for this book is available from the British Library.

Paperback ISBN 978-1-83561-298-9

Large Print ISBN 978-1-83561-297-2

Hardback ISBN 978-1-83561-296-5

Ebook ISBN 978-1-83561-299-6

Kindle ISBN 978-1-83561-300-9

Audio CD ISBN 978-1-83561-291-0

MP3 CD ISBN 978-1-83561-292-7

Digital audio download ISBN 978-1-83561-294-1

This book is printed on certified sustainable paper. Boldwood Books is dedicated to putting sustainability at the heart of our business. For more information please visit https://www.boldwoodbooks.com/about-us/sustainability/

Boldwood Books Ltd, 23 Bowerdean Street, London, SW6 3TN

www.boldwoodbooks.com

To friends

1

WALDEN, HAMPSHIRE, 1 MAY 1924

It turned out that Elijah's snail's pace was the ideal speed when trailing a procession of schoolchildren dressed as spring flowers. We sauntered along the side of the road, keeping out of the way of the crowds of parents lining the high street.

As *The Walden Herald's* only permanent reporter, I was usually assigned to cover the May Day pageant on my own. However, this year was different.

Reverend Childs had decided to combine the town's annual May Day festivities with the opening of Mill Ponds Hostel for Men. Elijah Whittle, the newspaper's editor, had received a personal request from the vicar to attend the event.

The hostel would provide temporary accommodation for unemployed and disabled men – many of them ex-soldiers and sailors who were suffering hardship due to the effects of war. Townsfolk were concerned at the arrival of these newcomers, and the vicar hoped an invitation to visit the newly refurbished mansion would help ease any tensions.

So, along with a good proportion of the residents of the small market town of Walden, Elijah and I followed the schoolchildren down the high street to the railway station, where a footpath led to Waldenmere Lake. At this point, things got a little tricky, as the procession was to join the lake path, which would allow for just two abreast.

Mrs Siddons, our local MP and only the third woman elected to parliament, led the parade, holding aloft a bright yellow parasol to make sure she was seen. It was unlikely anyone could miss her as she was wearing a startling lime green silk dress with a yellow scarf billowing behind her on the breeze. She'd become involved in politics after the death of her husband, and at the age of fifty-one had achieved her ambition of taking a seat in the House of Commons by winning the Aldershot by-election in 1920.

The mood of the crowd was jovial as they jostled along behind her on the narrow footpath. Once we turned onto the driveway of Mill Ponds House, people spilled out onto the freshly mown lawn, the smell of cut grass heightening the sense that summer had finally arrived. The children rushed towards a tall wooden maypole decorated with trails of ivy and colourful crepe paper flowers.

To my annoyance, the sun chose that moment to break through the clouds and shine down on the red bricks of Mill Ponds. It felt like everyone was giving the project their blessing. Everyone except me.

It's not that I was against the hostel – just the man the church had employed to run it.

'Archibald Powell is here to stay,' Elijah said as if reading my mind. 'And I'm afraid there's nothing you can do about it.'

He removed his homburg hat and mopped his brow with a handkerchief, grunting with relief as the May Day procession began to disperse. He was dressed far too warmly for the occasion as, for once, the first day of May actually was proving to be the start of summer.

'Don't be so sure about that.' I stared at the black-clad figure guiding each child to a long strand of ribbon dangling from the maypole. As usual, Archie was dressed in a dark shirt and trousers in an attempt to look like a vicar. But he wasn't one. Not any more.

'What do you mean?' Elijah rooted around in the pocket of his jacket for his cigarettes.

'Just that his stay in Walden might not be as permanent as he thinks.' I didn't yet know how, but I was determined to find a way to make Archie leave my hometown. I wouldn't sanction his presence at Mill Ponds as easily as some had.

As I said this, Archie's green eyes turned in my direction, and his lips widened into the malevolent wolfish grin he seemed to save just for me. It was part sneer, part threat.

The attraction I'd felt when I'd first met him in the autumn of 1922 had long since vanished. At the time, his contradictory personality had intrigued me, and I'd been drawn into his embrace on one too many occasions. Fortunately, I'd had the sense to draw back before the relationship could develop into something more serious. I'd begun to suspect that all was not what it seemed – and I'd been proved right.

At the time, he'd been the Reverend Archibald Powell of St Mary's Church in Deptford. His charitable work included running Creek House, a hostel that offered temporary accommodation to unemployed and disabled ex-servicemen. It was a property owned by the wealthy Timpson family, and he'd repaid their trust by turning sniper and firing a rifle at businesswoman Constance Timpson. He'd used the same tactic on Mrs Siddons, MP, in a bid to scare women from positions of power. As a result, he'd been detained at His Majesty's Pleasure in Winchester Prison, though his sentence had been cut short due to his exemplary behaviour.

Elijah waved his cigarette in my direction. 'You need to accept what you can't change.'

This was easy for him to say. He wasn't being blackmailed. Ever since New Year's Eve, Archie had been taunting me with a secret he knew I didn't want anyone to find out. He wasn't asking me for money. It was simply a case of leave him alone, and he'd leave me alone. But if I didn't comply, he'd tell my family and friends what he knew.

Four months on, I was sick of living with this threat hanging over me. It was Archie or me. One of us had to go.

2

'Are you alright?' Millicent mouthed as she reached out to stop a little girl's spectacles falling from her nose and into the path of the maypole dancers. With the other hand, she rescued a small boy from the ribbons he'd become tangled up in. As a teacher at Walden Elementary School, Miss Millicent Nightingale was adept at doing more than three things at the same time.

I'd been lodging with Millicent and her great-aunt, Ursula, since the previous summer. Millicent was the only one who knew of the close relationship I'd once had with Archie Powell, though I think both Elijah and Ursula suspected.

'I'm fine,' I mouthed back, feeling anything but.

I wasn't the only one horrified by Archie's decision to take up residence in Walden after his release from prison. The Honourable Constance Timpson was furious that her attacker was now living in her hometown and refused to have anything to do with him or the hostel. As a wealthy businesswoman, she'd been asked to become a benefactor and patron of Mill Ponds House – an invitation she'd declined.

However, Mrs Siddons had chosen to deal with Archie in her own inimitable way. And it was a method I was still uneasy about.

I said as much when she appeared by my side, peering at me through the lorgnette spectacles she'd taken to holding instead of wearing glasses.

'As a patron of Mill Ponds, I can ensure Mr Powell behaves himself.' Mrs Siddons closed her parasol and pointed it like a weapon. 'If he doesn't, I'm in a position to make his life extremely uncomfortable.'

I didn't doubt she would do just that. But if Archie thought he was under attack, especially from a woman, he'd retaliate. And that might lead him to reveal my secret to those people he knew I cared about most.

'Why do you think he came here?' I asked.

'To seek redemption,' she replied. 'Rather than running away from his crimes, he's facing up to them.'

'He's not. He's pretending.' But I knew it was hopeless. It was infuriating that she, along with everyone else in town, seemed to have fallen for Archie's act.

Only I understood him well enough to know he felt no remorse for his actions. His intention had been clear when he'd carried a rifle up to the tower of St Mary's Church and pointed it at Constance while she was giving a speech outside the factory opposite. He'd taken care to miss her, instead firing into a wooden display board behind her head. When he'd played the same trick on Mrs Siddons, Ben Gilbert, our local policeman and a childhood friend of mine, had been injured trying to protect her.

In court, Archie's barrister had blamed 'these unfortunate incidents' on shellshock, citing the commendations the Reverend Powell had received after serving as an army chaplain during the war. It was true Archie had risked his life to save others. It was also true he hadn't meant to physically harm Constance Timpson or Mrs Siddons when he'd fired those shots.

However, I knew Archie hadn't been suffering from shell-shock. Before his arrest, he told me he'd been 'trying to restore some of the natural order that was lost during the war'.

'I understand how you feel.' Mrs Siddons took my arm in a conciliatory gesture. We'd been friends for over ten years, since my mother's death in 1914, and this was our first serious disagreement. 'I wish he hadn't chosen to come here. But he has, and we must learn to accept the situation rather than fight it.'

Accepting things I didn't like was not my strong point, and I looked in vain to Elijah for support.

He shrugged. 'Mill Ponds was sitting empty. At least it's now being put to good use.'

'Don't worry, you have Mr Whittle and me to act as your chaperones and protect you while you're here.' Mrs Siddons must have seen the flash of annoyance on my face because she added, 'I'm not being flippant. I realise he makes you uncomfortable.'

This was an understatement. I pulled my arm away. 'I'm going to help Robbie,' I muttered, trying not to let my temper show.

Robbie Roper, *The Walden Herald's* photographer, stood out amongst the crowd of townsfolk gathered on the lawn. Six foot tall with copper hair glinting in the sunshine, he moved his camera easily amongst the children as they skipped around the maypole. He didn't need any assistance from me.

Millicent was still preoccupied with her pupils, and Archie was standing close by. Infuriated by his self-satisfied smirk, I turned my back on the throngs of people and wandered around to the side of the house.

The mill of the house's name was long gone and this section of the garden had an uninterrupted view of Walden-mere. The previous owner had planted a rose garden to enhance the scene and sweet-scented pink and lilac blooms provided bursts of colour against the silver backdrop of the lake. I breathed in their perfume, enjoying a peace I knew would be short-lived.

Sure enough, Archie appeared from around the side of the house, and I studied him as he approached me. He still had the physique of a soldier, and there was something animal-like about his narrow, intense eyes and sculpted jaw. He was tall, over six foot, though I noticed a stooping of his broad shoulders that hadn't been there before.

When we'd first met, his penetrating green eyes had scrutinised me with a lazy sexuality that had been hard to resist. His demeanour had been completely at odds with the dog collar around his neck. Nowadays, he looked at me with a mixture of resentment and triumph.

'Still dressing in black.' I couldn't resist taunting his attempt to replicate his former clerical garb. 'Doesn't quite cut it.'

I knew how much it had hurt him to be stripped of his ecclesiastical office – perhaps even more than the prison sentence he'd received. He blamed me for both. I'd gone to the police when I discovered he was the mysterious sniper, and he'd never forgiven me for that. He'd accused me of betrayal and been arrogant enough to believe he could persuade me to stay silent.

On his release from prison, Archie had headed straight back to the church, despite being unable to return to his former occupation. Instead, he'd become a verger at

Winchester Cathedral and joined the fundraising committee of their war fund. When the church purchased Mill Ponds House to use as a hostel, he was appointed manager due to his experience running Creek House in Deptford.

'How's the charming Mr Jansen?' Archie took a small diary from his trouser pocket and flicked through the pages. 'Here it is. Mr Marc Jansen, Tyler & Simcock, Chancery Lane.'

Four months ago, on New Year's Eve, Archie had revealed he'd been spying on me. On one of my regular trips to London, he'd seen me with Marc Jansen – a man I had a complicated relationship with. After following Marc back to his office, Archie had made a few discreet enquiries. It hadn't taken much detective work to find out that Marc was a solicitor – and that he was married.

Archie became convinced Marc and I were having an affair. Although this wasn't true, it was certainly a friendship I'd have trouble explaining to those closest to me. The secret nature of our meetings was enough to incriminate us in most people's eyes.

At the mention of Marc's name, I began to walk away, but Archie put out a hand to stop me.

'You haven't seen the rest of the garden yet. It's going to provide a form of therapy for our residents.' He turned and strode towards the rear of the house. 'We've acquired more land where we can grow fruit and vegetables. And we've started to dig the foundations for a greenhouse. It will be good for the men to have something to occupy them, and we can supply produce for the kitchen. Come and take a look so you can describe our plans in your article.'

'What article?' I followed him through the walled kitchen garden, curious to see the changes that had been made. The church had recently purchased a stretch of wasteland beside the railway line and enclosed it behind a tall wooden fence. You could now exit the extended garden of Mill Ponds via a gate that opened onto a dirt track leading up to an arched bridge over the railway line. On the other side of the track were rows of allotments owned by the railway company and rented out to their workers.

'You're going to write an article explaining our concept for Mill Ponds.' Archie made a show of opening the double doors to a large newly built shed. 'And I'll let you know when you can call in for a chat with our first three residents. It will be one morning next week.'

'And if I don't?'

Archie turned and gave me his familiar wolfish smile. 'I have nothing left to hide. Everyone knows what I did. What about you?'

I shrugged. Elijah had already asked me to write a feature on Mill Ponds. It would look odd if *The Walden Herald* didn't cover such a newsworthy event. However, Archie couldn't control what I wrote.

I was about to say as much when something caught my eye. He'd pushed open the shed's wooden doors to reveal racks of gardening tools and shelves lined with plant pots.

I peered inside, my breath catching in my throat. Leaning against the wall was a Lee-Enfield rifle. I knew the make from Archie's previous escapades with a gun. It was probably an old army rifle used in the war.

My hands balled into fists. 'What the hell are you doing with that?' I knew this was why he'd insisted on showing me the garden – just so I would see it.

'I still like to go hunting now and again.' He was watching me with malevolent glee, clearly enjoying my reaction. He stepped into the shed and lifted up the rifle. When he turned, he pointed it in my direction. 'It's to deal with pests.' His lips curled into a cruel smile. 'I don't intend to let vermin ruin my hard work.'

I said nothing and held my ground. I doubted he'd risk firing it with so many people around. Yet... Hadn't he done exactly that when he'd shot at Constance and then Mrs Siddons?

Laughing, he placed the rifle back against the wall. 'Don't worry, it's only to kill rabbits and pigeons. And possibly women who need to be reminded of their place.'

3

I turned away from Archie, tense with fear and anger. He was enjoying making my life a misery, and I felt powerless to stop him.

As I hurried through the garden, I caught sight of a man in a khaki army jumper, standing in one of the foundation trenches dug for the new greenhouse. He leant against his spade and stared at me, making no attempt to hide his curiosity. I wondered how much of our conversation he'd overheard. Surely, he couldn't have failed to notice that Archie had just pointed a rifle in my direction.

'I'll tell you when you can come and interview our first residents,' Archie called after me.

I ignored him and kept walking, glancing towards the strange man who was still watching us. He ran a hand through his dark blond hair as if confused. Had Archie just made his first mistake? Judging by the man's expression, he was shocked by what he'd witnessed.

Once I was back on the lawn with the other guests, I let out a long breath. Mrs Siddons shot me a concerned look, but I ignored her and went in search of Elijah. I found him standing with Robbie by the entrance to Mill Ponds.

'Can we go now?' I asked. 'I think I've seen enough for one day.'

'We haven't been in the house yet. I believe they've turned the general's old reception room into a communal lounge. I want Robbie to get a photo of it.' He took a last drag on his cigarette and stubbed it out in a plant pot by the oak front door. 'Let's see what they've done to the old place.'

My tension returned. I had no desire to go inside, and it had nothing to do with the presence of Archie Powell. It was because I had extremely unpleasant memories of the last time I'd set foot in Mill Ponds House.

During the war, the mansion had been used as a training academy for cadet officers. Its owner, General Cheverton, had welcomed terrified new recruits into his home and guided them through the brutalities of four years of war. I supposed it was fitting that it was now opening its doors to troubled men once again.

After the general's murder in 1921, Mill Ponds House had stood empty until Winchester Cathedral's Great War Fund had purchased it. They'd been able to buy it for a knock-down price thanks to the mansion's tainted history. General Cheverton's nephew had inherited the property, and his gambling debts meant he would have taken whatever was offered to be rid of it.

'I haven't been back here since we broke in,' Elijah whispered, holding open the door for me.

I smiled for the first time that afternoon, remembering what a hopeless pair of housebreakers we'd made. Shortly after General Cheverton's death, we'd illegally obtained access to Mill Ponds to search through confidential documents kept in the general's study. On that occasion, we'd gained access via the scullery and crept through the house with a torch. Now we entered the hallway to a very different scene.

'His Lord and Ladyship welcome you to their humble abode,' Robbie said in an undertone.

I had to stifle a laugh at the sight of Gordon and Jennifer Tolfree standing at the foot of the staircase, welcoming guests as if this was their stately home rather than a men's hostel.

Along with Mrs Siddons, Gordon Tolfree was a patron of Mill Ponds House, and as a committee member of Winchester Cathedral's Great War Fund, he'd influenced their decision to buy the old mansion.

'You'd think they owned the place,' I whispered. I suspected, like Archie, the Tolfrees saw their involvement with the hostel as a way of polishing up a tarnished reputation.

'Mr Roper,' Jennifer called when she caught sight of Robbie. 'I'm sure you'd like a photograph of my husband and me for *The Walden Herald.*'

Elijah grinned and nodded at Robbie, who duly obliged, positioning his camera on its tripod while Mr and Mrs Tolfree adopted their most regal expressions.

At one time, the name Tolfree had been famous across the globe. Founded by Isaac Tolfree in 1850, Tolfree Biscuits' decorative tins were sent all over the world. Even Captain Scott had taken Tolfree Biscuits on his expedition to the South Pole as the tins preserved the biscuits inside.

After the war, Tolfree Biscuits' fortunes declined as the price of ingredients rose. The business was on the brink of collapse, when Timpson Foods bailed out Gordon's father, Redvers Tolfree, adding the Timpson name to the famous brand at the same time. A furious Redvers had sought revenge by embezzling from Tolfree & Timpson – then died of a heart attack before the case went to trial.

Gordon and Jennifer, an attractive couple in their thirties, were endeavouring to repair the damage Redvers had done to the family name. Gordon owned a successful motorcar dealership in Winchester and had made generous donations to church funds since Redvers' death. He was a well-built man of thirty-five, who bore a strong resemblance to his late father, sporting the same neatly trimmed chestnut hair and beard in the style of King George. His wife, Jennifer, was a few years older but looked younger. Whenever I saw her around town, she was always dressed in the latest fashions and her blonde hair was generally rolled into an elaborate chignon, a style that suited her elegant neck.

'Is that...?' Elijah whispered, indicating with his eyes to a figure across the hall.

Standing to one side of the staircase was Gordon's mother, Gertrude Tolfree. Since her husband's death, Gertrude had become a reclusive figure. I generally only saw her on my rare visits to church on Sunday morning, where she ignored me. To be fair, she ignored most people, but in my case, she had a particular reason for avoiding me.

I'd helped my friend, Constance Timpson, uncover Redvers Tolfree's embezzlement. For a long time, Gordon had blamed me and Constance for his father's downfall. More recently, he'd come to accept Redvers' guilt, and we'd declared an uneasy truce. However, I had a feeling his mother wouldn't be so forgiving.

Gertrude was a tall woman with iron-grey hair and a long nose that gave the impression she was looking down on you. Her grandchildren stood next to her. I remembered Millicent telling me that Daisy was the older of the two, aged ten, and her younger brother, Luke, was nine.

To my surprise, when Gordon took his children's hands and

led them out into the garden, Gertrude came over to talk to me. I turned to Elijah for support, only to find he'd wandered off with Robbie to admire the general's old grandfather clock, still standing in the corner of the hallway.

'Miss Woodmore.' Gertrude's grey eyes studied my attire with disdain. This was clearly a woman who would never embrace the latest fashion for trousers.

'Mrs Tolfree, how nice to see you.' I self-consciously pulled at my pleated navy slacks, feeling out of place. Gertrude looked very much at home in Mill Ponds, her lavender scent mingling with the beeswax floor polish to create an atmosphere of fusty gentility. I wondered how the homeless and unemployed residents would feel in this refined setting.

'I'm pleased you felt you could come here today.' Her tone implied that she wished I hadn't. 'We're glad to welcome you.'

I felt like pointing out that I was a guest of the vicar, not the Tolfrees, but I said nothing and smiled politely.

'I'll come straight to the point. I appreciate that Mr Powell may not be your favourite person after what he did. However, he's paid for his crimes and is trying to atone for past mistakes. He's shown what can be achieved with charity and compassion, and I think it's time to forgive and forget and let him do what he does best.'

I'd heard this before and wasn't about to relent. 'Mr Powell may have helped many people in the past,' I agreed, then added, 'But he's harmed plenty of others.'

Over her shoulder, I saw Archie come through a door at the back of the house. He caught Jennifer Tolfree's eye, and the pair disappeared into the study together. I was tempted to point out to Gertrude that, as well as his criminal acts, Archie had a history of behaviour that, although not illegal, was certainly morally dubious. He had a predatory nature when it came to women, and I suspected Jennifer was his latest victim.

'I'm sure none of us are perfect.' Gertrude looked me up and down as she said this. 'Perhaps in time you'll learn to be more charitable. My son and Mr Powell have worked hard to get this place up and running, and it's destined to help many men rebuild their lives. I trust *The Walden Herald* will support them in their endeavours.' With that, she turned and walked away.

It seemed Archie wasn't the only one who saw Mill Ponds as a ticket back to respectability. I was beginning to wonder how much the hostel had been set up to help the men housed there or simply the people running it.

It was clear the Tolfrees were intent on re-establishing themselves as one of the prominent families in Walden. And I had no doubt Archie was enjoying exploiting their desperation to regain their social position. He was a master manipulator. I could picture him playing up to each member of the Tolfree family. However, I had a feeling he may have taken things too far with Jennifer.

I rejoined Elijah and Robbie, and we sauntered through the hallway, which was much as I remembered it. The walls had been freshly papered, but the old furniture was still in place. It was of good quality, although, like the mansion, it had seen better days, having taken a battering during the time Mill Ponds House was a training academy.

Elijah winked at me as we passed the door to what had been General Cheverton's study. This was the room we'd searched three years earlier, falling over in our attempts to light the gas lamp to see what we were doing. It was lucky we hadn't set fire to the carpet.

I wondered if Archie was still in there with Jennifer Tolfree or if they'd left by the French doors and gone out into the garden. If there hadn't been anyone around, I'd have pressed my ear to the study door to listen.

Instead, I followed Elijah into the large reception room, which the general had used to welcome military dignitaries during the war. It was now a communal lounge, fitted out to be more functional than stylish with plain, comfortable sofas and lots of small tables. The most eye-catching features were the beautiful paintings on the walls. I recognised them immediately.

Robbie began taking photographs while Elijah examined them with interest, his eyes widening with astonishment when I told him Archie had painted them.

He pointed to a particularly bucolic scene. 'They seem completely at odds with the man.'

I nodded, remembering the first time I'd seen Archie's paintings. He'd been staying in a cottage near Crookham Hall, working on a landscape of the surrounding countryside. Like Elijah, I'd been surprised by their serenity. There was a spiritual quality to how Archie depicted nature, with vast open spaces and lots of natural light.

I'd told Archie about the pictures I'd seen by soldiers who'd taken up painting as a way of coming to terms with the horrors they'd endured in the trenches. Some had painted desolate landscapes, while others depicted gruesome scenes of mud, blood and barbed wire in harsh blocks of colour.

Archie had said that, through his faith, he'd made peace with his time on the battlefields, and his art celebrated the healing powers of nature.

I showed Elijah some of the landscapes painted on the Crookham estate. 'These aren't the work of a disturbed mind. When Archie claimed to be suffering from shellshock, I knew it wasn't true because of what he'd told me about his paintings. They represent how Archie thinks the world should be, and if something doesn't conform to that, he tries to change it.'

'Using brute force, if necessary,' Elijah remarked.

I shuddered, thinking of the rifle propped up against the wall of the shed.

4

───────────

After work the following day, I headed to the Tolfree & Timpson biscuit factory. I'd promised to call on Constance Timpson and tell her about the Mill Ponds open day. Unlike Mrs Siddons, she had no intention of forgiving Archie Powell for the shot he'd fired at her, and I considered her one of my few allies.

The sprawling factory had been built by Gordon's grandfather, Isaac Tolfree, in 1850 and was situated on the outskirts of Walden on the banks of the Basingstoke Canal. At one time, its produce had been transported along the waterway, but Constance now used the services of a road haulage company. Like canals across the country, commercial traffic was in decline and pleasure boating had taken its place.

When I entered the factory, I sensed immediately something was wrong. It took me a moment to realise what it was. The workers were all still and unnaturally silent. A second later, I realised why. Shouts were coming from the offices above, and they were trying to hear what was being said above the noise of the conveyor belts.

I hurried over to Nora Fox, who I'd become friends with two years earlier, when I'd helped Constance investigate Redvers Tolfree's double-dealing.

'What's going on?'

'Archie Powell walked in bold as brass with another bloke, and they went upstairs to Miss Timpson's office.' Nora's face was flushed from the heat of the machines, and her white muslin cap stuck damply to her crimped hair. The air around us was clammy as clouds of steam spread the sickly-sweet smell of baking biscuits.

'Is she on her own?'

Nora shook her head. 'Lord Timpson is with her. He's been doing most of the shouting.'

I bounded up the stairs two at a time. Daniel Timpson was the most placid of creatures; I'd never heard him so much as raise his voice. Shouting didn't bode well.

'How dare you come here?' he was yelling when I entered the office.

Daniel was slim and of medium height, while Archie was around six feet tall and muscular in build. This didn't deter Daniel from squaring up to him, his face red with anger.

Constance stood behind her brother, reaching out to restrain him. The other person in the room was holding on to Archie, trying to pull him away. I realised it was the chap I'd seen in the garden the previous day. He was dressed in the same working clothes of dark corduroy trousers and an old army jumper.

'Isn't it about time we put our grievances behind us?' Archie was saying.

I walked past him and picked up the telephone on Constance's desk. 'Could you put me through to the station house, please,' I said to the operator.

Archie turned on me. 'You're calling the police?'

'That's right. Sergeant Gilbert made it clear he would arrest you if you harassed your former victims.'

'I'm not harassing anyone. I'm merely enquiring about the possibility of employment for one of my men.'

I noticed the proprietary way he said, 'my men'.

His companion noticed it, too, and raised his eyebrows. 'I think we should leave,' he said, pulling Archie by the arm. 'I'm sorry to have upset you, Miss—'

'I'm not going anywhere.' Archie tried to shrug him off. 'I haven't done anything wrong.'

'You shot at my sister and nearly killed Ben,' Daniel yelled. 'Why don't you get the hell out of Walden?'

'Walden is my home. I'm sorry if—'

'Ben, it's Iris,' I said, even though the operator hadn't yet put me through. 'I'm at the Tolfree & Timpson factory. Archie Powell is threatening Miss Timpson. He doesn't appear to be armed, although I know he keeps a rifle at Mill Ponds House. Can you come immediately?'

'This is ridiculous. I'm not threatening anyone,' Archie snarled, but this time he allowed his companion to drag him away.

Daniel made to follow, and I quickly replaced the mouth-piece in its cradle and made a grab for him, slamming the door closed as I did.

'Is Ben coming?' Constance flicked a stray lock of glossy dark hair over her shoulder.

'I hadn't actually been put through.'

She smiled and slumped into the chair behind her rosewood desk.

'The sheer bloody arrogance of the man,' Daniel muttered, pacing the room. 'What the hell are we going to do about him?'

I let go of his arm, wishing I had an answer to that.

Constance looked up. 'You said Archie had a rifle?'

I nodded, wishing I hadn't thrown that into my imaginary conversation with Ben. Constance had every reason to be afraid of Archie, even though I didn't think he'd risk targeting her again.

'I saw it yesterday. In a shed at Mill Ponds. On my way home, I stopped at the station house to tell Ben. He said he'd talk to Archie about it. He's probably taken it away by now.'

What Ben had actually said was that he'd check the rifle's ownership, and if it had a certificate, there wasn't much he could do about it.

Constance raised her hands to her temples. 'Who was that man with Archie?'

'I hoped you might be able to tell me that,' I replied. 'I saw him yesterday in the garden at Mill Ponds. I suppose he must be one of their first residents.'

'Archie tried to introduce him, but I didn't catch his name.' Constance glanced at Daniel as she said this.

'I told them to get out as soon as they walked in.' Daniel was still pacing the room. 'I'd only popped in to pick up Constance. Good job, too; otherwise, she would have had to face them alone.'

I saw by Constance's face that, had she been on her own, she would have handled things differently. For a start, she wouldn't have caused a row that her whole factory could hear.

She stood up. 'I've had enough for one day. Come on.' She took Daniel's arm. 'Let's go home.'

Home for the Timpsons was Crookham Hall, the ancestral estate Daniel had inherited – along with the title of Lord Timpson – on his father's death. The Honourable Constance Timpson had inherited the family business from her mother,

Lady Timpson, two years earlier. Despite the prejudices she faced as a woman in her mid-twenties running a large empire, she'd succeeded in making Timpson Foods even more profitable than it had been in her mother and grandfather's day. I was the same age as Constance and was in awe of her ability to stand up to her mostly older and male business rivals.

Pulling on an elegant navy cape that covered her formal work suit, Constance led the way downstairs, where her workers were preparing to go home. They had the sense not to mention the row they'd just overheard. She wished them a good evening and walked through the conveyor belts and out into the yard.

'Would you like me to drive you home, Iris?' Daniel asked as he opened the door of the Daimler that had once belonged to his mother.

'Yes, please. Millicent should be back from school by now. Why don't you pop in to see her?'

'I don't want to intrude—'

'I'd like to see Ursula,' Constance said in a tone that settled the matter. She knew Millicent was far better at calming Daniel than she was.

One of the many things I liked about Daniel was that he'd fallen in love with my good friend, Millicent, despite the disparity in their social positions. Although Millicent reciprocated his feelings, if she were to marry, she'd have to give up her job as a schoolteacher. So far, they'd yet to reach a solution to this impediment to their relationship.

When we reached 13 Victoria Lane, I showed Daniel and Constance into the parlour and went in search of Millicent and Ursula. I found them in the kitchen and told them briefly what had happened.

Millicent dashed from the room to go to Daniel, and a few

moments later, Constance joined Ursula and me in the kitchen. Ursula turned off the stove and started to hunt around for the sherry. I pointed to the lowest shelf – she was a diminutive woman and would take us to task if we placed any vital supplies, such as sherry bottles, out of her reach.

Ursula poured us each a glass, and we sat around the kitchen table, Constance describing what had happened before I arrived at the factory.

'It was the way he walked in, without even knocking, as though he had every right to be there. No acknowledgement, let alone an apology for what he did,' she told Ursula.

I noticed how she often looked to the older woman for guidance. She had no parents to turn to, and running Timpson Foods on her own was a lonely business. Although Constance possessed a classically beautiful face and razor-sharp mind, this combination tended to intimidate men rather than attract them.

In a male-dominated world, Mrs Siddons was her only ally in business matters, but, like me, she'd fallen out with her over Archie. Ursula, who'd led an adventurous life that included many lovers and no husbands, was a trusted adviser when it came to personal matters.

'Archie's arrogant.' Ursula propped her glasses on her head, causing her mane of grey hair to spring up even further. 'He thinks he can force people into accepting the situation – and that will be his downfall. He's being too brash, too forceful. If he went quietly about his business and made a success of this hostel, people would, in time, come to forgive and forget. I suspect that's what the Tolfrees are hoping for.'

I nodded. 'Even Gertrude was there yesterday. I get the impression she thinks Mill Ponds will redeem the family name.'

'At least they're civil to me nowadays,' Constance said. She'd become the sole owner of Tolfree & Timpson Biscuits when Redvers Tolfree was forced to sell his remaining shares to her. At the time, there had been some resentment on the part of the Tolfree family. However, they now recognised Redvers' financial situation would have been far worse if Constance hadn't bailed him out.

'Gordon Tolfree has indicated he'd welcome me as a patron of the hostel,' Constance continued. 'And I'd happily offer my support if it wasn't for Archie Powell. We've got to get rid of him.'

'How?' I asked.

'Micky Swann's helping out at Mill Ponds, and his wife, Polly, has taken a job as housekeeper there,' Constance replied. 'Micky's going to keep an eye on things for me. If we can get anything incriminating on Archie, even something slightly unsavoury, the church will have to kick him out.'

Micky Swann was once a resident of Creek House in Deptford; the home Archie had run for unemployed and disabled ex-servicemen. Thanks to Constance, Micky now had a job at the Tolfree & Timpson factory, and thanks to Mrs Siddons, his family had a home in Walden. However, Archie had also helped the Swanns, and I wasn't sure how willing they'd be to cause trouble for him.

But Ursula thought it was a good plan. 'Archie's too conceited not to trip himself up at some stage. In the meantime, don't show any hostility to him. Avoid him by all means, though treat him civilly if you run into him in town. The more you rail against him, the more he'll portray himself as the injured party. Especially to the women of the parish.'

I knew what she was talking about. I'd seen how enamoured the Walden Women's Group were of the handsome former vicar. Jennifer Tolfree was a prominent member of the group and had been singing his praises to her cohorts. Ursula was right when she said the more we crossed him, the more sympathy he'd gain.

But it was easier said than done. When I was with Archie, it took every ounce of my self-possession not to slap his arrogant face, let alone be polite to him. And today, I'd infuriated him by my telephone call to the police. He wouldn't have liked being humiliated in front of one of 'his men'.

I took a swig of sherry, not daring to think how he might retaliate.

5

I waited for Archie to summon me to Mill Ponds to interview the first residents, but in the end, it was Micky Swann who persuaded me to talk to them.

I was strolling along the high street on my way home from work when I heard someone calling my name. I looked back to see Micky hurrying after me. It reminded me of how he'd once frightened me by following me along a dimly lit street in Deptford. He was a stocky man with sandy brown hair and strange amber eyes that had unnerved me when I'd swung around to find them staring at me in the dark.

At the time, I'd believed he was attempting to scare me into staying away from Deptford. As it turned out, he'd been trying to warn me to keep away from Archie. How right he'd been.

I strolled towards him. 'How's it going?'

'Never been better. Polly and the children love it here. The children even like going to school. Never thought I'd say that. You can tell your friend, Miss Nightingale, they think she's the cleverest person in the world.'

I smiled. 'I hear you and Polly are helping out at Mill Ponds?'

He nodded. 'Polly's working there as housekeeper, and I've gone over a few times to help settle the new residents in. There are three now. Will you come and talk to them like you did to us at Creek House?'

'Do they want to be interviewed?' I asked.

'You know what it's like. They might need a bit of encouragement.' He grinned. 'You won us over in the end.'

Not before the men had ridiculed the trousers I'd been wearing and intimidated me with a revolver. I hoped the newcomers to Mill Ponds wouldn't be so suspicious.

'Frank got his old job back thanks to your article,' Micky wheedled.

This persuaded me. I'd been proud of the pieces I'd written on Creek House and what they'd achieved. Even Elijah had praised them.

'Okay. I'll pay a visit in the morning.'

'Good girl.' Micky squeezed my arm and sauntered off.

The following morning, it was a relief when Polly Swann opened the door to Mill Ponds House. I didn't have the energy for another encounter with Archie.

'Jennifer Tolfree is here with our first three guests. Come for a chat in the kitchen afterwards,' she said before ushering me into the lounge.

'Miss Woodmore, so glad you could come.' Jennifer was still acting as lady of the manor. She waved an elegant hand, sending a waft of floral perfume in my direction. 'Polly, could you bring us some tea?'

'I've got to get a loaf in the oven first. Then I'll see what I can do.' Polly turned and winked at me before departing. She was a tiny woman with copper-coloured hair, a pretty freckled face and a wicked grin. Although roughly half the size of her husband, she was the one who ruled the roost, and Micky was happy to let her. Jennifer would soon learn that Polly wasn't a woman to be ordered about.

'Miss Woodmore, let me introduce you to Mr Vincent Owen.' Jennifer nodded toward the man seated next to her. 'Mr Hugh Alvarez.' She indicated the man standing by the mantelpiece. 'And dear Paul.'

At last, I had a name. Hugh Alvarez was the man Archie had brought to the Tolfree & Timpson factory. This was the first opportunity I'd had to examine him properly, although I'd already appreciated how striking he was, with fine features and intelligent brown eyes. There wasn't a speck of grey in his thick, dark blond hair, and I guessed him to be somewhere in his thirties, though it was difficult to tell.

The three men greeted me, and I wondered why Jennifer had introduced Vincent and Hugh by their full names while Paul was addressed as if he were a child. All were wearing starched white shirts, and I hoped they hadn't been persuaded to dress formally on my account.

'Vincent worked on my family's estate for many years. It was a sad day for all of us when my father sold Blackthorn Park.' Jennifer patted the hand of the man beside her. He was short with grey hair, sunken eyes and a protruding belly. I was sure I'd seen him before, though I couldn't think where.

I recalled Jennifer was the daughter of Lord Darrington and had once lived in a grand house just outside Winchester. However, like many stately homeowners, her father had been forced to sell his ancestral estate due to high taxes.

I got the impression Jennifer was a little bitter at having been let down by the men in her life, first her father and then her father-in-law. Although she'd married into trade, it had at least been a well-established business with a famous name. Tolfree Biscuits was a respectable company with a royal seal of approval. Redvers Tolfree had even been awarded an OBE for his war work. However, Gordon hadn't received the Tolfree inheritance Jennifer would have come to expect.

'It was a sad day when I left Blackthorn, ma... Mrs Tolfree.'

It sounded as though Vincent had just stopped short of calling her ma'am.

'Fortunately, I was able to find Vincent work at Sand Hills Hall. But when Mrs Thackeray moved to London, he lost his job again and now finds himself in reduced circumstances.'

I was grateful Jennifer hadn't mentioned the reason for the move to London. Florence Thackeray had been unable to bear staying at Sand Hills Hall after the death of her daughter and my closest friend, Alice. I realised I'd seen Vincent when he'd been working as a gardener and odd-job man at the hall.

'I'm sorry to hear that, Mr Owen,' I said.

Jennifer turned her attention to the fair-haired young man sitting in the armchair opposite. One leg of his blue flannel trousers was pinned up to cover the stump of an above-knee amputation. Leaning against the side of his chair were a pair of underarm crutches.

'And dear Paul.' Jennifer smiled at the man as if he were a toddler. 'Like so many of our brave young men, he lost a limb during his time in France.'

To my surprise, she then moved on to Hugh Alvarez as if there was nothing more to be said about Paul. I'd come here to interview the men myself, not to listen to her relate a potted history of each.

'Hugh is a lorry driver. Was, I should say. At present, he's unemployed.'

Hugh was watching Jennifer with a sardonic expression on

his face. Like Paul, he didn't bother to react to her brief account of his life.

'I'm sorry you lost your job. Where did you work?' I asked.

'I travelled all over the country. I have good references and a few contacts in the trade, so I don't think I'll be here long. As soon as I'm offered a new position, I'll vacate my room for someone who needs it more.'

He had a soft, well-educated voice that had surprised me when I'd first heard him speak at the factory. Afterwards, I'd chastised myself for my preconceived ideas of what a homeless man should look or sound like. The war and subsequent high levels of unemployment had left people from all walks of life in unfortunate circumstances.

'Of course you will,' Jennifer assured him in a tone that seemed to suggest this was unlikely.

Hugh ignored her. 'May I ask what it is you intend to write? I'm curious to know the reason for your article.'

Jennifer appeared disconcerted by this, but I was happy to answer his question.

'Two reasons. First, Reverend Childs asked my editor to publish a story on the purpose of Mill Ponds. While most townspeople are supportive of the hostel, some are anxious at the thought of newcomers to the town. It's a fear of the unknown. The vicar feels that the more knowledge they have, the more accommodating they'll be of the hostel's aims.'

Hugh gave a slight nod. 'And the other reason?'

'The article might encourage more support. And I don't just mean financial donations to help with the upkeep of Mill Ponds. If I can write a little about your personal histories and former occupations, it might assist with your search for jobs. We have good levels of employment in this area of Hampshire, better than in some cities. Business owners may come forward with offers of work.'

As I said this, I realised I'd helped kick him out of Constance Timpson's office the previous day when Archie had taken him there to look for a job.

I decided to switch my attention to Paul. 'I'm sorry, I didn't catch your surname.'

We all knew it was because Jennifer hadn't given it.

'Richardson. I'm a mechanic. I can take any engine apart and put it back together again. But people take one look at this...' he indicated his pinned trouser leg '...and they think I'm no longer capable of manual work. I've learned to adapt and can do everything I did before. I'm just a little slower at completing tasks than I used to be.'

His insistence that he could still work told of years of rejection. He and Vincent carried an air of defeat – as if all hope of getting a job had been knocked out of them. Hugh, on the other hand, was confident this was only a temporary setback. Perhaps that was because he hadn't been unemployed for as long as the other two.

I nodded at Paul, making swift notes as he spoke. 'Is that what you'd like to do? Go back to working with cars?'

'Car, lorries, vans – I can fix anything.'

I couldn't help thinking that Gordon Tolfree, owner of Tolfree Motors, a large car dealership, would be in an ideal position to hire Paul. Yet obviously no offer of employment had been forthcoming.

At this moment, the door opened, and I was glad of the interruption – until I saw who it was. Polly came in with a tea tray, followed by Gertrude Tolfree.

'Please carry on.' Gertrude took a seat. 'Don't let me interrupt.'

Her air of superiority told of a privileged upbringing. She came from well-bred stock, like her daughter-in-law. And, like Jennifer, she'd married into trade and probably come to regret that decision.

After Redvers' death, she'd been left penniless. Her home, Sycamore Lodge, had passed to Gordon because Isaac Tolfree had stipulated when he built the property in 1860 that it must be handed down to the eldest male relative. Although Gertrude still lived there with her son and daughter-in-law, I got the impression neither she nor Jennifer were entirely happy with the arrangement.

I was reluctant to carry on the interview with both Tolfree women present. All three men appeared uncomfortable, and I suspected they'd be even more disinclined to speak than before.

I decided Hugh was the most confident of the three and asked if his surname was Spanish. He replied with a nod.

'Are you in contact with your family?'

Another nod.

I wanted to know the circumstances that had led these men to Mill Ponds, but it was too stilted an environment to ask personal questions. Before I could suggest I talk to each of them in private, Gertrude butted in.

'I'm sure your readers will also want to know a little about the people behind the hostel.'

I managed a slight nod. So far, *The Walden Herald* hadn't included a single mention of Archie Powell in its pages. Mainly because Elijah knew that I'd walk out in disgust if the newspaper gave one ounce of publicity to that man. However, it wasn't Archie that Gertrude was thinking of.

'My son, Gordon, has worked tirelessly to get this project off the ground. As a committee member of Winchester Cathedral's

Great War Fund, he was instrumental in securing church funding for the acquisition of Mill Ponds House.'

I scribbled a few random notes. We'd already covered this in the newspaper when the vicar had first announced plans for the hostel.

'But it was Mr Powell who identified Mill Ponds as a property with the potential to be used for such a purpose,' Jennifer pointed out, seeming keener to praise Archie than her husband.

This was news to me, although it didn't come as a complete surprise. I'd long suspected that Archie had been the brains behind the scheme. Gordon had just been one of many local businessmen who'd made donations to the cathedral's war fund, which provided support for veterans across Hampshire.

'Yes, my dear.' Gertrude flashed her daughter-in-law a look of irritation. 'We have much to thank Mr Powell for, though it was Gordon who had the vision and determination to see the project through to completion.'

I snapped my notebook shut and returned it to my bag, tired of this backslapping.

'I have all I need for the time being.' I stood up and hurried to the door, not caring if I appeared rude. 'I can see myself out.'

I caught Hugh's amused expression. He didn't say a lot, but I got the impression he didn't miss much and seemed to enjoy observing the goings-on at Mill Ponds.

If I wanted information on what Archie was up to, Hugh would be the one to ask. However, I had a feeling Mr Alvarez would be reluctant to reveal any secrets.

6

After shutting the lounge door behind me, I headed for the kitchen, deciding Polly might be a better source of information.

'How did it go?' She poured me a mug of tea before going back to chopping carrots. The kitchen smelt of freshly baked bread, and judging by the diced beef, vegetables and ball of pastry, Polly was preparing a meat pie for dinner. I was glad the men were being well fed. It was some sort of compensation for having to be patronised by Jennifer and Gertrude.

'Frustrating.' I took the tea and sat at the kitchen table. 'First, Jennifer didn't let the men speak for themselves, then Gertrude came in to sing Gordon's praises.'

'Jennifer's set herself up as mistress of the house.'

'And is Gordon its master? After all, he's the one who's a patron. Not his wife or mother.'

She shook her head. 'He's not here much. Archie's the master, and I think Jennifer likes that.'

I wasn't surprised by this.

'How are you getting on here?' I glanced around the kitchen, noting it looked much the same as it had in General

Cheverton's day. The ancient cooking range was still in place, as was the old oak table and sideboard.

'I'm not keen on being ordered about by Mrs Tolfree, either one of them. But the first three residents are pleasant enough. Micky came to settle them in, and I think it helped them to know he was once in the same boat as they are.'

Micky had been a resident of Creek House in Deptford after Polly had kicked him out of the family home due to his drinking. Micky had turned to the bottle after he'd been unable to find work due to a weak chest and wounded left arm. He'd been desperate to support his family and, with help, had been able to improve his health. Although he'd never regain the strength he had before shrapnel had torn into his arm, he was now capable of working the machines at the Tolfree & Timpson biscuit factory.

'It would have been better if Micky had been here instead of Jennifer and Gertrude.' I lowered my voice as I heard the sound of footsteps and conversation outside in the yard. 'The men seemed reluctant to speak, not that they were given much opportunity.'

'That will be them escaping to the garden to work on the greenhouse. If you want them to talk to you, that's the place to go. Paul and Vincent are uncomfortable in the house. It's too grand. I think it will be better when there are more occupants, and it doesn't seem as formal.'

'How do they get on with Archie?'

'Paul looks up to him. I'm not so sure about Vincent or Hugh.' She smiled at my expression. 'I know you don't trust him, and I don't blame you. What he did was despicable. But he's always been kind to us. I know we have Miss Timpson and Mrs Siddons to thank for Micky's job and finding us a place to live. But if Archie hadn't given Micky a room at Creek House and helped him get well again, we might never have got out of London. We lived in a cramped basement flat with nowhere safe for the children to play. Now we live in a lovely house in a friendly town, and the children are doing well at school.'

I didn't bother to argue. What she said was true. Archie had helped families like the Swanns. No doubt, the hostel would give him the chance to help others. I just wasn't sure I could stick around to watch while he did.

'I hope he can do the same for these men. I'll go and see if they're any more talkative without Jennifer and Gertrude to speak for them.'

I wandered through the kitchen gardens and out onto the stretch of newly acquired land, where I found Hugh, Paul and Vincent preparing the site for the greenhouse. The stiff white shirts had been replaced by khaki jumpers and, in Vincent's case, a buttoned-up grey cardigan – I suspected because he could no longer fit into his old army clothes.

Watching them, it was clear Paul could handle manual work. He'd learnt how to manoeuvre himself around by propping a single wooden crutch under one arm; the other was lying nearby on a patch of grass. While Vincent turned over the soil, Paul raked it and meticulously levelled it out.

Polly had been right – they were happier in this environment and chatted more freely having escaped the confines of the house. Paul was more confident and talked about his days as a mechanic before the war, working for a local garage in Greenwich. After he'd been discharged from the army, he'd done odd jobs but hadn't been able to find any permanent work.

He was a likeable young man with a pleasing manner and soft voice, and it was wretched to hear him say, 'No one wants to employ someone like me.'

'Why did you move from Greenwich? Don't you have family there?'

'I didn't want to be a burden. My parents are getting on a bit. I had a fiancée. We got engaged ten years ago on the day war was declared.'

'How old were you?' After speaking with him, I was reassessing his age. His youthful face had led me to believe he was in his twenties. I guessed now he was slightly older.

'I was twenty. I'd just joined up.'

'Do you still see her?' I wondered if this was an insensitive question. Had she broken off their engagement?

He shook his head. 'I told her I couldn't marry her. Not like this. It wouldn't be fair. That's why I moved out of the area. I didn't want to keep seeing her.'

He turned away at that point and began his slow, laborious raking. I didn't ask any more questions even though I was desperate to know how his fiancée had felt about his decision to end their engagement. Had she been heartbroken or relieved? I guessed the answer to that depended on the depth of her feelings for Paul.

I sensed he was deliberately hiding his face from me, so I moved away to talk to Vincent. The older man seemed happy to take a break from digging and put down his spade and took a pipe from his cardigan pocket. He looked to be in his late fifties with a tanned face that spoke of years of outdoor toil.

His tale was also one of sorrow, although Vincent told it in gruff tones with no show of emotion. He blew out aromatic smoke as he described being a man of all work for Jennifer Tolfree's father, Lord Darrington, at Blackthorn Park near Winchester.

'My wife and I lived in a tied cottage on the estate. She died of influenza in 1918, just before I was discharged. By the time the war was over, Lord Darrington was nearly bankrupt. I left the army with nothing to come back to. No wife, no home and no job. The estate was up for sale, and the family were moving out.'

'That must have been dreadful. I'm so sorry.' My words sounded hollow. What could you say that would offer any comfort?

Vincent took several puffs of his pipe before continuing. 'Then Miss Darrington, I mean Mrs Tolfree, said the Thackerays were looking for someone, so I managed to get a job at Sand Hills Hall for a few years. Then... well, you know what happened.'

My dearest friend, Alice, had lived at Sand Hills Hall. After her tragic death three years ago, her mother, Florence, had decided to leave Walden and move to London. The hall had been empty since then.

'I'm so sorry about Miss Alice.' Vincent's face crumpled, and he rubbed his eyes. 'She was a beautiful girl in every way. So kind.'

'She was,' I said in a choked voice and took out my own handkerchief. Even after three years, tears still rose whenever anyone mentioned Alice. I hastily wiped them away and thought of the times I'd seen Vincent working in the gardens at Sand Hills Hall. At the time, I'd had no inkling of what he'd been through. I wondered if Alice had. She'd been the kindest person I'd known and had a knack for discovering someone's sorrow and trying to make it better. As she was no longer around, I felt compelled to help Vincent on her behalf. 'What sort of work do you enjoy?'

'I used to love working in Lord Darrington's stables. I miss the horses. I couldn't ride, but I knew how to look after them. I hoped the new owner might keep me on.' He shrugged. 'In the end, they broke up the estate and sold off most of the land.'

'I'll mention your previous experience in my article. There are plenty of stables around this area.'

Vincent nodded but didn't look hopeful. I thanked him for his time, and he went back to digging. While talking to him and Paul, I'd been conscious of Hugh working nearby, listening to our conversations. Yet when I turned to him, he put down his spade and motioned me away from the others, walking over to a bench by the shed. The door was shut, and I wondered if the rifle was still inside.

'I want to apologise about what happened at the factory,' he said when I sat beside him. 'It wasn't my intention to upset anyone. I had no idea when Archie took me to see Miss Timpson of... of what he did to her. Polly told me later. I would never have dreamt of going there if I'd known. Would you pass on my apologies to Miss Timpson?'

'I'm sure she doesn't hold you responsible. She knows what Archie's like.'

'She's a remarkable young woman. I'd like to call on her again myself, but I wouldn't want to seem presumptuous.'

'I'll pass on your message.'

Hugh appeared very much taken with Constance. However, I doubted she'd welcome another visit from him.

'Archie Powell is certainly a contradictory man.' Hugh gave me a sideways look. 'Polly seems to think he's paid his dues and should be forgiven. I gather you and Miss Timpson don't feel the same?'

I chose my words carefully before speaking. 'I don't believe Archie is repentant. And I don't believe his actions were due to any type of war neurosis or shellshock. He knew exactly what he was doing when he decided to fire his rifle at my friends. So, no. I don't forgive him. And neither does Constance.'

He nodded, then said softly, 'Constance? That was my mother's name.'

I leapt at this opening to discover more about his past.

'Do you have any other family? A wife or children?'

He shook his head but didn't elaborate.

I persevered. 'What about your father? Was he from Spain?'

'My grandfather was from Valencia. He was a wine merchant and travelled around Europe before settling in Winchester.'

'Is that where you're from?'

'It's where my mother was from. She died earlier this year. I live, lived, in London.'

'What made you come here?'

He shrugged. 'Seemed as good a place as any.'

I was about to ask more when Paul lost his balance and stumbled onto Vincent. The two men fell to the ground, and Hugh rushed over to them. He bent down to pull them up, but they were laughing too hard to take his outstretched hand.

I smiled, deciding to leave them to it. Hugh hadn't been particularly forthcoming, and I got the feeling further questioning would be fruitless. Besides, I wanted to concentrate on Paul and Vincent. Hugh seemed to think losing his job was only a temporary setback, and I hoped he was right. By contrast, the other two men appeared to have given up hope of ever finding work. I needed to put their stories in front of people who might be able to help.

I was strolling back towards the house when I realised Gertrude was sitting on a bench under an arbour in the kitchen garden. I wondered how long she'd been there and if she'd been listening to my conversation with Hugh.

'I understand your dislike of Mr Powell. But I hope you'll be professional enough not to allow your feelings to affect what you write about the hostel. My son has worked hard to get this place off the ground. It would be churlish to let your prejudice stand in the way of the good that can be done here. This place can't function without Mr Powell.'

She obviously had been listening and was making no attempt to hide it.

'I have no intention of mentioning Mr Powell in my article,' I assured her. I didn't add that I wouldn't be mentioning her son, either. I gave a polite smile and walked away. I'd had quite enough of the Tolfrees for one day.

Rather than go back into the house and face another conversation with Jennifer, I went through the yard outside the scullery and was about to turn the corner when the sound of Archie's voice made me stop. The study was on this side of the house, and its French doors led out to the rose garden.

I moved closer to the wall and peered around the corner. Archie was standing outside the study, having an intense discussion with someone I couldn't see. He had his back to me, blocking my view of whoever he was talking to. I watched as he reached out his hands to the person. When they pulled away from his grasp, I saw it was Jennifer Tolfree. And she was crying.

I ducked out of sight and let a few moments pass before curiosity got the better of me. I cautiously peeked around the wall to see Jennifer striding across the lawn. Archie had stayed where he was and was watching her go. When he moved to turn around, I withdrew, deciding to go through the gardens where the men were working and out of the back gate onto the track by the bridge over the railway line. From there, I could join the lake footpath.

Part of me wanted to go and confront Archie about what I'd witnessed. But how could I when I wasn't sure exactly what I had seen?

Since Archie's arrival in Walden, Jennifer hadn't made a secret of her admiration for him. It occurred to me that the attention she paid Archie might be her way of getting back at her husband. The reversal of the Tolfree family fortunes wasn't the only thing Jennifer had cause to be bitter about. The previous year, an investigation into the death of one of Gordon's employees had revealed he'd been involved with a young woman.

Could Jennifer have turned to Archie for comfort? He'd probably been happy to lead her on but may have baulked at entering into an actual affair. After all, would he have the nerve to blackmail me over adultery if he was committing it himself? With Archie, you could never tell.

Whatever the situation, it looked like his relationship with Jennifer had soured. With any luck, Gordon and Gertrude would be the next ones to see what sort of man Archie really was.

7

Although I was sure Archie had long since given up following me, I was always careful when I went to London.

In fact, I realised as I took a seat on the train and glanced at the other occupants of the carriage, I often found myself looking to see if Archie could be lurking nearby. I'd almost forgotten what it was like not to have his insidious presence in my life. This strengthened my resolve to do whatever I could to escape from Walden.

When I reached Waterloo Station, I hopped on a bus that stopped close to the offices of *Time & Tide* magazine at 88 Fleet Street. I'd arranged to meet Freda Bray at a café nearby to see if the magazine was hiring reporters. I'd had a few articles published in *Time & Tide* about the work of Constance Timpson and Mrs Siddons and wondered what my chances were of obtaining a permanent position.

Time & Tide was a weekly journal, run by women, founded in 1920 by Margaret Haig Thomas, now Viscountess Rhondda, who'd been in the same suffragette group as my mother. And, like my mother, she'd spent time in prison, where she went on

hunger strike in protest at being held as a common criminal
rather than a political prisoner.

I'd first met Freda when she'd worked for Constance
Timpson at the Tolfree & Timpson biscuit factory. Since then,
she'd moved to London and begun working for *Time & Tide*,
first as an assistant, helping to manage the office for Lady
Rhondda and now combining that role with writing regular
features.

Freda cut a striking figure as she strode along Fleet Street.
She was a tall, angular woman with high cheekbones, a strong
jawline and a shingled bob. She moved with easy confidence
through the throngs of people crowding the pavements, occasionally waving a hello to someone she knew.

Watching her, I felt a twinge of excitement at the prospect
of working in a city that was always alive, no matter what the
time of day or night. It was a far cry from Walden high street.

'Are you planning to move back to London?' Freda asked
after the waitress had left us with two coffees and a plate of
sandwiches. It was a warm day, and we'd chosen a table outside
underneath the café's awning. 'I thought you liked working at
The Walden Herald.'

'I just feel like a change.'

'Does this have anything to do with Archie Powell? I heard
about the Mill Ponds House project.'

'He doesn't make my life any easier. Nor Constance Timpson's.' I told her what had happened at the factory.

'That man is unbelievable. I see it time and time again.
Violent men say they're sorry, and everyone forgives them. I'm
surprised Mrs Siddons hasn't run him out of town.'

'Legally, there's nothing she can do. And she's up against
the church. She seems to have decided to make the best of the
situation.'

'I don't blame you for wanting to get away, though I'm afraid I can't help much. *Time & Tide* mainly uses freelancers. I'm sure if you were here in London, there would be more for you to cover. But...' She hesitated. 'I can't pretend it's easy. The magazine's not doing well, and I can't guarantee how long it will run. I'm worried I'll soon be looking for work, too.'

'I suppose I could try to get more work as a freelancer.' I gazed out at the busy street. 'Though I guess not much has changed around here.'

When I'd lived in London during the war, I'd tried and failed to get a post with any of the big newspapers. After the war, my father was keen to move back to my childhood home-town. I was less enthusiastic, but when he persuaded Elijah to take me on at *The Walden Herald*, I relented, and we returned to Walden in 1919.

'If you apply for a job with one of the dailies, it will have to be as a typist.'

I nodded. Although it was what I'd been expecting, it was dispiriting to hear, nonetheless.

My mood was low as I walked to St James's Park to meet my secret lover. Only he wasn't my lover. Archie was wrong about that. Marc was more than just a friend, though, and when I saw him standing by the lake, I felt the familiar spark of longing run through me.

I took my time walking towards him, trying to hold a picture of him in my mind. I wanted to imprint the image of his straight back, square shoulders and strong jawline. More than anything, I wanted to memorise his smile and the intensity of his soulful brown eyes as they welcomed me.

By the time I reached him, I was almost in tears at the thought of never seeing him again.

He raised a hand to touch my cheek. 'You look sad. I hope it isn't because of me.'

I shook my head and tried to steady my voice. 'I met a friend earlier to talk about getting a job on Fleet Street. But newspapers will only employ women in admin roles.'

'You're planning to move to London?' Marc led me to a bench by the wooden bridge that crossed the lake. 'I thought you were happy in Walden. You have so many good friends there.'

And one enemy. I'd never mentioned Archie to him. It was a problem he didn't need in his already complicated life. And I refused to allow anything or anyone to invade the precious time I had left with Marc.

'I fancied working somewhere more exciting. Perhaps I will one day, just not now.' I tried to make light of it, but his concern made me want to cry. 'You mustn't worry about me.'

He sighed. 'I do worry. My only comfort is that you have your family and friends close to you in Walden. When I leave, I want to picture you safe and happy.' His voice faltered. 'And loved.'

'I am.' I gulped back the tears that were threatening. He hadn't yet told me when he was returning to Belgium, and I avoided asking.

'Your face tells me otherwise,' he murmured, pulling me close.

I snuggled into him, breathing in his warm, citrus smell, wishing I could bottle the scent.

I'd fallen for Marc in June 1917 when he'd arrived at the Park Fever Hospital in Lewisham, searching for his family. The hospital had been given over to housing Belgian refugees who'd fled after Germany's occupation.

Marc's wife and parents had travelled to Britain in 1914, and he'd stayed behind to fight in the Resistance. When he was finally forced to leave, he'd come to England to try to find them.

I'd just turned eighteen and was working for a Voluntary Aid Detachment at the hospital. Still grieving the loss of my mother, I was often overwhelmed by the stories I heard each day from refugees fleeing the horrors of war. I'd go and hide in the water tower in the grounds of the hospital to escape for a few moments. One evening, Marc had been exploring and found me there. He was twenty-four years old yet seemed to carry the burden of a much older man.

At first, we simply exchanged our stories. He'd just completed his law degree when the Germans invaded in August 1914. In an attempt to keep his loved ones safe, he'd married his childhood sweetheart, Annette, in a rush ceremony before helping her and his parents escape their war-torn country. In turn, I told him about my life in England and the death of my suffragette mother.

Our meetings in the water tower became more frequent, and intimate conversations led to passionate kisses. In the weeks we spent together at the hospital, our feelings intensified, perhaps because we could never allow them to leave the confines of the tower.

I helped Marc track his family down to Exeter in Devon, and he left to be reunited with them before joining the Belgian army. I thought our last lingering kiss in the water tower was the end of our story. And it had been, until our paths had crossed the previous summer, when I'd visited Devon for my father's wedding. I had no idea Marc and Annette had settled there after the war. They were about to embark on a new life in London as Marc had been offered a job in a city law firm.

Before I left Devon to return to Walden, Marc asked me if

we could meet occasionally. When his first letter arrived, I found myself looking forward to seeing him with far too much longing.

Although we'd been careful not to allow our feelings to spill over into the kisses we'd shared during those chaotic weeks of the war, we'd still become closer than propriety allowed. It was a doomed relationship, and we both knew it. In some ways, it had been foolish to let the fire between us reignite.

As if reading my mind, he said, 'I don't regret it. Even though it's painful. I'll always be glad we found each other again.'

'I'll miss you.'

'I wish I didn't have to go. You know I don't—'

I held up a finger to silence him. I knew he didn't want to leave London. He loved his job and his adoptive country. As for me... well, we'd been careful never to talk about love.

'It will make Annette and my parents happy for us to be together again in Bruges.' He stared into the lake with a forlorn expression as if seeing his future.

And that was all there was to it. With no family of her own, Annette was dependent on Marc. She'd been only twenty when they married, and she'd come to Britain under the protection of his parents. Nearly ten years after their hasty wedding, Marc had admitted to me that both of them often wondered what course their lives might have taken if war hadn't intervened. Although they still loved each other, they felt their childhood romance may not have led to marriage if circumstances had been different.

'Annette thinks having children will give us what is missing from our relationship.' From Marc's tone, it was clear he didn't share this view.

'Perhaps it will. I hope you'll be happy. And Annette, too.'

He gripped my hands tightly. 'That's all I want for you. So many people love you. Your father and stepmother, Millicent and Ursula, all the friends you have in Walden. And Percy. If they knew about your relationship with me, they wouldn't approve. That's why I know leaving is the right thing to do.'

'Not yet,' I sobbed. 'Just a little more time.'

8

By the time my train pulled into Walden station, I knew I should have said a final goodbye to Marc. Even though he'd been as reluctant as me to make that day's meeting our last, it was wrong to keep prolonging the inevitable.

As I trudged across the station concourse, my mind was still in St James's Park, going over what we'd said and what we should have said. I was jolted back to the present when a young lad on a bicycle narrowly avoided colliding with me.

'Sorry, miss,' he shouted as he sped away.

It was Luke Tolfree, Gordon and Jennifer's son. I was surprised to see him out so late – it had gone seven-thirty. He must have lost track of time and realised he should have been home by now.

I joined the lake path, for once taking no pleasure in the sight of Waldenmere. If I left Walden, it was the place I'd miss most, as I had during the war when I'd lived first in Exeter, then London. I usually enjoyed walking by the water's edge, but after the day I'd had, I just wanted to go home and lie on my bed and cry.

'Did you enjoy your trip to London?'

My heart sank as I recognised the voice. Archie Powell was the last person I wanted to see. But as I crossed the station concourse and joined the lake footpath, there he was, standing on the jetty.

Had he been spying on me again and waiting for my return? I swallowed my unease and told myself it was just unfortunate he'd spotted me getting off the London train. I kept walking, trying to ignore him, but he stepped off the jetty, blocking my way.

'And how was Mr Jansen? Still sneaking away from the office to meet with his mistress behind his wife's back?'

'I am not his mistress.' I felt my face grow hot with anger.

'I'm sure Mrs Jansen will be relieved to hear it.'

'What do you want, Archie? I'm tired, and I want to get home.' I tried to push past him, but he held his ground.

'To help you, of course. I want you to see the error of your ways.'

'I don't need help, and if I did, I wouldn't come to you.'

'I think you do.' He smirked, prodding me in the chest with his index finger. 'Someone needs to remind you that adultery is a sin.'

I backed away, fury rising. 'What about firing a rifle at inno-cent people? Is that a sin?' I knew I shouldn't react to his provo-cation, but I was too upset to stop myself from shouting. 'Injuring a policeman when he's trying to protect a woman?'

'No harm was done,' he hissed into my face, and I could smell whisky on his breath.

'No harm? Ben had to have a bullet removed from his shoulder,' I yelled. 'You're evil and dangerous, and one day you'll get your comeuppance. I'll make sure—' I stopped, catching sight of some people coming toward us. To my dismay, the three residents of the hostel – Hugh, Paul and Vincent – were heading in our direction.

Archie swung around to see what had distracted me, his demeanour changing in an instant.

'Good evening, gentlemen.' He gave an ingratiating smile, stepping aside to let them by. 'I apologise for Miss Woodmore's display of temper. I'm afraid she finds it difficult to control her emotions.'

'Are you alright, miss?' Hugh Alvarez asked.

I saw Archie's flash of annoyance at Hugh's concern. Red with embarrassment, I murmured that I was fine. He nodded, and the three men shuffled past.

I tried to make my escape, too, but Archie wasn't finished.

He gripped my arm and said loud enough for the men to hear, 'Remember the Commandments. Thou shalt not commit adultery. End your affair and repent, and God will forgive you.' He released my arm and made the sign of the cross with his hand.

'How dare you...' Before I could stop myself, I slapped him hard across the face.

He gasped, and so did one of the men. I think it was Paul.

With a smile, Archie raised a finger to touch his cheek. 'You really must try to control your passions.'

Furious for having fallen into his trap, I ran back towards the station, cursing myself for my stupidity. I couldn't face taking the lake path along with Hugh, Paul and Vincent, so I headed up the main road into town.

When I arrived home, I had little chance to recover as a cold supper was already on the table. After a quick wash, I sat down to eat.

'How was London?' Ursula asked, pushing a bowl of salad in my direction.

I forced a smile. 'It was interesting.'

My mind was still reeling from my altercation with Archie. What would those men think? And more importantly, what would they say? I knew how gossip worked in this town. Would they go back to Mill Ponds and tell Polly what they'd witnessed? Would she go home and mention it to Micky that night? And would he say something at work the following day? Soon, everyone in Walden would be talking about me and branding me an adulteress.

'You said you were meeting a friend?' Millicent prompted as she passed me a plate of cold tongue.

I realised I should have prepared something to say in advance. I considered telling them about my meeting with Freda. But that would mean admitting I was thinking of leaving Walden – and I wasn't sure I was ready to have that conversation yet.

It had been kind of Millicent and Ursula to offer me lodgings in the first place, given my reputation. After the death of Alice, I'd run away with a man I thought I'd been in love with. I'd spent nearly a year travelling around Europe before returning to Walden – on my own and unmarried. They'd ignored the gossips and invited me into their home, and I'd always be grateful to them for that.

But what now? Would this latest incident prove a step too far?

I'd been happy lodging at 13 Victoria Lane until Archie had shown up. Now, although I longed to run away, there weren't many options open to me. Returning to my father and stepmother's house wouldn't solve the problem, as they lived in Walden, too. It was either stay put or go and live with my aunt and grandmother in Hither Green. Unless I could get a job in London, I couldn't afford to stay anywhere except with family.

Millicent must have sensed my reluctance to talk and didn't press me. Kind as ever, she filled the silence by chatting about the afternoon she'd spent with Daniel at Crookham Hall.

My appetite had deserted me, and I could barely manage a few mouthfuls of salad before placing my knife and fork on my plate.

Ursula touched my arm. 'Are you feeling unwell?'

Her gentle tone caused me to fight back tears.

'Just a headache. It was hot in the city and on the train. If you don't mind, I think I'll go upstairs to lie down for a while.'

'Of course.'

I went to pick up my plate, but Millicent told me she'd clear up once they were finished.

Gratefully, I rushed up the stairs and flung myself onto my bed, letting the tears flow. Soon I became too restless to lie there and got up again feeling hot and thirsty. After splashing cold water on my face, I went downstairs, glancing into Ursula's book room to see her dozing in her chair.

Millicent was still in the kitchen. The dinner plates had been washed and put away, and school exercise books were strewn across the table.

'How are you feeling?' she asked.

'Better,' I lied. I went over to the sink, filled a glass with water and drank it in one go.

Millicent put her pen down and gestured to the chair next to her. 'Do you want to talk about it?'

I shook my head and stood gazing out of the window. The sun was low in the sky, and the trees in the back garden were dappled in evening light.

'I think I'll get my cardigan and sit in the garden for a while.'

'You'd better hurry – it will be dark soon.'

I left the kitchen and was walking down the hallway when I saw a small package lying on the mat by the front door.

The postman only called first thing in the morning, so I assumed someone had dropped something in for Millicent or Ursula. When I got closer, I saw my name neatly written on the brown paper.

My breath caught in my throat when I recognised the hand-writing. I grabbed the parcel and opened the front door, peering up and down Victoria Lane. It was deserted, apart from the old gentleman who lived at the end of the road, walking his dog.

I closed the door and rushed upstairs to my bedroom to open the parcel in private. I tore away the wrapping, and a small box fell onto my bed along with a single sheet of paper. I read quickly.

My dearest Iris,

I was a coward today. I should have said two things.

First, I love you. I think you know that, although we've always avoided any sentiment. It's hard not to dream about what might have been if circumstances were different. But they're not, and we must make the best of the lives we have.

The second thing I should have said was goodbye. We've been putting it off for too long. Every time we meet, we know it should be the last time, yet we're never strong enough to take that final step. I decided it was simpler and less painful this way. We can never say what we feel when we're together.

I enclose a token of my love. I've had it in my pocket for some time now. Perhaps it will remind you of the times we've spent together in St James's Park, or perhaps it will make you think of your beloved Waldenmere.

Remember me with fondness.
My love, always,
Marc

I opened the box and found it contained a delicate silver brooch curved into the shape of a swan. After wiping away my tears, I pinned it onto the lapel of my dress, feeling sadness and relief in equal measure.

Marc was right. We couldn't carry on any longer. But I'd decided long ago that when the end came, I'd kiss him once goodbye. Was it too late?

The parcel had been delivered by hand, which meant Marc must have driven from London not long after we'd parted. Could he still be in Walden? Or would he drive straight back?

He'd never been to Walden before and knew nothing about it apart from my address. And my love for Waldenmere. If he was still around, that was where he would be.

I grabbed my shoes from where I'd tossed them under the bed, pulled on a cardigan and dashed downstairs. When I reached the high street, there was no sign of the tiny red Austin Seven motorcar that Marc drove. All was quiet apart from a few people at the end of the road walking toward the Drunken Duck. I headed in the opposite direction, turning onto Queens Road and taking a shortcut through the woods to the lake path.

It was darker than I expected, and I knew I wouldn't be able to walk home this way. I'd have to take the main road from the station back into town, as the streetlamps would soon be lit.

I passed a few residential roads that led away from the lake, but Marc wouldn't be familiar with these. It was more likely he'd park his car by the railway station. I practically ran along the footpath, stumbling in the fading light, until I saw the lamp posts illuminating the concourse.

My heart lurched when I spotted a red Austin Seven parked by the entrance to the station. I kept walking until I reached the jetty where Archie had accosted me earlier.

And there was Marc, standing motionless, staring out at the water. I rushed toward him, and he turned, looking startled, his cheeks wet with tears. Then he smiled and gestured to the lake. 'It's just as you described it.'

I wrapped my arms around him, and he pulled me close, our lips touching for one final kiss.

9

'You look terrible,' Elijah commented the following morning.

'Thanks. You look the picture of health.' To annoy him, I opened the windows in his office and mine, trying to alleviate the smell of stale tobacco.

He grunted and reached for his cigarettes. 'What's put you in a mood?'

'I'm not in a mood. I'm just tired.' I took my time brewing the coffee, not feeling up to conversation.

When I took a cup into his den, he eyed me warily.

'That's a pretty brooch. Is it new?'

I lightly touched the silver swan pinned to the front of my blouse. 'Yes, I bought it in London yesterday.'

He peered at it. 'Looks expensive.'

'It's not. I found it in a curiosity shop. It was tarnished, but I polished it up when I got home.'

'Hmmm.' He didn't seem convinced. 'What else did you do?'

'Walked around and shopped.'

'On a Sunday? Were many shops open?'

'A few.' I knew I should mention my meeting with Freda Bray, but I felt disloyal about looking for another job. 'I'm going to finish my article on the men I interviewed at the hostel.'

I went to my desk and began to type to avoid further comment. I was barely through the first paragraph when I made a mistake and had to pull the paper from the machine and start again. A few minutes later, I swore as I realised I'd typed the same sentence twice. I ripped the paper out, scrunched it into a ball and threw it into the bin.

'Remind me to order a fresh ream from the stationers,' I heard Elijah mutter.

I drained my coffee, poured a fresh cup and managed to concentrate long enough to finish the article. I collected the sheaf of papers and was about to take them to Elijah when we heard the clump of boots on the stairs. More than one set by the sound of it.

'Policeman's boots, unless I'm mistaken. Probably Ben and Sid come to scrounge some coffee.' Elijah looked as if he'd welcome the interruption.

He was nearly right. PC Sid King's boyish face appeared around the door and then, to our surprise, Superintendent Cobbe strode in. It was rumoured he was in line to be made Chief Superintendent of Hampshire and we rarely saw him since his move to Winchester police station.

'Mr Whittle, Miss Woodmore.' The superintendent nodded at each of us. 'I'm sorry to disturb you at work.'

Elijah rose from his desk. 'What can we do for you, superintendent?'

'I'd like to speak with Miss Woodmore.'

Elijah rolled his eyes at me in a 'what have you done now' manner. I shook my head to indicate I had no idea what was behind the visit.

'It's about Mr Archibald Powell.'

I managed to suppress a groan, but Elijah made a loud, exasperated noise.

'What about him?' he asked.

Superintendent Cobbe didn't reply. Instead, he took a few steps towards my desk.

'Perhaps you'd prefer to come with us to the station house so we can discuss this in private,' he said, gazing around the room.

There wasn't much privacy to be had in the headquarters of *The Walden Herald*, which consisted of two offices above Laffaye Printworks. My desk was in the main office and Elijah's in the other. The adjoining door was usually left open so we could talk to each other from our desks. Even closing the door of Elijah's den wouldn't guarantee the conversation couldn't be overheard.

I glanced at Elijah, and the look of concern on his face made me feel afraid. Sid was standing awkwardly by the door, staring down at his boots. Where was Ben, I wondered? Ben was a sergeant. Why hadn't he accompanied the superintendent?

I quickly weighed up my options. I had no desire to accompany Superintendent Cobbe to the station house. Nor did I wish to shut the door on Elijah and be questioned by the superintendent and Sid as we huddled around my desk.

I stood up and tried to appear calm. 'I'm happy for Mr Whittle to be present while you talk to me. Why don't you go into his office? I can heat up some coffee if you'd like some?'

'Thank you, Miss Woodmore. Coffee would be most welcome.' Superintendent Cobbe removed his hat and placed it on the hatstand, patting his grey hair to smooth it down. He and Sid pulled up chairs around Elijah's desk and waited for me to join them.

When I came in with the coffee, Sid nodded his thanks and gave me a half-smile. I could see how uncomfortable he was, and this only served to increase my apprehension.

I looked up at the clock. It was a quarter past eleven. What could Archie have said to cause the superintendent to drive over from Winchester that morning? Had he told the police I'd attacked him? I wouldn't put it past him. After all, it wasn't just his word; there had been three witnesses to the event.

I sat down in the spare chair, and as I did, Superintendent Cobbe stood up and closed the door. It suddenly felt very claustrophobic in the room. I saw Elijah's hand hover over his cigarettes, then grip his coffee cup instead.

The superintendent positioned his chair so that he was turned sideways to Elijah and facing me.

'You were overheard arguing with Mr Powell on the lake path by the railway station yesterday evening.'

So Archie had gone to the police. In that moment, my hatred for him grew, and I wished I'd slapped him even harder. In fact, I wished I'd pushed him into the water.

'Could you tell me what the argument was about.'

The heat that infused my chest and rose to my cheeks was a mixture of anger and embarrassment. On the one hand, it was reassuring to have Elijah with me rather than face this on my own. On the other, it was going to be uncomfortable to repeat the accusations Archie had made.

Should I say I'd changed my mind and ask to be interviewed at the station house instead? But what was the point? Tales of my quarrel with Archie would already be circulating around Walden, and Elijah was bound to hear them at some stage.

Before I could formulate a reply, Elijah tried to draw Superintendent Cobbe's attention away from me with a question. 'Perhaps you could tell us why you're asking? Has Mr Powell made some kind of accusation?'

The superintendent didn't turn to look at him. Instead, he kept his eyes fixed on my face as he said, 'Mr Powell is dead.'

10

The office fell silent.

I tried to arrange my features into some sort of appropriate expression, aware Superintendent Cobbe was watching me closely to gauge my reaction.

Shock, sadness, pity – perhaps all those emotions flashed across my face. Archie and I had once been close, and although I'd grown to hate him, I'd never wished him dead. I'd just wanted him gone from my life.

'Dead?' I croaked. 'How?'

'He was shot. With a rifle.' Superintendent Cobbe's eyes were still trained on me.

Of course. How else would he die? Somehow, it seemed obvious.

'His own rifle? The one in the—'

'She needs a drink. She's in shock.' Elijah was suddenly out of his chair and moving to the filing cabinet with a speed I hadn't seen him possess in years.

He poured us both a shot of whisky, then inclined the

bottle towards the superintendent, who shook his head. Sid did the same, albeit more reluctantly.

Elijah then returned to his seat and made a show of lighting a cigarette. He offered the packet to Superintendent Cobbe and Sid, who both declined. He even asked if I'd like one, though he knew I never smoked.

I understood what he was doing, and from the look on the superintendent's face, so did he. It was Elijah's way of trying to protect me. He wanted to give me time to gather my thoughts so I wouldn't say anything rash. I breathed in the peaty aroma of the whisky, using the few moments of quiet to calm my mind.

Superintendent Cobbe evidently decided this had gone on long enough, as he asked, 'What were you and Mr Powell arguing about yesterday evening? Had you arranged to meet him?'

'No.' I took a gulp of whisky, enjoying the burning sensation. I'd answer his questions as truthfully as I could, but with a degree of caution. 'I'd spent the day in London. My train arrived in Walden at half past seven, and I left the station and took the lake path. I usually walk home that way. When I got to the lake, Archie was standing on the jetty.'

'And you stopped to speak to him?'

'I tried to ignore him. I was tired and wanted to get home. But he stood in my way so I couldn't get past, and we ended up having a row.'

'What about?'

I shrugged, attempting to appear unconcerned. 'Any conversation I had with Archie usually turned into a quarrel. He was always trying to annoy me.'

'According to witnesses, he seemed to be accusing you of adultery.'

His words hung in the air, and I sipped my whisky, aware of the discomfort of those watching me. I let my eyes rest on each of them in turn. Sid's gaze dropped immediately to his lap. Elijah held my stare momentarily before looking down to stub out his cigarette. Even Superintendent Cobbe shifted uneasily in his chair.

'Archie seemed to believe I was having an affair with a married man.'

'And are you?' The superintendent's pen hovered over his notebook as if to suggest his questions were purely a formality.

'No.'

'What made Mr Powell think you were?'

'Archie blames me for his imprisonment and for losing his position in the church. Ever since he showed up in Walden, he's been trying to make life difficult for me.' I was aware this didn't answer his question.

'I can assure you that it was Mr Powell who was the aggressor,' Elijah interjected. 'Iris tried to keep out of his way and avoid any confrontation.'

Superintendent Cobbe ignored him. 'What was the reason for your trip to London?'

Elijah butted in again. 'Iris has relatives there; she often visits her aunt and grandmother.'

The superintendent smiled even though I suspected Elijah was trying his patience. 'Is that where you were yesterday?'

I shook my head. 'No. I met up with a friend.'

'A male friend?'

'No. Miss Freda Bray. You may remember her? She used to work for Miss Timpson.'

He nodded. 'I remember Miss Bray. Did you spend the day with her?'

'We had lunch together on Fleet Street. It's where she works now. I spent an hour or so with her and then took a bus to The Strand. I looked in a few shops and then got a train home from Waterloo.' I failed to mention that I'd walked from The Strand to St James's Park to meet Marc.

'How long did your argument with Mr Powell last?'

'Not long. Five minutes at most. I had no desire to talk with him, but he blocked my path.'

'Witnesses said they heard you shouting at Mr Powell. Apparently, you called him evil and said that one day he'd get his comeuppance.' He paused. 'And then you hit him.'

Elijah closed his eyes, and I could almost hear the groan he'd had to suppress. I wanted to defend myself, to tell him Archie had provoked me. But what was the point? It would only incriminate me even more.

Hugh Alvarez, Vincent Owen and Paul Richardson had told the police what they'd seen and heard, and I'd be an idiot to try to deny it.

'I was angry. I'd had enough of Archie and his... accusations.' I'd been about to say threats and stopped myself in time. 'I shouldn't have let him goad me into losing my temper. I'm sorry for how I reacted, and I'm embarrassed those men had to witness it. I did slap Archie across his cheek and immediately regretted it. I got away from him as soon as I could and went home.'

'Was that the last time you saw Mr Powell?'

I nodded.

'When was his body found?' Elijah's hand shook as he lit another cigarette.

'Not until this morning. When he didn't come down for breakfast, Mrs Swann went upstairs and knocked on his bedroom door. There was no answer, and as the room wasn't locked, she went inside in case he'd taken ill. There was no sign of him, and his bed hadn't been slept in. Mr Alvarez, Mr Richardson and Mr Owen began to search for him. It was Mr Alvarez who found Mr Powell's body in the garden – in a shallow trench that had been dug for the foundations of a greenhouse.'

'So he'd gone back to Mill Ponds House after his row with Iris?' Elijah sounded relieved.

'He must have done, although no one saw him return. The last sighting we have of him was when he was with Miss Woodmore by the jetty.'

'What time was he killed?' Elijah asked.

'I hope the pathologist will shed some light on that.' Superintendent Cobbe clearly wasn't going to share much more with us, but Elijah tried another question.

'Did anyone hear the shot being fired?'

The superintendent shook his head. 'That end of the garden is close to the railway line. It's possible the sound of trains muffled the noise. Or simply that no one was around when the rifle went off. There are no other houses nearby.'

'Could it have been an accident?' I asked.

'It's something we're looking into.' Superintendent Cobbe's eyes were fixed on me again. 'Earlier, you said, "his own rifle". Sergeant Gilbert tells me you complained to him that Mr Powell had a rifle in his possession. How did you know?'

'On the open day at Mill Ponds House, Archie insisted on showing me the work they're doing in the new garden. He wanted me to mention it in an article. He took me over to the shed and opened the doors. Inside was a rifle leaning against the wall.'

'Did you touch it at any point?'

I shook my head. 'I got the impression Archie had taken me there on purpose so that I'd see it. He knew it would shock me.'

'Did he handle the rifle?'

I swallowed hard, knowing what I was about to say would give Superintendent Cobbe even more reason to suspect me of being involved in Archie's death.

'He picked it up and pointed it at me. He said it was to kill pests. Rabbits and pigeons. And women who need to be reminded of their place.'

11

'Archie's causing trouble even in death.' I regretted the words as soon as they left my mouth.

Unable to bear the look Elijah gave me, I buried my face in my hands. He'd been silent since the policemen had left, Superintendent Cobbe warning me not to leave Walden as it was likely he'd need to speak to me again.

I heard Elijah strike a match and draw on his cigarette. 'You're not sorry he's dead? I thought you once cared for him?'

In truth, I had no idea what I was feeling. The facts had barely sunk in. I allowed myself to think back to the man I'd first met. The attractive and intriguing man who I'd had a physical longing for. He'd been exciting, unpredictable and charismatic.

But the man I'd argued with on the jetty had been mean and bitter. Was I sorry he was dead?

I looked up. 'I don't know how I feel about Archie. He was a contradictory man. I'm sure there are many who will eulogise him at his funeral. And they won't be wrong. He did try to help his fellow man. But there was another darker side to him... and I think he was finding it difficult to suppress that.'

'Did you hate him?' Elijah asked.

I nodded. 'I'd come to hate him because I felt he was driving me away from...' My throat became tight with emotion. 'From here. From people I love.'

'Is that why you met with Freda Bray? She works for *Time & Tide*, doesn't she?'

'I asked her to find out if there were any permanent positions at the magazine. It was just... I wasn't sure...' I stumbled over my words, feeling I'd betrayed him.

'You could have told me. I wouldn't have stopped you from going if that's what you wanted.'

This made me feel even worse. 'I'm not sure what I wanted. It was like I was being trapped by him, and I had to get away.'

'At the open day, when I said there wasn't much we could do about Archie's presence in Walden, you told me not to be so sure; that his stay might not be as permanent as he thinks. What did you mean?'

'I don't know.' I truly couldn't remember what I'd been thinking when I said that. 'I guess I had a feeling that something would happen to make him leave. That he'd trip himself up in some way.'

More clumping boots could be heard on the stairs, and I welcomed the interruption as long as it wasn't the police. It was, but I was relieved to see the sympathetic brown eyes of Sergeant Ben Gilbert peer around the door.

'Come in, lad.' Elijah looked relieved to see him, too. 'I guess this is an unofficial visit. Should you be speaking to us?'

'Strictly off the record.' Ben removed his hat and ran a hand through his cropped sandy hair. 'I'm not on the case. I can't be after what Archie did to me.'

Of course. Stupidly, I'd thought my friendship with Ben was the reason Sid had accompanied Superintendent Cobbe.

'Are you a suspect, too?' I asked.

Ben sat in the chair that the superintendent had recently vacated. 'Whether we're suspects will depend on what the pathologist comes back with. Once the time of death has been established, we're both likely to be asked where we were at the time.'

'Cobbe said Archie was shot with a rifle. Do you know the make?' Elijah stubbed out his cigarette and picked up a pen.

'Not yet. The pathologist will remove the bullet, and a ballistics expert will compare it to the one fired from the rifle we found in the shed.'

'What the hell was the man doing with a rifle in the first place?' Elijah waved his pen, splattering black ink over his desk. 'Surely the police weren't daft enough to give him a certificate?'

'After Iris told me what happened on the open day, I went to Mill Ponds and searched the shed. I couldn't find anything. When I asked Archie about it, he said you must have seen a hunting rifle that didn't belong to him.'

'Then whose was it?'

'He claimed it belonged to Mrs Jennifer Tolfree. When I spoke to her, she said she'd taken her rifle to Mill Ponds to help keep the garden free of pests. She and her husband attend shoots and have certificates for their firearms.'

Elijah whistled. 'It could have been her rifle that killed Archie?'

'We won't know until we check with our ballistics expert. Somehow, I doubt it. The rifle we found in the shed after Archie's death was a Lee-Enfield SMLE Mark III. That's a military weapon, not a hunting rifle. There are a lot of them about

since the war. It's the same type Archie used in his shootings.'
Ben turned to me. 'You're sure the rifle you saw in the shed was
a Lee-Enfield?'

I nodded. 'I think so. I don't know what mark it was.'

'It's unlikely Mrs Tolfree would take that type of rifle to a
shooting party. I think Archie knew you'd tell me about the gun
and persuaded her to cover for him by saying it was hers.'

'That wouldn't surprise me.' I told them about Archie and
Jennifer's conversation in the rose garden at Mill Ponds. 'Something was going on between them, although I'm not sure what.'

Ben's brow furrowed. 'I knew she was lying. I think the Lee-
Enfield rifle did belong to Archie – and I bet it turns out to be
the one used to kill him.'

No one said what must have been in all our minds.
Retribution. Archie had fired a rifle at two women. And hit Ben
with one of the bullets. Had someone decided to take revenge?
No doubt, Superintendent Cobbe would be thinking along the
same lines, which made Ben an obvious suspect.

'It was fired from a distance. According to Sid, it looked like
someone picked up the rifle in the shed and pointed it at
Archie, who was digging the foundations for the greenhouse at
the far end of the garden. He was hit in the back.'

I felt cold despite the warmth of the day and shuddered.
'Was it quick? His death, I mean.'

Ben hesitated. 'He bled to death. If he'd been found immediately, it's possible, with treatment, he might have survived.
Sadly, he wasn't. It's likely he'd lain there all night.'

I closed my eyes, grief finally beginning to hit me. I thought
back to the first time I'd seen Archie. He'd been standing on
the steps of St Mary's Church in Deptford, and I'd noticed his
muscular physique and lean features. When he'd turned to
look at me, I'd been struck by his intense green eyes – and the

dog collar around his neck. I remembered the instant attraction, the chemistry. The kisses. Then, later, the realisation of his true character.

'It's a shame no one heard the shot,' Elijah remarked.

'That end of the garden is close to the railway line. It's possible a train was going by at the time. Or no one took any notice of the noise. Shotguns are often fired in the woods around there, and gardeners sometimes use them to keep pests off their allotments. Superintendent Cobbe and Sid will be interviewing everyone at Mill Ponds again to see if they saw or heard anything.'

I closed my eyes, picturing Archie lying bleeding on the ground. I'd spent months hating him, wishing him gone. But not like this.

'Does the superintendent really think I could have shot him?' Over the years, I'd developed a thick skin. I'd had no choice. I knew people in the town considered me something of an oddity, and I could understand why. I didn't conform to their views of how a young lady should dress and behave. But I was horrified that anyone could believe I was capable of firing a rifle at someone and leaving them to die.

'You were one of the last people to see Archie alive. Superintendent Cobbe has to interview you. Whether he suspects you or not...' Ben trailed off. 'He isn't rushing to any conclusions. He's talking to everyone Archie had contact with. Particularly anyone who showed animosity towards him recently.'

I groaned as a thought occurred to me. 'A factory full of workers heard a blazing row between Daniel Timpson and Archie.'

Ben frowned. 'If the superintendent knows, I suspect his next visit will be to Crookham Hall.'

'It wasn't Daniel's fault. The way Archie behaved at times...'
I rubbed my temples, hoping to ease the throbbing in my head.

'Why did he accuse you of adultery?' Elijah's question felt
like a punch to the stomach. 'There are many things he could
attack you for. Why adultery? What did he know? Or think he
knew?'

'I'm not sure,' I croaked. My mouth felt dry, and the
hammering in my head and chest was getting worse. I had no
way of answering this without making things worse. If I told
them Archie had been following me, I'd have to explain what
he'd discovered. And I wasn't going to bring Marc into this
mess.

Elijah reached for his cigarettes. 'I'm trying to help you.
And, as usual, you're not making it easy for me.'

Ben glanced between the two of us, seeming hesitant to
speak.

I looked at him with tears in my eyes. 'Is that what you're
here for? To ask me if I'm an adulteress. Or if I killed Archie?'

Ben rose from his chair and came over to me, putting his
hand on my shoulder. 'I'm here to make sure you're okay. And
to advise you to talk to your family and friends. Rumours are
flying around town, and those closest to you are likely to hear
them. They also might be on the receiving end of some hostility. Archie was popular with many.'

It felt like blow upon blow was raining down on me. But
Ben was right. I had to face up to what was happening.

I breathed deeply, then wiped my eyes with my handkerchief. 'My father and Katherine are in Devon. They won't be
back for another month.'

Would all this be resolved by the time they returned? Even
if it were, rumours would still be circulating. My father was
oblivious to town gossip, but my stepmother, Katherine, was a

member of the Walden Women's Group. She'd almost certainly be subjected to remarks from some of the ladies who'd been smitten with Archie.

Ben knelt beside my chair. 'You need to speak to Millicent and Ursula. Millicent is likely to hear comments at school.'

I nodded, letting him pull me into an embrace. The repercussions of what had happened to Archie were just beginning to dawn on me. And the worst thing was, it wasn't only me who would be affected. Those closest to me were going to be dragged into this nightmare.

12

When I arrived home that evening, it was clear from Millicent and Ursula's faces they'd heard what had happened.

Millicent was usually well informed about the goings-on in town, courtesy of her pupils and their parents. As for Ursula, well, no one quite knew where she got her information from, but it was almost always accurate and up to date.

Without saying a word, the three of us convened in Ursula's book room, which was part library, part curiosity shop. It smelt of old books and sweet sherry. The furniture was an eclectic mix of styles. The most striking piece was a teak table embedded with jewels and decorated with carvings of elephants and tigers. It was an extraordinary piece of furniture Ursula's father had brought back from India a hundred years ago.

'Are they sure it wasn't an accident? One of the men larking around?' Ursula placed the sherry bottle and three small glasses on the table, then reclined in her favourite armchair, her feet resting on a foot stool.

'It's possible. Superintendent Cobbe wasn't giving much

away. He'll be questioning the occupants of the hostel again.' I slumped down into the cushions of a colourful chintz sofa.

Millicent poured us each a glass of sherry, then sat down beside me. 'I don't understand what all this has to do with you. The police can't believe you're involved.'

'It's the timing of the thing. I had a row with Archie on my way home from the station yesterday.' When I told them what had happened, they didn't seem surprised. 'You've heard the gossip?'

Millicent nodded. 'It's been hard to avoid. Most of it ridiculous.'

She said 'most', but not all, I noticed.

Ursula peered at me through her thick glasses. 'This rumour about adultery. Does it have anything to do with your London boyfriend? The one who doesn't have a name.'

Elijah had asked why Archie had chosen to throw that particular accusation at me. He had no inkling of my relationship with Marc. The same couldn't be said for Millicent and Ursula.

During the nine months I'd lived with them, they'd come to recognise the neat handwriting on the envelopes with a London postmark that regularly dropped through the letterbox. I told them they were from someone I'd met during the war, never mentioning a name. One morning, Ursula had examined the handwriting and decided the writer was a clever young man. Since then, they'd dubbed my secret correspondent my 'London boyfriend'.

'I've told you before. He's an old friend. Not a boyfriend.'

'Is he married?' Ursula wasn't going to back down.

I knew she and Millicent had long suspected this was the case. It was no wonder, as I'd refused to give my 'old friend' a name. The reason I hadn't is because Millicent had met Marc and his wife, Annette, the previous summer.

I sipped my sherry and closed my eyes, savouring the sweet flavour accompanied by the welcome kick of alcohol. I was buying time before answering, and Ursula probably knew it.

Lying was pointless, so I nodded. 'It's not an affair or anything like that.'

'But it's not a simple friendship, either, is it?' Ursula regarded me through narrow eyes. 'How did Archie find out about it?'

'Last year, he started spying on me. You remember I went to the Tolfrees' New Year's Eve party? I left early, and Archie followed me home. That's when he told me he'd seen me in London with... with my friend.'

'Did he follow you to London yesterday?' Ursula asked.

'I don't think so. I guess he was just making an assumption because I got off the London train. I'd been to Fleet Street to meet Freda Bray.' I knew I was lying by omission, but there would be no more letters from my London boyfriend, no more meetings, so why reveal his name now?

'The journalist at *Time & Tide*?' Millicent clearly remembered Freda. 'Are you looking for a new job?'

'I was curious to find out what my prospects were.'

'Do you want to leave here?' Millicent didn't appear happy about this.

'No. I don't. It's just...' I took a deep breath. 'Archie was making my life a misery. I wanted to get away from him. And now he's dead, and everyone knows about the argument we had; I wonder if I should go. Only I can't because Superintendent Cobbe might think I'm running away.'

Millicent put her arm around my shoulder. 'I shall put anyone right if they dare to suggest you had any involvement in what happened just because you quarrelled with Archie. I know I shouldn't speak ill of the dead, but the odious man must have had plenty of enemies.'

I refrained from saying that Daniel Timpson was one of them.

Ursula nodded. 'I'm sure he did. And I think when Superintendent Cobbe starts digging a little deeper, he's going to uncover them.'

She looked troubled, and I suspected she was worried about what else the police investigation would reveal. And so was I.

13

The following morning, I found a message from Elijah on my desk. It said he was having an editorial meeting with Horace at Heron Bay Lodge and wouldn't be in until later. I scrunched up the note and threw it into the wastepaper basket.

Horace Laffaye was the owner of *The Walden Herald* and Laffaye Printworks. I'd long come to realise he'd created the newspaper out of love – a gift to Elijah, his partner in more than just business. They shared a love forbidden by law, and although I knew the true nature of their relationship, it was a secret that was never mentioned.

Their editorial meetings usually took place in the afternoons, when they'd indulge in brandy, cigars and the latest gossip. I was surplus to requirements on these occasions. Today's early morning meeting reflected the seriousness of the situation and no doubt my suspected involvement in Archie's murder was top of the agenda.

I knew they'd be worried about me and felt another wave of guilt at the distress I was causing my friends. But I also felt a glimmer of hope. Horace Laffaye was a wealthy businessman, a former banker who'd traded on Wall Street. During his career, he'd built up a vast network of contacts, and if we ever needed information that was hard to come by, Horace would get one of his spies to do some digging. He'd been known to employ methods frowned upon by the police, though I wouldn't be averse to him using them on my behalf. Would it come to that, I wondered?

Rather than sit in an empty office and brood on this, I decided to take advantage of Elijah's absence and walk to the lake. I dumped my satchel on my desk, locked up the office and went back out onto Queens Road.

I hurried along the footpath that led to Waldenmere, my anxiety making me walk faster than was necessary. When I reached Grebe Stream, I slowed my pace and steadied my breathing.

I followed the curves of the stream as it wound its way into Waldenmere, the flow of water calming my heightened emotions. I had to view the situation dispassionately if I was to make sense of it.

Did Superintendent Cobbe believe I could have crept into the garden of Mill Ponds, shot Archie with his own rifle, and then gone home again? It was beyond belief. Yet it seemed that's exactly what someone had done. It felt like some kind of preposterous joke.

Perhaps it had been an accident – someone larking about with the rifle, firing it in the wrong direction with devastating consequences. I'd been replaying similar scenarios in my head all night, yet I still couldn't picture the circumstances.

Even though I knew visiting Mill Ponds would be risky, I kept walking in that direction. When I reached the railway line, I spotted a familiar figure standing by the gate to the allotments.

Ben smiled when he saw me. 'I guess you're thinking the same as me. You want to go in and take a look at where it happened.'

I followed his gaze. Another gate at the far end of the allotments took you to a track leading up to an arched bridge over the railway line. If you crossed the track, another gate led into the newly extended gardens of Mill Ponds.

'Is Superintendent Cobbe around?'

Ben shook his head. 'He's back at the station house with Sid.'

I pushed open the gate and went into the allotments.

'This isn't a good idea,' Ben said, following me anyway.

I glanced around at the neat rows of vegetable beds. Fresh green shoots were everywhere, an enticement to all sorts of garden pests, from slugs and snails to pigeons and rabbits.

'Could it have been an accident? A gardener trying to scare away birds eating the new growth?'

'Unlikely. Sid told me Archie had been digging out a trench for the foundations of the greenhouse. The shot was fired from the direction of the shed, and he fell forward over the spade in his hand.'

We walked out of the gate at the far end of the allotments and onto the track by the bridge. Vehicles coming across the bridge had to drive a short way along the track before taking a sharp right turn onto the driveway of Mill Ponds. We crossed to the garden gate and peered over. All was quiet.

'Someone could have done what we're doing and got into the garden through the back gate, either coming through the allotments or walking up the track from the lake path.'

'They could have, but that would have meant them walking past Archie to get to the position where the shot came from.' Ben pushed open the gate. 'The indications are he didn't see the person, as the shot hit him in the back. That meant it must have been fired from the end nearest the walled kitchen garden. The most likely scenario is that someone picked up the rifle in the shed.'

With trepidation, I followed Ben through the gate into the garden of Mill Ponds. 'What do you think the person did after they fired the rifle?'

'Put it back where they found it and walked through the house or around it. Or they left via this gate and walked down to the lake path or through the allotments.' Ben had clearly been thinking about this as much as I had, with the advantage of knowing details of the crime scene from Sid.

'If they had come this way, they would have passed the body.' I felt nauseous at the thought of Archie lying in pain.

'If they had, they would have seen he wasn't yet dead. According to the pathologist, he died of blood loss. It's tragic his body wasn't found until the next day. If he'd received medical attention immediately, there's a slim chance he might have survived.'

My voice was hoarse when I spoke. 'Someone must have hated him a lot to have left him to die.'

'If they went through the house, they may not have realised he was still alive.'

'But they must have known they'd shot him. They can't have mistaken him for a bird or an animal.'

'It seems unlikely,' Ben agreed. He walked over to where the foundations for the greenhouse were being prepared. 'He was found here. You'd have to be extremely short-sighted to have fired from the shed and not realised you'd hit a man.'

At that moment, we heard a train approaching Walden station. It got progressively louder as it got nearer. Ben looked at his watch and began to time it. We stood there listening to the sounds of the locomotive rolling over the railway tracks, the puffing of the steam blowing through the stack, and the metallic screech as the train came to a halt at the station. The slamming of doors lasted a few minutes before the train moved off again and chugged into the distance.

Ben took out his pocketbook to make notes. 'You wouldn't be able to discern rifle fire above the sound of a locomotive. Even when it was stationary, it still made a noise. A train stopping at Walden would allow someone at least five to ten minutes to take a shot, even one passing through would give them a few minutes.'

'There was one train an hour on the line from London on Sunday afternoon. It stopped in Walden at half past the hour. The last train would have come through at half past ten.' I'd checked the timetable as I wasn't sure how long I'd spend with Marc that day.

'The train from Southampton going up to London stops at Walden on the hour.' Ben made more notes. 'The last one came through at ten o'clock. So there would have been a train going through every half an hour until ten-thirty that night. Then there would be a gap until the paper train arrived at six-thirty.'

'I suppose no one in the house heard the shot?'

He shook his head. 'Our best bet is the allotments. Sid's going to speak to all the railway workers who rent an allotment from Southern Railway.'

'Was anything found by the body?' My nausea returned as I peered into the trench. It was obvious where Archie had lain by the dark stain in the mud.

'No. Sid didn't find anything, and he searched the whole garden. A more extensive search still needs to be carried out of the allotments.' Ben began to walk towards the shed. 'It looked like the shot was fired from a distance. Sid and I think from about thirty yards away.'

I hurried after him, glad to get away from the blood-stained trench and the dank smell that hung in the air.

'You think it was fired from inside the shed?'

Ben nodded. 'Or close to the doors. The rifle was found leaning against the wall. It must have been the one he pointed at you. Sid found a used cartridge next to it.'

A vision of the tower of St Mary's Church in Deptford came into my head. It was where Archie had fired a shot at Constance Timpson while she was giving a speech in the court-yard of the factory opposite. No weapon was found at the scene, but a single shell case had been left behind.

Ben read my mind. 'You're thinking of Deptford.'

I nodded. 'Is it possible this was a form of revenge?'

'If that's the case, then I'm going to be top of Superinten-dent Cobbe's list of suspects.'

I couldn't imagine the superintendent would seriously suspect Ben. It was true he'd been the only one physically hurt by Archie's attacks, but others had suffered as a consequence of them.

I glanced inside the shed. It was filled with the usual garden tools, plant pots and packets of seeds. Nothing looked out of place. 'Where's the rifle now?' I asked.

'In Winchester, being tested for fingerprints before being given to ballistics to check if it's the one that was used. The bullet removed from Archie's body will be taken for comparison.'

'What does Jennifer Tolfree have to say about this rifle? I'm presuming it wasn't hers?'

Ben shook his head. 'She's changed her story. She now claims she was mistaken about bringing her hunting rifle over to Mill Ponds. She says Archie once asked to borrow it to use on garden pests, and she thought she might have lent it to him. She assumed that was what I was referring to when I mentioned a rifle in the shed. However, later, she remembered that she'd decided against lending it to him, realising it might be inappropriate.'

I snorted. 'Did you believe her?'

He grinned. 'Not a word.'

'Did any of the Tolfrees see Archie on Sunday?'

'They all saw him at church in the morning but not after. Only Gordon has admitted to visiting Mill Ponds that day. He called in at nine o'clock that night to collect the accounts. Hugh Alvarez, Paul Richardson and Vincent Owen had returned from their walk at around twenty past eight and were eating sandwiches in the lounge when he arrived. He asked where Archie was, and they said they didn't know. He spent a short time in the study, only about five minutes, and then left.'

'None of them saw Archie after I did?'

'No one's admitting to it. I'm guessing he came out here shortly after his row with you. The fact he was digging indicates it must have still been light. We need to find out exactly what he'd been doing all afternoon. He was seen riding off on his bicycle at about a quarter to six, yet he didn't appear to have it with him later on at the lake. We haven't been able to locate it. Did you see a bicycle nearby when you argued with him?'

I thought back to the scene by the jetty. 'I don't think so. Where's it normally kept?'

'In fine weather, Archie would leave it leaning against the wall outside the study. If it were wet, he'd put it in the shed. Whoever shot him could have—'

A cough behind us made me swing around.

To my dismay, Superintendent Cobbe and PC Sid King were striding across the garden towards us.

14

Sid shot Ben an apologetic look as he and Superintendent Cobbe stopped by the open doors of the shed.

'Sergeant Gilbert. May I ask what you're doing here?'

'I was on my rounds, sir.'

The superintendent raised his eyebrows. 'And your rounds brought you here?'

'Curiosity brought me here, sir,' Ben replied. 'I apologise.'

Superintendent Cobbe considered him for a moment. 'You might as well help PC King search the allotments along the railway line.'

'Yes, sir.' Ben seemed pleased to be set this unenviable task.

The superintendent turned to me. 'Miss Woodmore. I've no doubt curiosity brought you here, too. It saves me a visit to your office. Come with me.'

With an apprehensive glance at Ben, I followed Superintendent Cobbe through to the kitchen garden. He walked around the side of the house to the French doors of the study, where I'd seen Archie talking with Jennifer Tolfree. I wondered how she was taking the news of his death.

In the study, Superintendent Cobbe sat at the desk that had once been General Cheverton's. I looked around, remembering the night Elijah and I had broken in, and spotted the burn mark on the carpet where we'd dropped a lit match.

'I'm sorry to have to interview you here. This room must hold painful memories.'

'It's fine.' The superintendent didn't know the half of it, and I wouldn't be enlightening him.

'I want to ask you a few more questions about your activities on Sunday the eleventh of May. What time did you catch a train to London?'

'Ten-thirty.'

'Did you see Mr Powell on your way to the station that morning?'

I shook my head.

'Mr Whittle mentioned you often visit your grandmother and aunt when you go to London. Why didn't you on this occasion?'

'I didn't have time. They live in Hither Green. I was meeting Miss Bray in Fleet Street.'

'You had all afternoon. You could have taken the bus there.'

'I wanted to go to the shops.'

'On a Sunday?' He didn't bother to hide his scepticism. 'What did you buy?'

'Nothing. Few shops were open.' I was aware I was floundering. 'I like browsing the shop windows in London. It makes a change from Walden High Street.'

'I imagine it does.' To my relief, he changed tack. 'When you saw Mr Powell, what was he wearing?'

'Black. He often wore black. Black trousers and shirt. I got the impression he was attempting to look like a vicar.'

He seemed amused. 'Did you ever say that to him?'

'I once asked him if he was missing his cassock.' I remembered the flash of fury that had crossed his face when I'd made the comment. He'd looked as though he'd been tempted to strike me but thought better of it.

The superintendent's lips twitched. 'When was that?'

'On New Year's Eve. Mr and Mrs Tolfree invited me to Sycamore Lodge for a party. I left early, and Archie followed me, wearing a black cloak.'

'Why did he follow you?'

I shrugged. 'I told you. Ever since he showed up in Walden, he tried to make life difficult for me, either by frightening me or goading me into an argument with him.'

He steepled his fingers together. 'Before his arrest in November 1922, had you been intimate with Mr Powell?'

I squirmed with embarrassment but decided to answer honestly. 'I'd been attracted to him. We'd... we'd kissed a few times. Then I became aware of what he was really like. When I found out what he'd done, I went to the police. He never forgave me for that. He thought he had a hold over me and could persuade me to keep quiet.'

I hadn't wanted to admit my infatuation with Archie, but I guessed Superintendent Cobbe already knew. When Detective Inspector Yates arrested Archie, the intensity of our relationship would have been apparent, and I suspected he'd shared this information with the superintendent.

'You had good reason to hate Mr Powell. He'd pretended to like you, yet he'd fired his rifle at two women you're close to. And his bullet hit your friend, Sergeant Gilbert. On the open day, he even pointed a rifle at you. Did you hate him?'

'I hated him being here in Walden. I was angry.'

'Yet you did nothing about it.'

'What could I do? Everyone seemed to think he was a reformed character.'

'But you didn't. You've admitted he either tried to frighten or goad you.' He paused, and I knew what was coming next. 'Why did he believe you were seeing a married man?'

This was a question I couldn't risk answering. If I said Archie had seen me with an old friend and made assumptions, the superintendent would want to know this friend's name. And I had no name to give him.

'I think he just liked to annoy me. He's never forgiven me for what I did.' I tried to sound dismissive but didn't quite pull it off.

'I get the impression there's more to this than you're saying.' Superintendent Cobbe leant back in his chair and sighed. When I was silent, he began again. 'Who was at home when you returned on the evening of the eleventh?'

'Millicent and her great-aunt, Ursula. We had supper together, and then I went to my room.'

'Did you go out again that night?'

I was tempted to lie, but if someone had seen me, I'd only get into more trouble. 'Yes. I had a headache and decided to take a stroll.'

'What time was this, and where did you go?'

'I suppose it would have been around half past eight, perhaps a little later. I walked to the lake to clear my head and then went home again.'

'Did you go to the jetty?'

'Yes.'

'Were you expecting to meet Mr Powell there?'

'No.'

'Wasn't it a bit late to be going for a walk on your own? It must have been dark.'

I shrugged. 'As I said, I had a headache. It was darker than I'd expected, so I went home by the main road. I think I got back at around twenty past nine.'

'Did you meet anyone on your walk?'

'No. It was quiet.' My face flushed at this outright lie, but a terrifying thought had occurred to me. Archie might have been murdered while Marc was in Walden.

After what Ben had said, it seemed likely that someone had killed Archie before it got dark. I'd been the last person to see him at the jetty at seven-thirty, and the sun was setting by eight-thirty. Marc must have been in Walden for some of that time.

Even if I told the superintendent that Marc knew nothing of Archie's existence, I didn't think he'd believe me. He'd want to question Marc, and that was something I couldn't allow to happen. Not when he was about to return to Belgium to embark on a new life with his family.

'Alright. We'll leave it there. For now,' he added.

I didn't need telling twice, and shot out of my chair, closing the study door behind me. In the hallway, I was about to head for the front door when I heard Vincent Owen's gloomy voice coming from the lounge.

'What do you think will happen to this place?'

I'd intended to escape from Mill Ponds before Superintendent Cobbe could change his mind. However, I lingered in the hallway by the open door of the lounge, curious to know how the three residents were feeling after Archie's death.

'They'll appoint a new manager, and it will carry on as planned.'

I recognised Hugh Alvarez's confident voice.

'I hope so.' Paul Richardson sounded as miserable as Vincent. 'I don't have anywhere else to go.'

'Archie wasn't indispensable,' Hugh said. 'And after what we saw, I don't think he would have lasted here much longer anyway.'

I heard murmurs of agreement from the other two men. Hoping the superintendent wouldn't suddenly emerge from the study and catch me eavesdropping, I moved closer to the door.

'The vicar had started to notice, too,' Paul muttered.

Notice what, I wondered?

'And he kept disappearing. Not telling anyone where he was going,' This was followed by the crackling sound of Vincent drawing on his pipe. The aroma of spicy tobacco drifted from the room.

I heard the curiosity in Hugh's voice as he asked, 'What did you mean the other day when you said he'd be off to the summerhouse again?'

'I meant he'd be working on the greenhouse in the garden.'

Even from outside the room, I could tell Vincent was lying.

'He didn't spend much time in the garden as far as I could see. And you said summerhouse, not greenhouse,' Hugh insisted. 'Besides, Archie wasn't going into the garden. He cycled out to the lake path and turned left—'

To my annoyance, I heard a movement from inside the study and had to run for it. I was too far from the front door to leave without being seen, so I dashed into the kitchen instead.

15

Polly, who'd been slicing calves' liver at the kitchen table, looked up with a start, brandishing the knife in her hand as I burst through the door.

'I'm sorry. I didn't mean to scare you.' I took a step back, realising she might actually believe I was a murderer. 'I'll go if you want.'

She let out a long breath. 'I didn't realise how on edge I was. Come in, love. I'm not frightened of you,' she said with a laugh. 'I don't believe the rumours. Not the ones about you shooting him anyway.'

Polly washed her hands at the sink before flopping into a chair. I pulled up another to join her, wondering which rumour she did believe. Probably the one about me seeing a married man.

'It must be horrible for you.' I tried to avoid looking at the bloody liver on the chopping board. Its earthy smell permeated the kitchen.

'I took the job because I was bored at home now the children are at school all day.' She gave a wan smile. 'I didn't think it would be this lively. Micky wants me to leave. But who'll keep this place going if I do? I've got three men to feed and more arriving at the weekend. They'll be homeless if they can't stay here.'

Polly was more indispensable than Archie, I realised. 'Do you know what's going to happen to Mill Ponds?'

'Reverend Childs, Mr Tolfree and Mrs Siddons said we should try to carry on as normal while they look for a new manager. They said it's what Archie would have wanted, and I think they're right.'

'What about Mrs Tolfree?'

'Which one? Jennifer hasn't been seen since it happened. I've got a feeling she won't be spending as much time here now.' She shot me a meaningful glance.

'Were she and Archie...?'

Polly shrugged. 'She was keen on him. I could never make out what he thought of her. Gertrude's been a tower of strength. Even helping me out with getting meals ready. She was always more practically minded than Jennifer. She and Gordon want to make sure no one suffers because of this.'

'Were they upset about Archie?'

'Gertrude was. Gordon less so.'

This was interesting. Archie and Gordon were once friends. When had their relationship cooled and why? Perhaps Gordon hadn't been as oblivious to his wife's feelings for Archie as he'd seemed.

'When did you last see Archie?' I asked.

'At lunchtime on Sunday. I'd cooked them a proper roast. Micky and the children came over to help me, and we roasted chicken and potatoes and boiled up cabbage and swede. Archie had lunch with the men, and when I went to clear the table, he thanked me as usual. Always polite.' Polly began to look tearful.

'How did he seem?'

'The same as normal. He'd been to church that morning and came back in good spirits. I told them all at breakfast I'd be serving lunch at two o'clock and not to be late. I'm not normally strict about the time if it's an informal lunch, but if I'm cooking a proper meal, I want it to be eaten when it's hot on the table. My youngest is a terror for disappearing just as I'm dishing up his tea.'

'What did Archie do after lunch?'

'He went into the study to finish the accounts to give to Mr Tolfree. I do all the shopping, and we have credit with the butcher, fishmonger, baker, greengrocer and Fellowes Emporium. They bill us at the end of each week, and when I took the receipts in to Archie, he said, "I don't know how you manage to feed us so well for so little." I told him I'd had plenty of practice.'

'I'm sure everyone here is grateful to you for looking after them.'

'Me and Micky know what it's like. Without help, we would never have got out of that damp basement flat. We've often said God must have brought us to Walden for a purpose. And now we know what it is. It's this place.' She gazed around the well-organised kitchen. 'That's why we brought the children over for a couple of hours on Sunday to help out. We want them to understand that you have to repay kindness with kindness.'

I smiled at the loaves of bread cooling on the rack and the colander of green beans resting on the draining board. 'I'm sure Archie would have wanted you to carry on his work here.'

'That's what I thought. I felt very proud when he said it was my household management that would keep this place going.' She sniffed. 'It was the last thing he said to me.'

'What time was that?' Not for the first time, I ruminated over what a contradictory character Archie Powell had been. He could be so kind to some people yet so nasty to others.

'Just before I left at about three-thirty. He was in the study, and Hugh, Paul and Vincent were in the garden working on the greenhouse. Micky had taken the children to play by the lake while I cleared up, and then we all cycled home. I didn't come back that night as there was enough food in the larder for the men to make themselves sandwiches. And Archie often spends Sunday evenings at the church with the vicar.'

'When did you come back?'

'Not until the following morning. I got here at seven-thirty, made breakfast and took it into the dining room. Hugh, Paul and Vincent were down by eight o'clock, but no Archie, which was unusual as he's normally up and about when I arrive. I went upstairs and knocked on his bedroom door. When there was no answer, I went in and saw his bed hadn't been slept in. I wasn't too worried because I saw his bicycle had gone.' Polly's face crumpled. 'I'm not sure if Hugh went into the garden to search for Archie or his bicycle. And there he was.'

At that moment, I could hear noises outside and looked up to see Hugh, Vincent and Paul pass the window. I got up and peered out into the yard. Once the men had disappeared through the gate into the kitchen garden, I couldn't see or hear them.

'I suppose you only know someone's in the garden if you see them walk past the window?'

Polly nodded. 'No one had any idea Archie was out there. It's horrible to imagine him lying there all night.'

I rejoined her at the kitchen table. 'Did he often work in the garden?'

She shook her head. 'I think he must have been in a mood.'

'What makes you say that?'

'He returned from church one Sunday and was...' She paused. 'Not angry, but not happy about something. He got changed, went outside and began digging. I suppose it was a way of getting out his frustrations.'

'When was that?'

'A few weeks ago. Around Easter time. In fact, I think it was Easter Sunday. I was upstairs with Jennifer, sorting out linen for the bedrooms, when we saw him through the window. She went out to talk to him, but I stayed where I was, watching them. She must have got short shrift as she came back in looking upset.'

I wondered what or who had caused Archie to take his frustration out on the garden this time. Had he been distressed by our confrontation earlier that evening? I got the impression he'd rather enjoyed his theatrical performance – and its outcome. So, if I wasn't behind his change of mood, who had prompted him to come back and start digging?

'Did all the residents get on with Archie?' I asked.

'Yes. Although...' Polly hesitated. 'I don't like to speak ill of the dead, but I think we'd all noticed he was drinking a bit too much.'

I nodded. I'd smelt it on his breath when we'd argued. It was something I'd forgotten to mention to Superintendent Cobbe. Is this what the men had been referring to when they said the vicar had noticed too?

'Did anyone ever comment on it?'

'I once overheard Hugh say something about it being a bit early for the hard stuff.'

'What did Archie say?'

'He tried to laugh it off. Said something like, "You don't know the morning I've had," though I could see by the look on his face he hadn't liked Hugh saying it.'

That sounded like Archie. He hated criticism.

'What about the others?'

'Vincent and Paul would never have dared to make a comment like that. They're too grateful to have a room here.'

'And Hugh's not?'

'He doesn't seem as desperate as they do.'

I knew what she meant.

'I could tell Paul was shocked by the changes in Archie,' Polly continued.

'Changes?' I sat forward in my chair. 'They knew each other before?'

'They've known each other for years. Paul was once engaged to one of Archie's sisters.'

16

I left Polly and went out into the kitchen garden, curious to discover what Hugh, Paul and Vincent had meant when I'd overheard them talking about Archie.

I found Paul and Vincent unravelling a ball of string to mark out rows in one of the vegetable beds. Hugh sat nearby on the bench under the arbour, sketching in a large drawing pad. I wandered over to him, and he moved a slim leather roll filled with pencils so I could sit down. He was making bold lines with deft strokes of a thick pencil.

'What are you drawing?' I asked.

'A plan for the layout of the new garden.' Hugh motioned towards the gate leading to the plot of land. 'We're not allowed in there until the police have finished.'

'Mrs Tolfree's been advising us where to position the beds to make the most of the sunlight and where to build trellises.' Vincent finished tying lengths of string to wooden pegs sticking out of the ground, then took his pipe out of his cardigan pocket and began to fill it.

'Jennifer?' I couldn't imagine her as a gardener.

Vincent shook his head. 'Mrs Gertrude Tolfree. She's very knowledgeable about plants. She's been bringing us packets of seeds and cuttings from Sycamore Lodge to get us started.'

'Archie mentioned the plan was to grow more produce for the kitchen.' I remembered his comments on the open day and his enthusiasm for the garden. How long ago that seemed now.

'He wasn't much of a gardener, but he knew a greenhouse would help get things going. That's why he was so keen to get it built.' Paul's eye drifted to the gate. 'I can't believe someone would harm him when all he was trying to do was to help people.'

I noticed Hugh exchange a glance with Vincent. Paul caught the look.

'I know he wasn't perfect,' Paul snapped. 'Far from it. But he never used to be... well, he never used to be that bad.'

Hugh closed his sketch pad and placed it under the bench along with his roll of pencils. He went over to a spade that had been plunged into the earth and began digging in one of the neglected vegetable beds, attacking the ground with vigour. He seemed to have energy to spare, and it made me think of what Polly had said about Archie taking his frustration out on the garden. I got the impression Hugh was feeling cooped up at the hostel and was itching to get out to work.

'Had you known Archie a long time?' I asked Paul as he came to sit beside me. Vincent took his crutch from him and laid it on the ground before joining us on the bench.

'Quite a few years. I was engaged to his sister, Teresa. She doted on him. So did her mother and the other sisters. They're going to be devastated. He was the man of the family, and everything revolved around him.'

I wondered where that would have left Paul if he'd married

Teresa. 'What was he like when he lived at home? It was Greenwich, wasn't it?'

Paul nodded. 'He was a good bloke. Always helping others. Well, that's what I'm going to say in the letter of condolence I write to his family.'

Vincent grunted.

'There was another side to him,' Paul admitted. 'I'd hear stuff in the garage where I worked.'

'What sort of stuff?' I was curious to hear about Archie's life before I'd known him.

Paul flushed a little. 'He was popular with ladies.'

'Married women?'

'Amongst others. It was always hushed up. His family made excuses for him.' Paul frowned. 'Even after he was convicted of those shootings, they wouldn't believe he'd done anything wrong. I thought his time inside might have sorted him out. If anything, it made him worse.'

'You mean he could have been seeing a married woman around here?' I tried for a shocked tone that ended up sounding sarcastic. Given what he'd accused me of, I couldn't help it.

Vincent was puffing on his pipe, but I could have sworn I saw the flicker of a smile.

Paul shrugged. 'I don't want to speak ill of him. He was always kind to me. Got me a room here.'

'When I was arguing with Archie, I could smell alcohol on his breath. Had you noticed anything?' I tried to make it seem like a throwaway question, hoping they wouldn't guess I'd overheard their conversation in the lounge.

Hugh stopped digging and shot me an inquisitive look. I didn't react, and he turned away, pulling his khaki army jumper over his head and throwing it to the ground. When he rolled up his shirt sleeves and resumed digging, I couldn't help glancing across at his broad chest and muscular arms.

Vincent nodded, not seeming surprised by my question. 'We all had. You could tell when he'd had a snifter and not just because of the smell. He'd get a bit belligerent. I'm not a pious man, but one of the hostel rules is that no alcohol is allowed. I think he should have set a better example.'

'I was shocked,' Paul admitted. 'He never used to be like that. He'd have an occasional pint in the pub with me, nothing more. I never saw him touch spirits. We debated whether to tell the vicar or one of the patrons about it.'

Hugh stopped digging and leant on his spade. 'There were other incidents that made us think he wasn't the best person to be running this place. I saw him pointing that rifle at you on the open day. And the way he gripped your arm when you were arguing by the lake.'

'Had you seen the rifle before?' I asked.

'Once. I noticed it when I went to get a spade from the shed. It was leaning against the wall. I was surprised someone would leave it there, but I presumed it was to deal with pests.' Hugh rubbed a stubbly chin. 'Then, after that scene at the Tolfree & Timpson factory, I started asking questions about Archie, and Paul told me his history.'

'I knew he could never have got a permit for that rifle.' Paul's brow creased. 'I wondered if I should tell someone. Then that policeman came. He asked Archie about it, didn't he?'

I nodded. 'Archie told him it must have been Jennifer Tolfree's hunting rifle.'

Vincent shook his head. 'Didn't look like the type of rifle she'd use.'

'She does have a rifle then?'

'Yes, and a shotgun for hunting grouse. She's an excellent

shot. Better than her father.' Vincent drew on his pipe, seeming unaware of the implications of what he'd just said.

By the sardonic expression on Hugh's face and the way Paul shuffled uncomfortably beside me, they both knew Jennifer might have reason to want Archie dead. And the means to do it.

'Who else knew about Archie's rifle?' To be fair to Jennifer, her husband would also be a suspect if he'd discovered something was going on between her and Archie.

'Anyone who worked in the garden would have seen it. I think he hid it for a week after the open day, but it's been back there for the last few days.' Hugh ran a hand through his dark blond hair. 'I regret not doing something about it.'

'I didn't mean to suggest you did anything wrong.' I decided to be frank with them. 'I'm the one the police seem to suspect. That's why I'm trying to find out when and why Archie was killed. Because no matter what the police might think, I never saw him again after our argument by the lake.'

'The only thing we did wrong that night was to take an illicit drink,' Hugh said, clearly deciding to reciprocate my frankness. 'We got back here shortly before half past eight, and there was no sign of Archie. We'd been discussing him on our walk, wondering whether to tell someone about the way he was behaving. We continued the conversation in my bedroom, where I keep a bottle of malt whisky hidden. We couldn't risk talking downstairs in case Archie heard us. Or saw us drinking.'

'You thought he was in the house?'

'At first, we assumed he'd gone back to the church for the evening. His bicycle wasn't outside. But when Vincent and I were in the kitchen getting glasses out of the cupboard to take up to Hugh's room, we saw the shadow of someone walking past the window.' Paul looked to Vincent for confirmation.

Vincent nodded. 'We thought it might have been Archie. We didn't want him to see us with the glasses, so we put them in our pockets and went upstairs. We came downstairs at nine o'clock to make coffee and sandwiches and took them into the lounge. Then Gordon Tolfree came in asking for Archie. When we told him we didn't know where he was, he went into the study for about five or ten minutes, then we heard his car driving away.'

'Could he have gone into the garden during that time?' I pictured the crime scene. 'He might have left the study through the French doors, walked to the back of the house, come through here and then through the gate to the shed where he found the rifle.'

Hugh began brushing mud from the faded black corduroy trousers he was wearing. 'Why, though? How would he know Archie was in the garden?'

I thought about this. 'You say he drove here? He would have had to come over the arched bridge. He might have been able to see the end of the garden from the top of the bridge.' I wasn't entirely sure if this theory would hold water.

'At that time of night?' Hugh shook his head. 'And why would he ask us where Archie was if he already knew?'

'It's possible, though, isn't it?' Vincent chewed his pipe meditatively. 'He could have been pretending not to have seen Archie to cover his tracks.'

'He seems like a nice man to me.' Paul looked at me anxiously. 'You won't tell anyone about the whisky, will you? I don't want to lose my room here.'

I shook my head. 'I'm not interested in getting anyone into trouble. My intention is to get me out of it by finding out who did that to Archie. God knows we weren't friends, but still...'

'Were you friends once?' Hugh was watching me with a

curious expression. 'Archie certainly seemed to have a preoccupation with you.'

I gave a rueful smile. With Archie's reputation, they'd no doubt guessed I'd once fallen for his charm.

'When I first met him, I was intrigued by him. But any attraction soon wore off when I discovered what he was like. I went to the police when I found out he was behind the sniper attacks on Mrs Siddons and Miss Timpson. I also told them where he'd hidden the rifle. He never forgave me for that. To his mind, I betrayed him.'

Hugh thrust his spade into the ground and walked over to me. 'He was threatening you, wasn't he? I saw it at the open day and then again by the lake.'

Reluctantly, I nodded.

'He certainly seemed to have it in for you,' Vincent remarked. 'That's what we were talking about in Hugh's room. It looked like things were getting out of hand. We were worried.'

'I didn't handle the situation very well,' I admitted, touched by their concern.

'You always were the feisty one. So different from Miss Alice.' Vincent's eyes became watery. 'I used to see the pair of you together. She wouldn't have wanted anything bad to happen to you.'

I bit my lip, not trusting myself to speak.

'We thought one of your spats would end with someone getting hurt. We'd imagined it to be you rather than him.' Hugh fixed me with a hard stare. 'Turns out we were wrong.'

17

When I returned home that evening, Millicent took one look at my face and poured me a glass of sherry. At this rate, I'd soon need to make a trip to Fellowes Emporium to replenish our dwindling supply.

'You may get a visit from Superintendent Cobbe,' I said as we joined Ursula for a pre-supper drink in her book room. It had occurred to me that the superintendent would probably want to check the information I'd given him.

'We already have,' Ursula informed me. She seemed unperturbed by the event, but Millicent appeared nervous.

'Did he ask you about the evening of the eleventh?'

'I told him you went out at half past eight and came back around three-quarters of an hour later, and I didn't know where you'd gone,' Millicent said in a rush. 'I'm sorry. I hope I didn't get you into trouble. One minute, you said you were going to get your cardigan and sit in the garden; the next, I heard you going out the front door.'

'You have nothing to be sorry for.' I felt unbearably guilty at what I was putting her through. 'I told Superintendent Cobbe I'd gone for a walk to ease a headache.'

Millicent sank into the cushions in relief, but Ursula sat forward in her armchair.

'Did you go anywhere near Mill Ponds?' she asked.

'I went as far as the jetty by the station. And I was only there for a few minutes before I came back.' I was lying by omission yet again, and it didn't feel good. 'It was darker than I realised.'

Millicent bit down on an ink-stained thumbnail – an action she would have reprimanded a pupil for. 'Superintendent Cobbe questioned Daniel, too. He wanted to know where he was on Sunday night. Daniel was out riding on the estate on his own. No one saw him between seven-thirty and nine o'clock. Will that matter?'

'It will if that's when they think the shooting took place.' Ursula twirled the sherry glass in her hand. 'It would have given him time to ride to Mill Ponds and back.'

'Ben thinks the murder must have taken place not long after Archie was last seen with me at seven-thirty. It was dark by nine and unlikely that he'd have gone out digging later than that. The pathologist is still examining the body, but it seems Archie had been there all night.'

Millicent ran a hand through her unruly curls, dislodging hairpins. 'Daniel refuses to shoot even a pigeon or a rabbit. He could never have done something like that, no matter how angry he was with Archie.'

'I know he couldn't. Besides, if he'd galloped into town on Marley, someone would be bound to have seen him.' I'd once ridden on the back of the giant black stallion, and he wasn't a horse you could easily miss. 'I'm sure Superintendent Cobbe doesn't believe he had anything to do with it.'

'What about you? Does he believe you?' Ursula pulled her turquoise fringed shawl tighter around her shoulders.

I shrugged. 'I've no idea what the superintendent thinks. Or the rest of Walden, come to that.'

'No one will believe you had anything to do with it,' Millicent said with a conviction I wished I shared.

And as we walked along Walden high street the following morning, I think Millicent's confidence in that statement was shattered.

It was hard to ignore the covert glances we received from everyone we passed. Jim Fellowes stood outside his store, hands on hips, watching us. Next to him, Ted Cox, landlord of the Drunken Duck, muttered something under his breath.

Before parting company with me at the turning to Walden Elementary School, Millicent squeezed my arm. This simple gesture brought tears to my eyes.

Walden was a place I loved, filled with my family and friends. I'd only wanted to leave because of Archie Powell. Now he was gone, I had every reason to stay. But at what cost? Millicent was a respected schoolteacher. She was also my best friend, and that association would do nothing for her reputation.

What of Elijah? And Horace? They'd weather the storm. So would Ursula. But would people start to shun my father and stepmother?

As fast as I wiped them away, more tears fell, and I hurried along the high street and down Queens Road. I tried and failed to compose myself before I walked into the office.

Without a word, Elijah rose from his desk and went to light the gas ring. I must have looked in a sorry state if he was actually going to make coffee himself.

'Has someone said something to you?' He placed a steaming mug of bitter-smelling dark liquid in front of me.

I shook my head. 'It's the way people stare at me. And Millicent.'

For once, he took a seat by my desk rather than the other way around.

'Rumours are flying. And unless you tell me the truth, it's going to be hard for me to defend you.'

I was stung by this comment. 'I don't know what else I can say.'

When I'd returned from Mill Ponds the previous day, I'd told Elijah of my visit to the crime scene and my subsequent interview by Superintendent Cobbe.

'From what you've said, Archie was killed not long after you were seen quarrelling with him. It was described as a heated argument. You even hit him. It's no wonder Cobbe is focusing on you.'

'I've told him everything I know,' I insisted.

'But you haven't, have you? You told him you were browsing shop windows on The Strand on the afternoon of the eleventh and didn't buy anything.'

'I didn't.'

'What about the swan brooch? You told me you'd bought it in a curiosity shop.'

I blushed at having been caught out in this obvious lie.

Elijah pressed home his point. 'I think the brooch was given to you as a present by a man you were meeting that afternoon. A man Archie Powell seemed to know all about. A man he suspected you of having an affair with.'

I wiped my eyes, knowing it was futile to deny it. 'The brooch was a present. Given to me by a friend. Not a lover.'

'A married friend?'

'He has nothing to do with this.'

Elijah looked as exasperated as the superintendent had the previous day. I braced myself for a lecture when we were interrupted by footsteps on the stairs. He closed his mouth, and I let out a long breath. An interrogation by Superintendent Cobbe would be preferable to Elijah questioning me on this particular subject.

To my surprise, a familiar pair of brown eyes beneath a fringe of floppy brown hair peeked around the door. Seeing us seated by my desk, Percy Baverstock sauntered in, dressed as if he were on his holidays, in baggy grey flannel trousers and a red polo shirt.

'Percy to the rescue. You look like you could do with the old Baverstock charm to cheer you up.'

At this, I burst into tears.

'It's a reaction I often get from women,' he informed Elijah. 'I blame my devastating good looks.'

Elijah smiled and went into his den to light a cigarette.

Percy took his place by my desk. 'Is this about Archie Powell? I heard what happened.'

I pulled out my handkerchief and wiped my eyes. 'Shouldn't you be at work?'

'I am. I'm on a field trip to Waldenmere.' Percy worked for the Natural History Museum and rented a flat nearby on Brompton Road. He was also a member of the Society for the Promotion of Nature Reserves and often travelled to sites around the country on their behalf. His family lived in Winchester, and he was a frequent visitor to Hampshire, even founding the Walden Natural History Group with Millicent. 'Come on. Tell me who they think did it. What's the gossip?'

'The gossip is that I had a row with Archie. A public one. I even slapped him across the face.' I winced at the memory. 'And now everyone thinks I murdered him.'

Percy laughed. 'I'm sure that's not true.'

He looked at Elijah, obviously expecting him to contradict me. When Elijah said nothing, Percy's mouth gaped.

'What was this row about?'

I buried my face in my hands. Percy was the last person I wanted to hear Archie's accusations.

'Archie used to provoke Iris whenever he could,' I heard Elijah say. 'Including pointing a rifle in her direction.'

I was grateful to him for his discretion. Over the last four years, my relationship with Percy had veered from friendship into a near romance and then back again. Elijah knew as well as I did that Percy's feelings, albeit fickle at times, would be hurt if he thought I'd been keeping secrets from him.

'He really was a—' Percy spluttered.

I held up a hand to stop him. 'Don't add yourself to the list of suspects. Superintendent Cobbe's been interviewing anyone known to be hostile towards Archie.'

'Cobbe needs his noddle examined if he thinks you could have fired a rifle. I'd like to see you try. Who else is in the firing line? If you'll pardon the pun.'

'Daniel.'

Percy flinched. From their army service together during the war, he was well aware that his close friend knew how to shoot. He also knew how angry Daniel had been with Archie because of what he'd done to Constance.

I described the scene at the Tolfree & Timpson factory.

'God, that man really did know how to cause trouble, though I would never have wished that on him.' Percy was silent for a moment, then said, 'What are the police doing apart from interviewing people who had every right to be furious with Archie?'

I told him about the previous day's events at Mill Ponds. 'Ben and Sid went to search the allotments next to the garden where Archie was found. Sid was going to talk to the railway workers to see if any of them saw or heard anything. It's difficult to know exactly when Archie was killed.'

Percy leapt from his chair. 'Come on. Let's go and see if they found anything.'

I shook my head. 'I don't want to risk running into Superintendent Cobbe again.'

But Percy was adamant. 'I'll drive us to the station house. If Cobbe's car is there, I'll drive away.'

'Go on,' Elijah urged. He knew Percy was probably the only person who could cheer me up in these circumstances. I guessed he was also curious to hear if anything had been found. 'You're no good to me here. I'm going to call on Horace, see if he's turned up anything.'

Percy brightened at this. 'Good oh! That's more like it. Mr Laffaye will find out where the skeletons are buried.'

As we made our way down the stairs, he whispered, 'Trust Horace to stick his beak in. He'll look after you.'

Although I took comfort in this, I couldn't help feeling I didn't deserve Elijah and Horace's kindness. I told myself they weren't only investigating Archie's death for my sake. They were fond of Ben, and Constance and Daniel, and would want to protect them from any false accusations.

Percy had parked his Model T Ford on the kerb outside Laffaye Printworks.

'This will all sort itself out, you know,' he said, opening the passenger door for me. 'Promise me you'll stay put until it does, though, won't you?'

As I suspected, the spectre of my flight abroad two and a half years before still rankled with Percy. Not that it had deterred him from producing a sprig of mistletoe at Mrs Siddons' Christmas party and drunkenly informing me we weren't getting any younger and should settle down. He hadn't been too disappointed when I'd rejected his half-hearted proposal.

Although Percy wasn't really ready to settle down, he didn't like the thought of me going off with someone else. I'd promised him I wouldn't run away with anyone – and I meant it. If I did move away, it would be by myself, and I'd let everyone know where I was going.

'No. I won't run away if that's what you think, though I may have to go and stay with Gran and Aunt Maud if things become unbearable here.'

'Heaven forbid.' He shuddered in mock horror, having previously experienced my grandmother's caustic tongue. 'The police will find out who killed Archie, and you can put it all behind you.'

'You're probably right.' My guilt over Marc increased. Some rumours might be easier to quell than others.

'Now I am worried. You've never told me I was right before. I rather like it.'

He drove up Queens Road and, at the junction with the high street, was about to turn left when I grabbed his arm.

'Go right. Could you drive us to Mill Ponds?'

'Is that a good idea?' he asked, but swung the car to the right nonetheless.

'I don't need to go into the house. I just want to look at the view from the arched bridge over the railway line.'

'I think I know where that is, although I don't believe I've ever driven across it.'

'You probably haven't. The only reason to take that road is to get to Mill Ponds House.'

It was a short drive down the high street, past the railway station, and then up a hill before we turned right onto the bridge.

'Gosh, I wouldn't take this at speed.' Percy drove cautiously onto the bridge. 'Those walls are low.'

'Stop here in the middle.'

He did as I asked, and we both got out of the car. I walked over to the side of the bridge, gazing towards Mill Ponds garden, and Percy followed.

'What are we looking at?' he asked, peering down at the railway track below.

'I'm testing a theory. Gordon Tolfree visited Mill Ponds at about nine o'clock on the night of Archie's murder. He spent around five or ten minutes in the study and could have gone into the garden during that time without anyone noticing. It seems unlikely he would have gone out there unless he knew that's where Archie was. I wondered if he could have spotted him as he drove over the bridge.'

Percy shielded his eyes with his hands and stared across to the garden. 'You can't see much from here in broad daylight. If it was nearly dark and he was driving, I doubt he would have seen him.' He must have sensed my disappointment as he added, 'It's possible, but I think he would have had to stop the car and look hard to be sure it was Archie. He might have very good eyesight.'

'Never mind,' I said, returning to the car. 'It was just a thought.'

'Is there somewhere I can turn around?' Percy asked, jumping back into the driver's seat.

'Only at Mill Ponds. Go over the bridge and along the track

and then take a sharp right.' I guided him to the driveway of the house, where he swung the car around, and we sped straight out again.

No one was in sight, and I was glad I didn't have to explain why I was there or what I'd been doing. Even to myself, it felt like I was desperate to shift the blame onto someone else's, possibly innocent, shoulders.

18

Percy and I drove in companionable silence to the station house where, to my relief, there was no sign of Superintendent Cobbe's car. Propped up against the wall was Ben's bicycle.

'We're in luck.' Percy pulled up and jumped out of the driver's seat.

I followed, and as we crossed the road, a familiar figure walked up the path to the station house.

'Victoria.' Percy dashed over and wrapped his arms around her. 'I was planning to drop in on you later.'

'Percy.' She hugged him tightly. Victoria Hobbs was the widow of one of Percy's old army pals, who'd died the previous year. 'How lovely to see you. Your mother said she was expecting you at the weekend. What are you doing here in the middle of the week?'

'I just wanted to see how Iris... how everyone was after what happened. What are you doing here?' Percy jerked his head towards the station house.

'I need to see Sergeant Gilbert. Everyone's talking about Archie Powell's death. He had a row with Iris—' She blushed when she saw me, and I dreaded to think what she'd heard. Or what she was about to say to Percy.

She turned to me. 'I've heard gossip in town. People are saying you were the last person to see Archie alive. But I think I might have been the last one to have seen him before he was killed.'

The wave of relief I felt at Victoria's words was short-lived. I may not have been the last person to have seen Archie alive, but I had been at the lake later that evening. I was still a suspect – unless Victoria had information that would shed some light on the exact time of Archie's murder.

'What time did you see him? Where was he—' I was interrupted by a cough from behind me.

Ben was standing at the door to the station house, watching us with a bemused expression. 'I ask the questions, remember?'

Percy slapped him on the back. 'Ben. Just the person we need. I've tried telling her to leave it all to you. You'll have it solved in no time.'

'I appreciate your faith in me. But I'm not officially working on this case. However...' he smiled at Victoria '...I can take a statement. Why don't you all come in?'

We all huddled into his tiny office, and Ben pulled out chairs for each of us before perching on the desk and reaching for his notebook.

'You say you saw Mr Powell on Sunday. What time was that?' he asked Victoria.

'At about a quarter to eight. I arrived at Mill Ponds as Archie was walking up the driveway. I'd taken a taxi because I'd brought a large bag with me. The driver was just turning the car around.'

Ben noted this down. 'Did you go into the house with Mr Powell?'

Victoria shook her head. 'He asked me to, but I didn't want to keep the taxi waiting. I'd told the driver I'd only come to drop off the bag and would be going straight home again.'

'What was in the bag?' I couldn't help asking, earning myself a reproving look from Ben.

'Clothes. My husband's clothes.' Victoria cast an apologetic glance at Percy as if she'd done something wrong. 'I thought they might come in useful at the hostel.'

Percy smiled. 'I'm sure Harry would have wanted that.'

'I'd seen the Swanns earlier that afternoon. They're neighbours of mine,' Victoria explained. 'They'd just come back from Mill Ponds, and Polly told me more residents were expected the following week. I mentioned Harry's clothes, and she said she was sure they'd be appreciated, so I decided to give them away. It was silly holding on to them, but I couldn't bear to part with them for a long time.'

'I understand,' Ben said. 'How long did you spend with Mr Powell?'

She hesitated. 'A few minutes. Five at the most. I gave him the bag, and he thanked me. He tried to persuade me to go with him to see the new garden, but I said I'd see it another day.'

'Were there any cars on the driveway of Mill Ponds? Or any coming over the bridge?'

Victoria shook her head. 'There were a few parked by the railway station. After that, we didn't pass any.'

'Did Mr Powell have a bicycle with him?'

Her brow furrowed as she tried to recall. 'No. I don't remember seeing one.'

'How did Mr Powell seem? Was he his usual self?' Ben asked.

Victoria blushed. 'He's been very kind to me since my

husband died. He said I could always call on him if I needed anything. I assured him I was fine and then left. I think that's all I can tell you.'

I sensed her unease and could guess why. Victoria was a beautiful woman, and Archie's infatuation with her had been obvious. The first time I'd met her, she'd reminded me of a damsel in distress in a Hollywood film with large dark eyes and bow lips. She'd been only thirty years old when her husband died the previous year, and Archie had cast himself in the role of her protector. I'm not sure Victoria welcomed this attention.

She looked relieved when Ben stood up and thanked her for coming. Percy stood, too, and asked if she'd like him to drive her home.

Victoria shook her head. 'I have some errands to run in town. I'll see you at your parents' on Saturday.'

Percy kissed her cheek and saw her to the door while Ben and I went to sit in the parlour.

Percy returned and began to nose around the room. 'You live here with Sid?'

Ben nodded.

'Very cosy. Nicer than my flat. Perhaps I should have become a policeman.'

'I'm not sure it's your vocation,' I remarked. 'Though Superintendent Cobbe might think differently.'

'I'd look dashing in the uniform.' Ben's hat was lying on the table, and he tried it on.

Ben sat back in his chair, watching. 'If you were a detective, who would you suspect in this case? As an outsider, you might have a less prejudiced view. You haven't witnessed any of the bad feeling Archie has been stirring up.'

Percy put the hat down and paced the room, considering this. 'I suppose I'd concentrate on the people at Mill Ponds. I can't see a complete stranger waltzing into the garden with a rifle and shooting him.'

'The rifle was already there,' Ben informed him. 'Our ballistics expert says the bullet and shell came from the Lee-Enfield SMLE Mark III kept in the shed. It's an old army rifle. We don't know how Archie came by it as the one he used in his attacks was confiscated.'

'Didn't stop him from getting another one,' I muttered.

Ben held up his hands. 'Old army rifles aren't hard to come by, though whoever owns them should have a certificate. We're trying to find out where this one came from. And how long Archie had owned it.'

'Has it been tested for fingerprints?' I asked.

'They tried, but the results weren't helpful. Only Archie's smudged prints were found on the barrel of the rifle. That doesn't mean it hadn't been handled by someone else, it just wasn't possible to discern a clear print.'

'The killer used his own rifle against him,' Percy mused. 'Sounds like a revenge attack to me.'

'It does. Hence, the direction of Superintendent Cobbe's investigation.'

That silenced Percy, and he finally stopped perusing the room and sat down. Archie's victims were Constance, Mrs Siddons, and Ben. They would have reason to retaliate. As would their family and close friends.

Percy steepled his hands under his chin. 'Iris would be hopeless with a rifle. She'd lose patience trying to figure out how it works and end up hitting him over the head with it. And you can rule out Daniel. He may be a competent marksman, but he hates violence and would never hurt anyone.'

'Neither would I,' Ben commented drily.

'No, of course not. I never meant to suggest—'

'And thanks for that assessment of my character. You obviously think I'm violent enough to kill him, but too stupid to know how to fire a rifle.'

Percy leapt up and put Ben's hat on again. 'Back to what I was saying about it being someone at Mill Ponds. Tell me who spends most time there.'

Ben described the three current residents, the Swanns and the hostel's patrons.

'Don't forget the vicar,' Percy reminded him. 'I'd like to rule him out, but remember Archie was once a man of the cloth. Let's concentrate on the residents and the Tolfrees for the time being. What were they doing that day?'

'Hugh, Paul and Vincent went with Archie to church that morning. The Tolfrees were all there, too. Polly and Micky Swann and their children arrived at Mill Ponds during the morning to cook lunch, which was served at two o'clock. After lunch, Archie was in his study, and the men worked in the garden until they went for a walk at half past seven. They returned shortly before half past eight and didn't go out again that night.'

'What did the Tolfrees do after church that day?' I asked.

'They had lunch together at one o'clock. At three o'clock, Mr Tolfree went into town to play cricket. Following the match, he went to the Drunken Duck with some of the other players. Jennifer was at home until half past five when she went out for a walk by herself. Shortly after, Luke asked if he could go out to play. By all accounts, his grandmother is more indulgent than his mother. Gertrude felt the boy had been cooped up all day and said he could go out as long as he was back by seven o'clock. When he wasn't home by half past seven, Gertrude went to look for him. I think she was worried her daughter-in-law would be cross with her for allowing him out so late.'

'I saw Luke on his bicycle when I was leaving the station. He nearly ran into me.'

Ben nodded. 'The stationmaster saw that and told Gertrude when she called by later. Luke's often at the station. He likes watching trains and sometimes leaves his bicycle there when he goes to play by the lake. He was home by the time Gertrude returned.'

'What time did Jennifer get back from her walk?' Percy asked. 'And where had she gone?'

'She says she went to the lake but only as far as Heron Bay, and she's not sure of the time. No one saw her return. Gordon got back from the pub at about a quarter to eight. He says he saw his wife not long after. Gordon went out again, driving to Mill Ponds at around nine o'clock to pick up the accounts. He was surprised Archie wasn't there. He went into the study for a while and then took the books away with him.'

Percy took off Ben's hat and scratched his head. 'Gosh. This is confusing. It seems to me that the three residents would all have had the opportunity. As would the Tolfrees. Jennifer or Gertrude could have gone into the garden of Mill Ponds when they were out walking. And Gordon when he was there at nine o'clock.'

Ben smiled. 'Thanks. That's a big help.'

Percy flopped into a chair. 'Victoria saw him at a quarter to eight. Does her evidence help at all?'

'It explains the bag Sid found in Archie's room. And tells us that he returned directly to Mill Ponds after his row with Iris. I expect he went into the garden shortly afterwards. The pathologist thinks he probably died before ten o'clock that night.'

'Did you find anything when you searched the allotments?' I asked.

'Nothing. Sid spoke to all the railway workers who rent an

allotment, and none of them were there on Sunday evening. A few had been there that morning but hadn't seen anything out of the ordinary.'

'What about his bicycle?'

Ben shook his head. 'No sign of it. Nor his pocket diary. If we could find that, it might tell us if he'd planned to meet with anyone that evening.'

I felt a tightness in my chest as I remembered the little black book Archie had taken from his pocket at the open day. He'd flicked through its pages, pretending to look for something.

Then he'd recited Marc's name and address.

19

When I arrived in the office the following morning, Elijah told me not to bother taking my coat off because Horace Laffaye had summoned us to a meeting. Expecting a trip to Heron Bay Lodge, Horace's lakeside home, I was surprised when Elijah said the three of us would be going to Crookham Hall.

I peered out of the window to see Horace's chauffeur-driven Daimler pulling up outside.

As usual, Horace was immaculately dressed in a blue woollen suit with trousers pressed to perfection. Whereas Elijah's brown homburg hat had seen better days, Horace sported a new blue Fedora above his well-cut jacket. Seated beside each other in the back of the Daimler, they made an eccentric-looking couple.

At Crookham Hall, we were shown into a large reception room I was familiar with, yet every time I saw it, I still marvelled at the décor. It was expertly decorated to blend in with the surrounding landscape. Silk paper, patterned with trailing wisteria, adorned one wall while the others were painted the palest of greens. Silk-damask curtains flowed down to the polished mahogany floor, framing tall windows that showed the rolling pastures to the side of the hall.

Daniel Timpson, dressed in a smart navy morning suit, stood as we entered. Constance stayed seated beside Mrs Siddons on one of the green velvet sofas.

Horace waited until Miss Grange, the Timpsons' housekeeper, had finished serving tea and left the room before he began.

'I thought it prudent under the circumstances that we meet to discuss the repercussions of Mr Archibald Powell's unusual death.' He turned to Daniel. 'I gather Superintendent Cobbe has interviewed you?'

Daniel nodded. 'Constance, too.'

'What?' I didn't know why this should surprise me. If Superintendent Cobbe considered me a likely candidate for shooting Archie, then there was no reason to rule out the Honourable Constance Timpson.

In fact, when I thought about it, I regarded her as a more likely suspect than Daniel. He was a gentle creature who abhorred violence. He would never kill an animal, even though hunting was part of his family's tradition. I remembered when I'd first met him, in this very room, four years earlier. He'd been standing by the windows, gazing out at the three thousand acres of farmland, woodland and pastures that surrounded the hall, and I'd known that was where he'd rather be – with just his horse for company.

Constance was a different matter. She was a shrewd businesswoman notorious for demolishing any obstacles that stood in her path. However, she wasn't impulsive. If she'd wanted to kill Archie, she would have employed other means.

Horace turned to Mrs Siddons. 'Dare I ask if you've been interviewed, too?'

The thought of Mrs Siddons as the killer brought a smile to my face. It was a preposterous idea. Surely even Superintendent Cobbe couldn't suspect our local MP of murder?

I pictured her dressed in silk and jewels, perhaps wearing one of her more exotic hats, wielding a rifle. The outfit she wore, hunter-green silk with emerald drop earrings, would be perfect for the occasion, though the dangling emerald bracelet might prove to be a hindrance.

'I have not,' she replied. 'Although I wouldn't want to be considered above suspicion. I'm sure Superintendent Cobbe will get around to me at some point. He probably has a long list of suspects. Archie was good at making enemies.'

'From what Ben said about the method of killing, it doesn't sound like the work of a professional marksman. Or woman.' Elijah took a cigarette from the silver box Constance pushed in his direction. 'More like someone saw an opportunity and took it.'

I nodded. 'It must have been a spontaneous act. No one could have known he'd be in the garden at that time.'

'To pick up a rifle and shoot him while he worked would suggest someone in an emotional state.' Elijah lit one of the long, expensive cigarettes using a match from an old box he kept in his pocket rather than the ornate silver lighter on the table. A sulphuric odour overpowered the delicate rose pot-pourri that scented the room.

'Did they know the rifle was there?' Horace pondered. 'Or did they spot it and take a chance?'

'It was there on the open day,' I said. 'If anyone had gone into the garden and opened the shed door, they would have seen it leaning against the wall.'

Horace tutted. 'Including the dozens of children who were present.'

'I can see why Superintendent Cobbe is focusing on people known to have recently argued with the deceased.' Elijah let out a long spiral of smoke. 'Someone who was angry and perhaps had been angry for some time suddenly sees the rifle and acts impulsively.'

I realised that could apply to me. I'd spent the last four months feeling furious at Archie's intrusion into my life. If I'd wanted to kill him and had walked into the garden and seen an opportunity, would I have taken it?

I shook my head, remembering what Percy had said about my abilities with a rifle.

Elijah waved his cigarette in my direction. 'You disagree?'

'No. I think you're right. It's just that I've never fired a rifle, so it wouldn't be my impulse to pick it up.' I saw their doubtful faces and added, 'This sounds like I'm trying to prove my innocence. What I'm saying is a Lee-Enfield SMLE Mark III is nearly forty-five inches long. It's unlikely someone unfamiliar with a rifle would have been tempted to use it.'

The same could not be said for Daniel, who had experience of handling firearms during the war, and I hoped he didn't think I was attempting to shift the blame in his direction.

'I know how to fire a rifle,' he responded. 'But I have no desire to do so. I was furious with Archie, after everything he put Constance through and then to come here with no regard for her feelings...' Colour rose to his cheeks. 'I still get angry when I think about it. I don't deny I wanted to pop him on the nose, as Percy might say.'

Elijah smiled. 'No one would blame you if you had. That's a far cry from shooting a man in the back.'

'The Tolfrees can all fire a rifle.' Constance gestured with a slim hand, causing the draped sleeve of her white silk dress to shimmer. Her elegant ensemble put my own knitted cream cardigan and black trousers to shame.

'Even Gertrude?' I asked, remembering I'd once suspected Redvers Tolfree of the attacks on Constance and Mrs Siddons after discovering he enjoyed shooting. It hadn't occurred to me that his whole family would have joined him at weekend shooting parties.

Constance nodded. 'Both Gertrude and Jennifer are considered pretty decent shots. Gordon isn't as good and often sits it out.'

'Presumably, the three men currently staying at the hostel have firearms experience from when they served.' Elijah tapped his cigarette in the ashtray Miss Grange had made a point of placing in front of him. 'What do we know about them?'

'Paul Richardson was once engaged to Archie's sister. He broke it off when he lost his leg,' I said.

'Interesting,' Horace commented. 'Although I'm not sure what sort of motive that gives him.'

'Who was it that Archie brought to the factory?' Constance asked.

'Hugh Alvarez,' I replied.

'What's his background?' She seemed as interested in Hugh as he had been with her.

'He recently lost his job as a lorry driver. I'm not sure how he ended up at Mill Ponds. Paul got a room through Archie, and Vincent Owen once worked for Jennifer Tolfree's father.' I thought about the three men. 'Of all of them, Hugh is the most confident.'

'One of them could have known Archie during the war,' Elijah said. 'Or even before. Perhaps they had an old score to settle.'

'Does that fit in with the seemingly spontaneous method of killing?' Horace pondered.

'Why look a gift horse in the mouth?' Elijah retorted. 'A train was passing; the gun was there. Murder made easy.'

'Perhaps we should be examining Archie's background,' Mrs Siddons suggested. 'It could have been someone from his past. Or someone he met in prison.'

I could understand why she hoped it wasn't someone staying at Mill Ponds. It would hardly bode well for the future of the hostel if one of its first residents murdered the man who was running it.

'True.' Horace nodded. 'As you know, I did a little investigation when Mr Powell began to show his face in Walden. After what his solicitor described in court as "unfortunate incidents", namely firing his rifle in your and Miss Timpson's direction, he was sentenced to a year's imprisonment but released after ten months. He served his time in Winchester Prison, where he was deemed to be an exemplary prisoner who helped his fellow inmates to learn new skills.'

Horace's network of contacts included senior figures on the court circuit and in the police force. He also had the ear of several high court judges.

'During his time in prison, he became friends with the prison chaplain and made the acquaintance of the bishop of Winchester Cathedral,' Horace continued. 'On his release, Archie was given the job of verger at the cathedral, and his friends within the church found him lodgings nearby. Through his work, he was invited to join the committee of Winchester Cathedral's Great War Fund.'

'What about Archie's family?' Elijah asked.

'They live in Greenwich, where Paul Richardson's family live. Archie once mentioned how his mother and sisters used to fuss over him. He was always the man of the house as his father left when he was young, and he never saw him again. He described him as being a drinker. It seems that in the last year, Archie has followed in his father's footsteps.' I told them what I'd learned from Hugh, Vincent and Paul. 'They suspected the vicar had noticed Archie's drinking, too.'

Mrs Siddons made a tssking sound. 'Reverend Childs failed to mention it to me. If he had, I would have started to search for a new manager at once. As it is, we have several other men due to take up residence this weekend, and I need to find someone soon.'

'Now Archie's gone, I'm willing to get involved with the project.' Constance placed her teacup on the table. 'And I have a suggestion: Micky Swann could manage the hostel.'

Mrs Siddons held her lorgnette spectacles to her eyes. 'You think he's capable?'

'With guidance, I believe he could be. He's a hard worker and copes well at the factory despite the weakness of his left arm. His fellow workers like him, and he gets things done because he knows how to talk to people. I have a feeling he'd enjoy taking on a new challenge. The only problem is, I don't think he'd be willing to live in like Archie did, as he has a family.'

Mrs Siddons nodded. 'I'm sure we could accommodate that. I suggest we hold a meeting with the vicar and Mr Tolfree. I'd like to get something in place before the new residents arrive.'

Horace coughed. 'To return to the murder of Mr Powell.'

Daniel leant forward in his seat. 'Surely the most likely candidate is someone who lives or spends time at the hostel.

That means the three residents, the Tolfrees, the Swanns and the vicar.'

'I think we can rule out Reverend Childs,' Mrs Siddons replied. 'And I don't see what motive the Swanns or the Tolfrees would have. I've spoken mainly with Gordon and Gertrude, and they both felt Archie was vital to the success of Mill Ponds. They gave me the impression they were grateful to him for helping them to restore the Tolfree name. Thanks to the hostel, Gertrude seems to have regained a sense of purpose since Redvers' death.'

'Jennifer was also highly enamoured of Archie but for different reasons.' I told them of the intense conversation I'd witnessed outside the study at Mill Ponds. 'If he had given her the brush-off, she might have been upset and angry.'

By the silence that followed, I gathered no one gave much credence to Jennifer as the murderer.

'I guess I'm still the main suspect then,' I said, trying not to sound sulky.

Horace exchanged a glance with Elijah before saying, 'I think it would be prudent not to do anything that might further damage your reputation.'

Daniel shifted in his seat, then said in a stilted voice, 'I don't believe you killed Archie. But I can understand why you're under suspicion. The rumour is you're having an affair with a married man, and he was blackmailing you.'

'I... that's not... I wasn't—' I felt winded and unable to respond. It was the first time someone had said this directly to my face, and that it should come from mild-mannered Daniel hurt me more than I cared to admit.

'Whatever the truth of the matter, I don't think it's right for you to carry on lodging with Millicent. She's respected in the town, and it's not fair that she should be...' Daniel cleared his throat. 'Be dragged into all this. Couldn't you go back to live with your father?'

I blinked, determined not to let the tears fall, aware that all eyes were upon me.

'Perhaps you're right,' I croaked.

20

To our surprise, not long after we'd returned from Crookham Hall, Elijah and I received a note from Mrs Siddons asking us to attend a meeting at Sycamore Lodge the following morning.

The Tolfrees' family home had been built by Isaac Tolfree in 1860 when Tolfree Biscuits was in its heyday. It was a large, colonial-looking house designed to impress, with sweeping steps leading up to a pair of tall oak doors flanked by white stone columns. Two rows of symmetrical windows sat in white-painted walls beneath a red-tiled roof.

It appeared Isaac wanted to emulate the aristocracy by creating a family home he could pass down to future genera-tions of Tolfrees. Perhaps anticipating his son's fecklessness, a caveat in Isaac's will ensured that the house passed to Gordon rather than being lost to Redvers' creditors.

In addition to copying the colonial-style architecture of the eighteenth century, the interior was contrived to look like it was from a similar period. However, it didn't quite succeed, espe-cially as Gordon had modernised some aspects but not others, giving the place a somewhat eccentric feel.

Elijah and I were shown into a reception room where Mrs Siddons and Constance Timpson sat opposite Gordon and Jennifer Tolfree. Gertrude Tolfree occupied an upright chair between the two sofas, making her look like an umpire. Her expression was impassive beneath her helmet of iron-grey hair.

Reverend Childs perched on an occasional chair, and the maid brought over two more for Elijah and me. I couldn't help remembering my last visit to Sycamore Lodge on New Year's Eve. That was the night Archie's threats had begun. I'd left before the clock struck midnight, preferring to welcome in 1924 on my own with a sherry in Ursula's book room. But any thoughts of celebrating the new year vanished after Archie had followed me home from the Tolfrees' party and told me he knew all about Marc.

'Thank you for coming,' Gordon said once we were seated. He wore a modern fitted suit that showed off his sturdy frame. 'Given recent events, there's been speculation in town over the future of Mill Ponds. Mrs Siddons, Reverend Childs and I are determined the hostel should carry on as planned and we'll be welcoming new residents tomorrow. I'd be grateful if *The Walden Herald* could continue to support us in our efforts and report on what we have planned.'

'Of course,' Elijah replied.

Mrs Siddons added, 'We're as committed as ever to the objectives of the hostel. And we're fortunate that Miss Timpson has generously offered to support our cause by coming on board as a patron of Mill Ponds House.'

Gordon smiled at Constance, but I noticed Gertrude purse her lips. I doubted she'd fully forgiven Constance Timpson for her part in Redvers' downfall. However, she was canny enough to recognise that if she wanted to redeem the family name, she would have to rise above any remaining grievances.

'Miss Timpson has made the excellent suggestion that Mr Swann steps in for the time being to act as manager,' Mrs Siddons continued. 'He's familiar with the running of the place, and, of course, Mrs Swann is already doing an admirable job as housekeeper. I feel confident Mr Powell would wish us to continue with a project that was so close to his heart.'

Gordon and Gertrude nodded in agreement, but I noticed Jennifer flinch at these words. As usual, she was immaculately dressed and her face powdered, though when I looked closely, there were subtle changes. Her blonde hair wasn't quite as perfectly styled as usual, and there was tension around her eyes and a slight tremble to her lips. These were barely noticeable details but enough to suggest she was anxious.

Was it simply shock at Archie's gruesome death? Or could there be something else behind her distress? Had she heard that Archie's pocket diary was missing? I guessed she would share my concern over its contents.

'We owe much to Mr Powell's endeavours.' Reverend Childs blinked behind his round spectacles, seeming to feel more should be said about Archie's contribution to the establishment of the hostel.

No one responded. Interestingly, even Jennifer no longer seemed compelled to praise Archie, and the room fell silent.

Constance placed her cup on the small table beside her and shifted in her seat. I wondered what she made of the décor. Grand as it was, Sycamore Lodge was no Crookham Hall.

'In the past, Timpson Foods has tried to offer employment to those in need. With Mr Powell gone, I'm now willing to offer that support where possible to residents of Mill Ponds House.' The steel in her voice was unmistakable. Although others may have forgiven Archie, she never would. And I didn't blame her.

The vicar turned a little pink, but Gordon seemed unfazed by this statement.

'Excellent.' He beamed at Constance.

Gertrude inclined her head. 'That's most kind of you,' she said, sounding as if every word had to be forced out.

Jennifer stayed silent. She hadn't spoken during the whole meeting.

Mrs Siddons stood up with a swish of her full-length silk skirt. 'I'm going to visit Mill Ponds now to introduce Miss Timpson to the current residents and inform them of our plans.'

Gertrude and Jennifer stayed in the reception room while Gordon showed us all to the front door, pointing out various features of the house to Constance on the way. He was evidently proud of his family home.

Outside, Elijah lit a cigarette and told me he'd stroll up to the church with the vicar. He gave a slight jerk of his head towards Mrs Siddons and Constance, who were walking over to the Timpsons' Daimler parked on the driveway of Sycamore Lodge.

I nodded in response. I'd already decided to tag along with them, curious to see how the hostel's residents would react to the latest news.

At Mill Ponds, Polly Swann showed us into the lounge and said that Hugh, Paul and Vincent were working on the greenhouse. She offered to fetch them, but Mrs Siddons told her we'd go into the garden.

I was glad to see the foundation of the greenhouse had been completed and a low supporting wall built over the area where Archie had lain. There was no trace left of the blood that had stained the ground.

The three men stopped working when they saw us approach.

'You have been busy. This is marvellous.' Mrs Siddons clapped her hands in appreciation. 'I can't believe how much you've achieved already. I won't keep you long, I just wanted to introduce you to Miss Timpson, who'll be joining Mr Tolfree and me as a patron of Mill Ponds House.'

Constance stepped forward and greeted each of the men individually. I noticed that when she and Hugh locked eyes there was no hint of awkwardness over their previous encounter, only curiosity on both sides.

'I also wanted to inform you that Micky Swann has kindly agreed to take on the role of manager temporarily,' Mrs Siddons continued. 'Reverend Childs, Mr Tolfree, Miss Timpson and I will be on hand to support him. We'll see how the arrangement suits all parties before we make any permanent appointments. I hope that's acceptable to you?'

Paul and Vincent nodded without speaking.

'Seems sensible,' Hugh said, his gaze still resting on Constance.

She returned his look, and I detected a certain challenge in her eyes.

'Excellent. Four more gentlemen will be taking up accommodation tomorrow. Mr Swann will be here to help them settle in. I hope you'll make them feel welcome.'

'Of course,' Hugh replied. 'We'll be happy to help.'

Paul and Vincent nodded their agreement.

'Can we continue to work on the garden?' Paul asked. 'We're making good progress.'

'You most certainly can,' Mrs Siddons replied. 'You're doing an excellent job. If you require any more materials, please let one of us know, and we'll see what we can do.'

Mrs Siddons turned to leave, but Constance hadn't finished. 'One other matter. It concerns Mr Alvarez.'

Hugh looked at her inquisitively.

'Mr Powell asked if I could find you employment at the factory. If you're willing to undertake manual work, I'd be happy to employ you in Mr Swann's role while he's occupied here.'

Hugh seemed surprised, and I saw the corners of his mouth twitch as if he was suppressing a smile. Would he think this role beneath him? He certainly appeared too well-educated and well-spoken for the job she offered. Yet he'd said he was a lorry driver, so was this comparable? I didn't know.

'That's very kind of you, Miss Timpson. When do I start?'

21

Millicent placed the morning post on the breakfast table, and I instinctively looked at the envelopes to see if I could spot Marc's handwriting. Then felt a crushing weight of sadness as I remembered there would be no more letters. We'd agreed on a complete parting of the ways with no further correspondence.

I felt Ursula watching me and concentrated on peeling the shell from my boiled egg.

Millicent put down the letter she'd been reading and turned to me. 'Percy's coming to see us tomorrow. He's suggested we go for a picnic by the lake.'

I stopped buttering my toast. 'I'm not sure that's a good idea under the circumstances.'

'He said you'd say that.' Millicent pushed the letter, in Percy's distinctive flamboyant writing, over to me. 'He thinks you need cheering up, and he's right. Why shouldn't you go out?'

'Because...' I sipped my tea, trying to find the right words. 'It might seem disrespectful. Everyone believes I had something to do with Archie's death. If they see us out enjoying ourselves, it could make things worse.'

'Worse for whom?' Millicent reached for the teapot.

'For you. Perhaps Daniel's right. It might be better if I go back to live with my father and Katherine. At least until this has all blown over.'

'What?' Millicent stopped pouring, teapot hovering in mid-air. 'When did he say that?'

'Oh. I thought...' I paused, realising I'd made a blunder. I'd assumed it was something he'd discussed with Millicent. 'He was worried about you. And perhaps he's right to be.'

This only seemed to infuriate her more.

'I'll decide what's right for me.' She spoke quietly, but there was no mistaking the fury in her voice.

I'd never seen Millicent angry before and was beginning to comprehend why her pupils rarely misbehaved. I sank low in my chair, glancing nervously at her.

'You will not move out. And we will go on a picnic with Percy tomorrow afternoon.' She pushed her cup away in a violent gesture, splashing tea on the table.

I looked to Ursula for support. Or at least a comment. After all, she owned the house, and it was her decision who lived in it.

But she smiled at Millicent and carried on eating her boiled egg.

'Okay,' I muttered.

'Good,' Millicent replied and strode from the room.

'I'll bake a cake for your picnic,' Ursula called after her.

'I'm only thinking of Millicent. She's respected in Walden. I'm... I'm not a suitable friend. Couldn't you speak to her?'

Ursula shook her head. 'Millicent is twenty-seven years old and perfectly capable of deciding who she wishes to be friends with. People respect her because of her good sense and compassion. I don't think she's the one who needs talking to.'

This silenced me.

'What would you do if you were me?' I asked.

'I would accept the support your friends are offering. And not keep secrets from them.' With that, Ursula stood up and began clearing the table.

I got to my feet, knowing I'd been dismissed.

* * *

On Sunday afternoon, the toot of a horn told us that Percy had arrived. We tried to persuade Ursula to come with us, but she claimed that if she sat on the ground, she'd never be able to get up again.

It was a wise decision, as Percy insisted on leading us along a rough woodland track that even Millicent and I had trouble navigating. I was glad I'd worn trousers as Millicent's linen skirt kept getting tangled in spirals of bramble.

'Is this some kind of military training course?' I asked, remembering the army camp that had been based on the shores of Waldenmere for the duration of the war.

'I've worked out the precise location to give us the best view of the lake,' Percy replied, tripping and nearly falling headfirst into a patch of stinging nettles. 'I just didn't expect it to be as overgrown as this.'

Eventually, he stopped in a grassy glade by the water's edge, and I guessed the secluded location was for my benefit. I had to admit, I felt more relaxed knowing we couldn't be seen by anyone taking an afternoon stroll around Waldenmere.

Percy was sweating, having lugged a heavy picnic basket through the undergrowth. He put it down and mopped his brow with a polka-dot handkerchief, taken from the pocket of his navy flannel blazer.

He opened the picnic basket, fished out a bright red gingham tablecloth and laid it on the ground with a flourish.

'Be seated and admire the view.' He made a sweeping gesture with his hand. 'Didn't I promise you this would be the perfect spot?'

Millicent and I did as we were told, conceding that he'd chosen well. You could see the width of the lake, surrounded by swathes of reeds swaying in the breeze. A pair of swans glided up to see if we were likely to throw any food in their direction.

I peered into the picnic basket. 'How many were you expecting?'

'I'd hoped to persuade Daniel to come along.' Percy handed me a glass of beer. 'But he said he was busy.'

Millicent flushed. I guessed they'd had a row, and I was the cause.

'I popped in to see Ben, too. And guess what?' Percy brandished a bottle of beer in my direction. 'He was all spruced up and about to go on a date. Who is she?'

'Her name's Laura and she's a nurse at the cottage hospital,' I told him.

'Good for him.' Percy poured himself a beer, then delved into the basket for plates, knives, forks and napkins.

'Did you pack all this yourself?' I asked in wonder.

'Mother obliged.' Percy indicated the bowl of salad and home-baked pie he was cutting into slices. 'She sends her love.'

I remembered Victoria had said Percy would be staying with his parents in Winchester this weekend.

'Didn't Freddie come down from London with you?' Millicent accepted the slice of pie Percy offered.

'He did. But the boy's such a swot, he brought his books with him. I couldn't persuade him to give studying a swerve and come out. He told me to save some food to take back with us tonight.'

We chatted about Percy's younger brother as we ate. After winning a place at architectural school, Freddie had moved into Percy's London flat. The pair of them made an odd couple. Both had inherited a daft side from their mother and a serious side from their father, although Freddie was more studious and less gregarious than Percy.

'He met a lovely girl at the Foxtrot Club. I think she was quite sweet on him. But he became enamoured with another girl who was seeing a racing car driver. Freddie didn't stand a chance. The boy has an unfortunate habit of falling for women who have no interest in him.' Percy took a swig of beer. 'Anyway, he's decided to give romance a miss and concentrate on architecture instead.'

Percy waited until we'd started on Ursula's cake before asking for the latest news on Archie's murder. I told him about the get-together at Crookham Hall and the subsequent meeting at Sycamore Lodge.

'What do you know about the three chaps living at Mill Ponds? To my mind, one of them is most likely to have done it as they were there at the time. Although don't ask me why.'

I told him what I knew of Hugh, Paul and Vincent.

'This Hugh seems a bit suspicious to me. Paul sounds least likely, though don't discount him because of the leg. I've seen men fire rifles when they've been shot to bits themselves.' His face clouded, and Millicent and I knew he was thinking back to his time in the trenches.

'Vincent sounds harmless enough,' Millicent remarked.

'I'm not sure. I did overhear something a bit odd. It was just after Superintendent Cobbe questioned me at Mill Ponds. As I was leaving, I heard the men talking in the lounge.'

'Of course you did.' Percy laughed. 'You have a talent for loitering and eavesdropping.'

'I admit, I was. I'm suspected of murder. You can't blame me for wanting to find out the truth.'

'Fair enough,' he replied. 'So what did you hear?'

'Hugh was asking Vincent what he'd meant by a comment he'd made about Archie going off to the summerhouse again.'

'Summerhouse?' Millicent wrinkled her brow. 'I didn't think there was one at Mill Ponds House.'

'There's not. They're building a greenhouse in the new garden, but that's not a summerhouse. When Vincent claimed that's what he meant, Hugh challenged him, saying he'd clearly said summerhouse, not greenhouse, and that Archie hadn't been going into the garden. Apparently, he'd cycled down the driveway to the lake path and turned left.'

'Have you mentioned this to Ben?' Percy asked.

'No. Because...' I hesitated.

'Because what?'

'Well, if you come out of Mill Ponds onto the lake path and turn left, it takes you around to Willow Marsh. Above that is Sand Hills Hall – where there's a summerhouse that overlooks the lake.'

Percy brushed crumbs from his lap. 'You think that's what Vincent Owen was talking about?'

'He once worked for the Thackerays. And it's the nearest summerhouse to Mill Ponds.'

Of the four large houses situated around the lake, Sand Hills Hall was the only one unoccupied. Mrs Siddons resided in Grebe House, Horace Laffaye in Heron Bay Lodge, and the hostel had given Mill Ponds a new lease of life. Sand Hills Hall stood vacant and had been boarded up. Somehow, I found that fitting, given the tragedy that had befallen the Thackerays.

'And you don't want to tell Ben because of Alice?' Percy knew Ben had loved Alice Thackeray as much as I had.

I nodded. It had taken Ben years to come to terms with what had happened, and I didn't want to remind him of it now. Not when he was seeing a girl for the first time since we'd lost Alice.

'I may be completely wrong. Sand Hills Hall has been empty since Mrs Thackeray moved to London. It's on the market, but I don't think there's been much interest. I can't see why Archie would want to go there, unless he had some sort of plan to expand his empire, although I doubt the church would stump up for another old mansion.'

'But Vincent specifically said summerhouse,' Millicent commented.

'Let's go and take a look.' In typical Percy style, he leapt to his feet and started throwing the remains of our picnic into the basket, waving Millicent away when she tried to help him pack it in some sort of order. Freddie needn't have worried that we'd scoff all the food. We'd barely made a dent in the huge chicken and ham pie that Hetty had baked, and there was still plenty of Ursula's cake left.

We trekked back through the undergrowth and onto the road where Percy had parked his car. After storing the picnic basket in the boot, we rejoined the footpath that circled the lake and set off for Sand Hills Hall.

It was a place I hadn't visited in years. After Alice's death, her mother had found it too painful to stay in Walden and had shut up the hall and moved to London. Since then, I'd avoided going there.

When we reached Willow Marsh and the foot of Sand Hills,

we climbed the slope up to the gates of Alice's old home. The rotting wooden jetty that had once dominated the marshes had been demolished the previous year and white blooms of water lilies filled the space it had occupied.

The hall was an imposing Victorian mansion that over-looked Waldenmere on the eastern side of the lake. The Thack-erays were a military family, and Alice's grandfather had bought Sand Hills Hall in 1854 when the army had first settled in nearby Aldershot.

Percy went over to the iron gate set into the grey stone walls that surrounded the hall and gave it a tug. 'It's locked.'

Millicent's relief showed. 'Perhaps that's for the best. I'm not sure this was such a good idea.'

'There's another way in.' I began to walk alongside the moss-covered stone wall. 'The wall doesn't quite encircle the hall. There's a long gap on this side of the garden so that you can see down to the lake.'

The summerhouse was situated at the edge of the grounds of Sand Hills Hall, perched on top of the slope that dropped down to Waldenmere. It was positioned to offer a view of the shimmering water in the distance but set far enough back not to be seen from below.

The scent of a tall conifer and the sound of doves cooing on the roof conjured up memories of sunny afternoons spent there with Alice. We'd gather strawberries from the kitchen garden and sit in the summerhouse, eating them from our laps as we chatted.

Tears pricked my eyes when I saw how neglected it was. In the years since Mrs Thackeray had left, ivy had grown over its walls, partially obscuring the large windows.

'I don't think anyone has been here,' I murmured, regret-ting our decision to come.

'I wouldn't be too sure of that.' Percy was peering through the tarnished glass windows. He walked around to the door, where an ornate iron key was sitting in the lock. It turned easily in his hand, and when he pushed the wooden door, it swung open with no creaking.

'Look.' Millicent pointed to the trunk of a thick oak tree that towered over the summerhouse.

Leaning against it was a man's bicycle.

22

'Is it Archie's?' Percy asked.

I examined the bicycle. 'I can't tell, but it's a bit of a coincidence that his is missing.'

He went over to the summerhouse and tried locking and unlocking the door several times. 'I think someone has oiled the lock and hinges.'

'Perhaps a caretaker did it, although they haven't tended the garden.' Millicent gazed at the neglected flowerbeds and patchy lawn.

I'd expected the summerhouse to smell musty, but inside, the air was fresh.

'Someone's been here recently.' Percy ran a finger over the clean window ledge. 'There's no dust and the floor's been swept.'

The summerhouse was exactly as I remembered it. The Thackerays' wicker sofa and chairs were still there, the rose pattern of the cushions faded by sunlight. The same beige hessian rug covered the stone floor. I sniffed and imagined I caught the scent of freshly picked strawberries. Then I wrinkled my nose as I realised the aroma was the lingering traces of a ladies' sweet perfume.

I knew at once that Archie had been here with a woman, and a wave of fury washed over me. It was yet another violation of a place that was dear to me. When I looked down and saw the heavy iron doorstop in the shape of a duck, I burst into tears. I had a vision of Alice dragging it across the floor to prop open the door on a hot afternoon. How dare he touch something that had once belonged to my dear friend?

Percy put his arm around my shoulder and held me close, stroking my hair as I sobbed into his chest.

'I'm sorry,' I mumbled when I pulled away.

Percy said nothing, dismissing my apology with a sweep of his arm.

Millicent handed me a fresh handkerchief. 'We know how much you miss her.'

'It's the thought of him being here, amongst her things.'

'We can't be sure it was Archie who's been coming here.' Percy poked around the cushions on the sofa to see if anything telling had been left behind. 'Why would he?'

'To meet someone in secret?' Millicent suggested. 'What about Victoria Hobbs?'

Percy pulled a face. 'She would never look at a man like Powell.'

'He looked at her,' Millicent replied.

I thought about this. Victoria was a widow with her own house. If she had wanted to meet with Archie, they could have made excuses for him to call on her at home, though neighbours' curtains might have twitched. Like Percy, I didn't want to think Victoria would fall for a man like Archie, but it was possible. However, there was another more likely candidate.

'Let's assume it's a married woman. That's why they had to meet here in secret.' I glanced down at the cushioned sofa.

Percy followed my gaze and raised his eyebrows. 'Do you have anyone in mind?'

'Jennifer Tolfree. She knows about the summerhouse as she's friends with Florence Thackeray.'

'It's possible, I suppose.' Millicent sounded doubtful.

Whoever it was, I was sure I was right about Archie meeting a woman here. And I hated him for it. I closed my eyes, trying not to let my feelings for Archie grow into something that would eat away at me. He'd been a flawed man. Nothing more. He was dead, and it was time to forgive and forget.

When I opened my eyes, I inhaled sharply at the sight of a tall figure dressed in black walking across the Thackerays' unkept lawn. For a heart-stopping moment, I imagined it was Archie coming towards me.

As the figure approached, I realised it was Hugh Alvarez, dressed in dark trousers and a black jumper, carrying a sketch pad.

'Hello there.' He peered inside the summerhouse as if it was the most natural thing in the world that we should be meeting in the grounds of a hall that had been empty for years.

'What are you doing here?' I asked.

'Same as you. I'm guessing you listened in to my conversation with Vincent Owen.'

'She does that,' Percy observed. 'I've tried to break her of the habit but she will eavesdrop.'

I elbowed him in the ribs.

Hugh laughed and introduced himself. 'Are you the married man? Or the one Archie assumed was married?'

Millicent made a gulping noise.

'No,' I almost yelled. 'This is Percy Baverstock. An old and annoying friend of mine.'

'What do you—'

Millicent cut in before Percy could continue. 'How did you know about Sand Hills Hall? You're not local, are you?'

Hugh shook his head. 'I asked around about summer-houses. Someone at the factory mentioned this place.'

'Have you worked in a factory before?' I asked, desperate to keep the conversation away from the subject of married men.

'Not in one. But I've done my share of loading and unloading lorries in factory yards.' Hugh took in the interior of the summerhouse. 'Looks like someone's been making them-selves comfortable here.'

I nodded. 'How did Vincent know this was where Archie was heading?'

'I think Vincent sometimes comes here to keep an eye on the place out of loyalty to the Thackerays. I suppose he must have seen him.'

From the gleam in his eyes as he scrutinised the summer-house, he suspected what had been behind Archie's visits.

I pointed to the bicycle leaning against the oak tree. 'Is that Archie's?'

Hugh let out a low whistle and went over to it. 'Yes. I think it is.'

'We'll tell the police about it.' Millicent tugged at my arm and shot a glance at Percy, who was watching Hugh with a puzzled expression. 'We should go now. After all, we're trespassing.'

'You're right,' Hugh agreed. 'Although I'm going to make a quick sketch of the hall before I leave. It's an impressive building.'

As we made our way out of the garden, Percy looked back at

Hugh, who was now inspecting the outside of Sand Hills Hall. 'What did he mean about me being your married man?'

I took my time answering, gripping Millicent's arm as we walked around the moss-covered wall.

'Well?' Percy demanded.

'Hugh, Paul and Vincent overheard the row I had with Archie on the day he died. Archie was implying I was having an affair with a married man.'

Percy didn't reply immediately, and the three of us clambered down the slope in silence.

Once we were walking along the lake path by Willow Marsh, Percy asked, 'Is it true? Are you?'

'No. Of course not.'

'Then why didn't you tell me?'

'There's nothing to tell.'

'Did you know about this?' he asked Millicent.

'Superintendent Cobbe mentioned it when he called on Ursula and me. I told him I had no idea who Archie could have been referring to.'

It was a diplomatic answer. But I could tell Percy wasn't satisfied.

When we reached Heron Bay, I was glad to see Ben standing by the shore with Laura, a pretty young woman who was bound to distract Percy.

To my surprise, Ben whispered something to Laura, then left her by the water's edge while he hurried over to us. He clearly wasn't intending to introduce her. Was that my fault, I wondered? Perhaps he didn't want to risk her being associated with me.

Millicent told him about the summerhouse and the bicycle we'd found.

'At Sand Hills Hall?' He frowned. 'I'll get Sid to go up there and take a look.'

Percy nudged him. 'I say, is that your new girlfriend? She's jolly pretty.' He gave Laura a smile and one of his inane waves, and she smiled and waved back.

My relief that Ben and Laura had diverted him from the subject of my married man was short-lived.

'Before I left the station house, Superintendent Cobbe telephoned Sid to say he's coming over from Winchester to speak to you,' Ben told me.

'What's she done now?' Percy flapped his hands in exasperation.

'I haven't done anything.' But I knew I had. I'd lied about Marc.

'You told the superintendent you didn't meet anyone on your walk on the night of the eleventh. Yet someone claims they saw you kissing a man on the jetty by the railway station at around nine o'clock.'

23

'You're on the run from the police?' Freddie was just beginning to grasp what was going on.

After Ben had told us Superintendent Cobbe was on his way over to interview me, I'd persuaded Percy to take me back to London with him. I explained to Millicent and Ursula that I needed to speak to the man I'd been seen with before I could answer the superintendent's questions. They'd agreed to tell him I was staying with friends in London and would return in a day or so.

I'd packed an overnight bag, and as Superintendent Cobbe drove from Winchester to Walden, we drove from Walden to Winchester to pick up Percy's younger brother.

In the car, Freddie had presumed Percy would drop me off somewhere. Only when we were all standing in the living room of Percy's first-floor flat on Brompton Road did he realise I'd be staying the night with them.

'No. I'm not on the run. I just need a little more time before I talk to the police again.'

Freddie stared at me with round, dark eyes that were so like his brother's. He had the same floppy brown hair and hand-some features as Percy, although his face was thinner and more boyish.

Percy had gone quiet, and I knew he was starting to regret what we'd done.

'Of course, you're welcome.' Freddie pushed his floppy fringe back from his brow, his cheeks flushed with embarrass-ment. 'I'm just not sure it's seemly for you to stay here with us.'

Percy was shuffling from foot to foot. 'Perhaps it would be best if I take you to your grandmother's.'

'It's only for tonight.' I hoped this was true. It depended on whether I was successful in tracking down Marc the following day. After I'd spoken to him, I could decide what to say to Superintendent Cobbe. 'No one will know I'm here.'

Percy shrugged and picked up my overnight bag. 'You can have my bed. I'll sleep on the sofa.'

'Thank you.' I reached out to squeeze his arm, but he brushed past me and took my bag into the bedroom.

For supper, we sat around the table in the tiny kitchen and shared the remains of the picnic with Freddie. Hetty had packed the leftovers in a large bag along with other essential supplies, probably realising the flat contained little more than a loaf of stale bread and a few bottles of beer. After supper, Freddie went to his room to study, leaving Percy and me to share a bottle of beer in the living room.

'What are you planning to do?' Percy asked.

'Go to where my friend works to speak to him.'

'I suppose you can't visit his home if he's married.'

I flushed at this. I didn't like to admit that I didn't know where Marc lived. I knew it was near Chelsea, but not exactly where. I'd always written to him at his work address.

'Did you kiss him that night on the jetty?' Percy was holding the neck of the beer bottle between his fingers and swinging it as if trying to appear nonchalant.

'He... we... we were saying goodbye. I've known him for a long time, and we won't see each other again. We were close, but we weren't having an affair.'

I could tell he didn't believe me. 'Then why haven't you told Superintendent Cobbe his name?'

'Because he'd want to interview him. He might think he had something to do with Archie's death.'

'Are you certain that he didn't?'

'He wasn't even aware of Archie's existence. He knows nothing about what's been going on in Walden. It wouldn't be fair for me to give the police his name without telling him what's happened first.'

When Percy didn't reply, we sat in awkward silence until I said I was going to turn in. For a long time, I lay awake on Percy's bed, listening to him shuffling around in the living room. I wanted to go to him and apologise, but I knew I was only likely to make things worse.

The following morning, I rose at dawn and crept into the bathroom, careful not to wake Percy or Freddie. I needn't have worried, as even the noise of a cat jumping in through the kitchen window and knocking over an empty beer bottle failed to rouse them.

I shooed the cat out and closed the window, then went into the living room. From the bedroom, I could hear Freddie's snores. Percy was sprawled along the length of the sofa, his long legs dangling over the end. I smiled at the sight of his floppy hair spread across the cushions.

Silently, I left the flat and walked to the bus stop on Brompton Road. When I got to Chancery Lane, I sat on a bench close to Tyler & Simcock, the law firm where Marc worked, and waited for him to arrive.

The street got busier as the hours passed, and I watched a stream of men in dark suits and bowler hats enter the austere grey stone building. By ten o'clock, there was still no sign of Marc, and I began to grow impatient, peering up and down the road.

I got up and strolled along Chancery Lane, all the while keeping an eye on the entrance to Tyler & Simcock. When I couldn't stand it any longer, I took a deep breath and went up the steps of the building and opened the door.

Glancing around for any sign of Marc, I walked over to the reception desk. The young woman behind it greeted me with a smile. 'Good morning. Do you have an appointment?'

'No. I'm looking for a...' I referred to a piece of paper in my hand as if I was unfamiliar with the name. Quite why I'd felt the need for this subterfuge, I wasn't sure. 'Mr Jansen.'

'I'm afraid Mr Jansen no longer works here.'

'Oh.' I felt a thud in my chest. I hadn't anticipated Marc would leave so soon. I'd imagined it would take months for him to work his notice and make arrangements.

'He left recently and has returned to Belgium. That's where he's from,' she added. 'Perhaps one of our other solicitors can help you?'

'Thank you. I'm here on behalf of my... aunt. I'll consult with her first and then come back to you.' I turned and walked out of the building, feeling bereft.

Although we'd agreed to have no further contact, I'd taken comfort from the fact that Marc was still in the country. It was a shock to know this wasn't the case, and I had no address for him in Belgium.

I returned to the flat expecting to find it empty, but Percy was seated in the living room, waiting for me.

'Shouldn't you be at work?'

'I've been into work. I told them I was going to spend the day back at Waldenmere.' He scrutinised my face. 'What did this chap say?'

'He's gone.' I dumped my bag on the floor and slumped into an armchair.

'Gone where?'

'Abroad. I knew he was going, but I hadn't expected him to leave so soon.'

'What are you going to do now?'

'Go home. Talk to Superintendent Cobbe.'

'Will you tell him who this man is?'

This was the question that had been playing on my mind since leaving Tyler & Simcock. What would happen if I told Superintendent Cobbe the truth? Would he contact the police in Belgium and ask them to interview Marc? After all, he'd been in the vicinity at the time they suspected the murder had taken place.

How would that look to Marc's new employer? And to his wife and parents? His new life, his fresh start, would be tainted forever by what happened when he was in England. I couldn't do that to him. And I didn't want to do it to us. To Marc and me. I wanted to keep the ending we'd had. That final, loving kiss by the lake.

'No,' I said with a finality that I hoped would deter him from arguing. Of course, the matter might be taken out of my hands if the police found Archie's diary and Marc's name appeared in its pages.

Percy looked at me for a long time before saying, 'Tell Cobbe you were kissing me that night.'

It took me a moment to realise what he was saying. 'I can't do—'

'It would solve everything.' Percy came over and knelt by my armchair. 'Tell him you met me on your walk. It would give you an alibi and stop him from questioning you about this married man. We kissed, and then I walked you home. That way, you'll have an alibi for the whole evening. Millicent and Ursula know you were in the house the rest of the time.'

I rested my head in my hands and let the tears flow. I couldn't believe he would consider doing such a thing for me. Eventually, I raised my head and wiped my eyes on the handkerchief he'd offered.

'I can't let you do that.' He made it sound so easy, but I knew it would be far too dangerous.

'Why not?'

'Because you'll get into trouble.'

'How?'

'Where were you on the night of Sunday the eleventh of May?'

He had to think about it. 'Here with Freddie. We went to the pub on the corner for a quick one, but he wouldn't stay out long. Can't keep him away from his books.'

'So if you lie to Superintendent Cobbe and he checks, Freddie will have to lie and say you weren't here when you were. One lie will lead to more lies, and even more people will get dragged into this mess because of me.'

'It's not your fault. You didn't murder Archie.'

I took a deep breath. 'No. I didn't. But... I am guilty of allowing my behaviour to affect others. This is my responsibility to sort out.'

He didn't reply, just sat kneeling on the floor, looking up at me. I leant forward and kissed the top of his head.

'Thank you for... for everything.' I saw his lip tremble and stroked his hair. 'Freddie's right. It's not seemly for me to be here. Can you take me to the station?'

He shook his head. 'Pack your bag. I'll drive you back to Walden.'

24

'Iris.' PC Sid King's face was a picture when he opened the door of the station house and found me standing there with Percy.

Superintendent Cobbe had called at 13 Victoria Lane on Sunday evening. When Ursula had informed him I was staying with a friend in London, he'd requested that I visit the station house on my return.

Percy had insisted on driving me there straight away, probably afraid I'd get cold feet and end up back at his flat.

'I had a message to say Superintendent Cobbe would like to speak with me?'

Sid glanced over his shoulder. 'I'll let him know you're home.'

'Did you want me to come in and wait?' I'd expected him to drag me in and tell me to stay put until the superintendent arrived. Instead, he seemed to want to get rid of me.

'No. That's not necessary. We'll let you—' Before he could finish, a tall woman with long blonde hair appeared behind him and pushed past.

I tensed, noticing the resemblance to Archie in the curve of her jaw and the intensity of her green eyes.

'Iris Woodmore?' she asked.

I took a step back. 'Yes.'

'I'm Teresa Powell. Archie's sister. My brother told me about you.'

Whatever Archie had said, it hadn't been good.

'I'm... I'm sorry for your loss,' I mumbled.

'No. You're not. You're glad he's dead. You tried to destroy him, and you finally succeeded. And I'm going to make sure you pay for what you did.' With that, she strode away, stifling a sob.

Ben appeared and jerked his head at Sid, who nodded and hurried down the path after her.

'Miss Powell,' Sid called. 'Let me take you to Mill Ponds House.'

Ben pulled me into the station house, and Percy followed, his arm around my shoulder.

'What has she been saying?' Percy demanded. 'Why is she so hostile to Iris?'

'She's insinuating Archie was shot with his own rifle as some kind of vengeance,' Ben replied. 'By Iris or someone in cahoots with her.'

'Did she know he had a rifle?' I asked.

'She did. And she didn't think it worth mentioning to the police.' Ben shook his head in exasperation. 'After his time as an army chaplain in France, Archie returned home with two rifles.'

'Two!' Percy spluttered. 'Good grief. Didn't he have enough of all that on the battlefields? I certainly did.'

'As well as the one we confiscated at the time of his arrest, there was a second one kept at his family home. After his conviction, they didn't want to get him into any more trouble, so they kept quiet about it. When Archie moved into Mill Ponds, he visited the family home to collect a few things, the rifle being one of them. He told his sister that it was for shooting pests in the garden.'

Percy was wandering around the parlour again. 'Given his conviction for a firearms offence, wasn't she concerned about this?'

'Apparently not. She claims he wouldn't hurt a soul. Obviously, now she regrets not reporting it to the police.'

'No doubt she considered him to be a reformed character.' I sank into an armchair, feeling Teresa Powell was hardly in a position to throw accusations at me. And Archie most certainly hadn't been either. 'Was that Archie's bicycle up at Sand Hills Hall?'

Ben nodded. 'It seems he went out for a ride and, for whatever reason, left his bicycle by the summerhouse.'

'I think we know the reason,' Percy sniggered.

'I'm not so sure.' Ben perched on a chair beside me. 'Teresa Powell said that Archie was planning to settle down. She believes you decided to put a stop to his happiness.'

'Settle down?' I queried.

'In his last letter to his sister, Archie told her he'd recently asked someone to marry him.'

I snorted. 'Who?'

'Archie didn't give her name but said she was a widow. She turned him down, saying it was too soon after her husband's death. Archie told his sister that, in time, he hoped she would agree to marry him.'

'Victoria Hobbs, I bet,' I said.

Percy's mouth dropped. 'No. I can't believe that.'

'I told you he liked her.'

'And I told you, she would never look at a man like Powell. Not after Harry.'

'She turned him down,' Ben pointed out. 'So it appears she didn't reciprocate his feelings.'

Percy seemed mollified. 'She never mentioned it when I saw her at the weekend.'

This didn't surprise me. The Baverstock family had been close to Harry Hobbs, and I could imagine Victoria's reluctance to tell them about a proposal, particularly an unwanted one.

'Why don't we call in and see her?' I suggested. I expected Ben to object to this, but to my surprise, he nodded.

'Sid or I will be speaking to Mrs Hobbs. However, I appreciate this is something she might feel uncomfortable talking about. As you're her friends, she might reveal more to you. If she does, tell me. In the meantime, I'm going to telephone Winchester police station and let Superintendent Cobbe know you came here. He'll probably want to see Miss Powell first, so he may not speak to you until tomorrow.' Ben gave me a stern look. 'Do not leave Walden until he does.'

* * *

Victoria Hobbs lived in one of the new houses on the Crookham estate, not far from Crookham Hall.

In the years following the Great War, the site had become a makeshift campsite, with caravans and shacks providing inadequate accommodation for poor families. After being elected Member of Parliament for Aldershot in 1920, Mrs Siddons replaced the dwellings with affordable housing under the national building scheme. Micky and Polly Swann had benefited from this and had been able to rent one of the houses when they'd moved to Walden from London.

The previous year, Victoria Hobbs and her husband had moved into a house nearby. Sadly, Harry had died shortly afterwards.

Victoria showed us into the lounge, and any fears Percy may have had that she'd consigned her husband to the past were soon put to rest by the array of photographs on display. I saw Percy getting teary-eyed as he looked at them and went to make tea while he and Victoria reminisced about Harry.

I rather liked the compact kitchens of the new houses. They were cleverly designed with built-in larders and sleek gas cookers, a far cry from the old cooking ranges that I was used to. Victoria's kitchen was spotlessly clean and smelt of laundry soap. I couldn't help thinking it wouldn't be so pristine if Harry were still around. Even less so if they'd had the children he'd longed for.

When I returned to the lounge with the tea tray, Percy had already introduced the subject of Archie.

'I didn't want to say too much about him in front of your parents,' Victoria was saying. 'Archie did propose. And I turned him down. I couldn't marry again. Not after...' She gestured around at the photographs, and it was obvious where her heart lay.

'Harry would want you to be happy.' Percy hesitated. 'If you ever met someone special, I'd be delighted for you. And so would my parents and Freddie.'

Tears sprang to Victoria's eyes, and to my surprise, I found myself hastily wiping my cheeks. To hide my face, I bent down to pour the tea.

Victoria's hand trembled when she took the cup from me. 'When I turned down Archie's proposal, I tried to make it clear that it wasn't just because of Harry. I didn't love Archie and never would.'

Yet according to what he'd written to his sister, Archie had hoped to one day win Victoria's hand. This didn't surprise me. That was Archie's nature. When he decided something should be a certain way, he did all he could to change the situation – including pointing a rifle at someone.

'Did Archie ever ask you to meet him somewhere? A summerhouse, for instance?' I asked.

Victoria shook her head. 'I generally only saw him in church on Sundays. When I knew he was developing feelings for me, I tried to distance myself from him. It was a shame, as I wanted to help out at Mill Ponds – to honour Harry. He would have been the first to lend a hand to a fellow soldier suffering because of what they'd been through in the war. But I rarely went to Mill Ponds after... after Archie told me how he felt about me.'

Percy was shaking his head, clearly fuming with Archie. 'When did he ask you to marry him? Bloody presumptuous of him.'

'At Easter. We were in the church, and I was collecting the hymn books after the service on Easter Sunday. The vicar was outside speaking to his parishioners, and Archie and I were alone.'

Easter Sunday. Polly had mentioned that day. I recalled our conversation in the kitchen at Mill Ponds when I'd asked if Archie often worked in the garden. She'd said the last time had been on Easter Sunday. He'd come back from church in a mood and seemed to be digging as a way of getting rid of his frustration.

'Did Archie ask you again? Perhaps on the day he died?' I suggested.

Victoria placed her teacup on the table, her hand still trembling. 'He told me that his feelings hadn't changed and he hoped in time I'd come to realise that we should be together. He said something about it being God's will. That's when I became angry.'

'How did Archie react?' I knew from experience he didn't like women defying him.

She flushed. 'All I'd wanted to do was hand over the bag of clothes I'd brought and go away again. When Archie said we needed to talk, I told him there was nothing to say. He grabbed my arm.' Hesitantly, she rolled up the sleeve of her pink cotton summer dress. A ring of greenish bruising encircled her upper arm.

Percy clenched his jaw. 'That bloody man. He really was the limit.'

I reached for Victoria's hand. 'That must have been frightening.' Although Archie had never physically hurt me, on more than one occasion, I'd suspected he was on the brink of lashing out.

'For a moment, I thought he was going to strike me. Then, he seemed to come to his senses. When I told him he was hurting me, he let go of my arm at once.' Victoria said it almost apologetically, making Percy's jaw clench even tighter.

'You should tell Sergeant Gilbert what took place.' I didn't know how relevant this information was to what happened to Archie, but it gave us an insight into his frame of mind at the time of his death.

She nodded. 'I'm sorry for not saying anything earlier.'

'You have nothing to be sorry for,' Percy said gently. I could tell he was trying to appear calm lest Victoria think he was angry with her and not Archie.

'It's just I was so furious. When he tried to apologise, I told him to go to hell and ran to the taxi.' Tears returned to Victoria's eyes. 'Those were the last words I said to him.'

25

I spent the following day with a knot in my stomach, waiting for Superintendent Cobbe to appear.

Elijah wasn't impressed that I hadn't shown up for work on Monday. He threatened to sack me unless I told him where I'd been. As we both knew he wouldn't carry out this threat, it wasn't much of an inducement for me to explain why I'd fled to Percy's flat.

However, with Ursula's advice in mind about not keeping secrets from my friends, I told him why I'd suddenly decided to go to London with Percy and Freddie on Sunday night. The only information I omitted was the name of the man I'd hoped to see while I was there.

'If I were you, I'd tell Cobbe everything and have done with it.'

But he wasn't me. And I wasn't entirely sure I believed him. If he were in a situation where he had to protect Horace, I reckoned he'd stay silent, too.

I didn't have the nerve to suggest this and instead put up with his nagging for the rest of the day. It wasn't until I was tidying my desk and preparing to head home that I heard the sound of boots on the office stairs. PC Sid King poked his head around the door.

'Superintendent Cobbe is at the station house. He'd like a word.'

'I'll be over shortly.'

Sid nodded and disappeared again.

Elijah stubbed out his cigarette. 'Do you want me to come with you?'

I shook my head. After his moaning and groaning, I appreciated the fact that he was still willing to help me. However, this was something best tackled alone. I picked up my bag and cardigan and left the office, walking slowly up to the high street. By the time I reached the station house, I'd decided what I was going to say.

Sid opened the door and gave me a cheery grin as he showed me into the office. He'd trusted me not to run off again, and I guessed he was relieved I'd shown up. There would have been questions to answer if I hadn't.

Superintendent Cobbe was seated behind the desk Ben usually occupied. He stood up as I walked in but didn't smile. He gestured for me to sit down and told Sid he could go on his rounds as he wouldn't be needed.

Sid looked a little disappointed. I think he'd hoped to hear the next instalment of this saga. He nodded at the superintendent and closed the door, leaving me to my fate.

'Miss Woodmore. You told me that when you went for a walk on the evening of Sunday the eleventh of May, you didn't meet anyone. Yet I have an eyewitness who saw you kissing a man on the jetty by the railway station.'

I wondered who the witness was. Could it be Hugh Alvarez? Was it conceivable he'd gone out without Vincent or

Paul noticing? If he had, it was feasible any of them could have slipped into the garden and shot Archie without the others seeing.

Hugh had a habit of appearing at the worst possible moment. First, he'd witnessed the scene between me and Archie at the open day. Then he'd overheard our row by the lake. He'd even shown up at the summerhouse of Sand Hills Hall. Why was he so nosy? Could Archie have told him to keep an eye on me? Yet why would he comply, particularly now Archie was dead?

'I did meet someone in London on the afternoon of the eleventh. A friend who came to Walden later that evening. When we said goodbye, we kissed briefly.' All of that was true, except perhaps the word 'brief'. I had no idea how long our kiss had lasted. All I knew was that I hadn't wanted it to end.

'Why didn't you tell me about this man sooner?'

'Because it's not relevant.'

The superintendent made a strange noise, which I took to be a growl of annoyance.

'I'll decide what's relevant. All you have to do is tell the truth. The whole truth,' he added, obviously seeing I was about to protest.

'He's an old friend of mine. We meet up sometimes just to talk.' I emphasised these last words.

'How did Mr Powell know about this man?'

'You remember I told you Archie had followed me home from Sycamore Lodge on New Year's Eve?'

He nodded.

'It wasn't the first time he'd followed me. In the months before that, he'd been spying on me. He'd even get on the same train as me if he saw me at the station. At least once, he followed me to London. That's when he saw me with this man.'

The thought of Archie watching me all those months still made me feel sick. And angry. How dare he invade my life like that.

'What was he hoping to discover by spying on you?'

'Me doing something I shouldn't.'

'Not an unfeasible expectation,' he said drily. 'How did Mr Powell know this man was married?'

'One afternoon, Archie followed him back to his place of work. He asked around and managed to find out who he was.'

The superintendent fixed me with a severe look. 'You must understand that if Mr Powell had this man's name, I need it too.'

'He has nothing to do with all this. I've never mentioned Archie to him.'

'I don't care.' His voice was harsher than I'd ever heard it. 'He was in Walden at the time of Mr Powell's death. He might have witnessed something. He could also provide you with an alibi for at least some of the time.'

This left me in no doubt that I was still a suspect.

'He was only on the jetty for a short time before he got into his car and drove back to London. Didn't your eyewitness see that?' As I said it, a dreadful thought occurred to me. Whoever saw the car might have made a note of its registration number.

Superintendent Cobbe ignored this. 'Is that where he lives? London?'

'It was. He's since moved abroad. And I don't have an address for him.'

'A name will do,' he snapped. From the look on his face, he was struggling to keep his temper.

I didn't reply, and we sat in silence for a few moments.

When he spoke again, it was in a softer tone. 'Mr Whittle said that Mr Powell was the aggressor. Sergeant Gilbert has also taken a statement from Mrs Victoria Hobbs regarding her encounter with Mr Powell shortly before he died. Was Mr Powell ever violent towards you?'

'Not physically, unless you count pointing a rifle at me, though I doubt he intended to fire it. But he liked to threaten me, and if he saw an opportunity to scare or annoy me, he'd take it.'

'Was Mr Powell blackmailing you about your relationship with this married man?' the superintendent asked bluntly.

I shook my head. 'Not exactly.'

'What's that supposed to mean?' He began tapping his pen on the desk in a gesture of frustration.

'He didn't ask me for money.'

'What was he asking for?'

'He didn't want me to disrupt his plans for the hostel.'

Superintendent Cobbe scrutinised me while he digested this. 'Presumably, he threatened to tell people about your relationship with this man if you didn't co-operate? A relationship you claim is wholly innocent, yet one you're determined to keep a secret.'

'Yes.' I was beginning to regret sharing as much information as I had with the superintendent. Everything I'd told him proved I had good cause to want Archie dead.

'Mr Powell seems to have made your life extremely unpleasant since he was released from prison. I'm sorry for that. I wish you'd come to me. Or confided in your friend, Sergeant Gilbert. We would have done what we could to help you. However, we now find ourselves in this situation.' He took a deep breath. 'As reluctant as I am, if you refuse to give me the name of this man, this "friend", I will be forced to arrest you.'

I felt a tremor run through me. Although the superintendent's tone was now kindly, there was no mistaking the resolution behind his words.

'I didn't kill Archie Powell.' It was all I had left to say.

'We're going around in circles. All I want—'

'Sir.' Ben barged in without knocking. 'We have a missing child. The Tolfrees' son, Luke, hasn't been seen since this morning.'

26

'How old is this boy?' Superintendent Cobbe asked, getting to his feet. 'And when did he go missing?'

'Luke is nine years old,' Ben replied. 'He hasn't been seen since around a quarter to nine this morning. He walked to school with his mother, Jennifer Tolfree, and his older sister, Daisy, who's ten. Mrs Tolfree watched the children go through the school gates, and then she walked home. Daisy ran off to play with her friends and then went into her classroom. She didn't see her brother for the rest of the day. She's in the year above, and her lessons take place in a different part of the school. She assumed Luke had gone into class with his friends as usual. But none of his friends or schoolteachers saw him that day. When Mrs Gertrude Tolfree walked to the school this afternoon to collect her grandchildren, only Daisy was there.'

The superintendent glanced at his watch, and I looked up at the station clock. It was now after seven, which meant that nearly ten hours had passed since Luke was last seen.

'Any ideas where he might have gone?' Superintendent Cobbe asked.

'His favourite places are the lake and the railway station. He likes to watch trains. As we have no sightings of him in town, I suggest we organise a search from Mill Ponds House.'

The superintendent nodded. 'Let's do what we can before the light fades. Where are the Tolfrees?'

'They're already at Mill Ponds.'

'Right, let's get going.' With that, Superintendent Cobbe strode from the room with Ben in tow.

I hurried out of the station house after them. 'I can help search.'

I was ignored, Ben cycling off while Superintendent Cobbe got into his car. I was tempted to tap on the window and ask for a lift to Mill Ponds, but as he'd been on the brink of arresting me, I decided it might be safer to walk.

When I got to Mill Ponds, a crowd had gathered on the lawn. I wasn't surprised to find Millicent amongst them.

'Could Luke's disappearance have anything to do with Archie's death?' she said in an undertone when I reached her side. 'I've noticed he hasn't been himself recently in class. Do you think he might have witnessed something?'

'I saw Luke at the station on the day of Archie's death. It was as I was walking across the concourse. He came by on his bicycle and nearly—'

'What are you doing here?'

I turned to find Teresa Powell scowling at me.

'I've come to help with the search.'

Paul Richardson tugged at her arm. 'Now's not the time.'

I expected Teresa to shrug him off, but her face softened, and she allowed him to take her arm.

'I had nothing to do with your brother's death,' I said to her retreating figure as Paul escorted her into the house.

'So that's the sister,' Millicent whispered. She was about to say more when Superintendent Cobbe appeared. He nodded to Ben before ushering Gordon, Jennifer and Gertrude Tolfree into Mill Ponds.

Once they were inside and the door closed, Ben held up his hand to address the gathering.

'Thank you all for coming to assist in the search for Luke Tolfree. Many of you will know Luke by sight. For those who don't, he's nine years old, of slim build, with short, wavy blond hair and blue eyes. He's just under five foot tall. Luke loves being by the lake, particularly Heron Bay, and he also likes to watch trains. He usually stands on the pedestrian footbridge over the railway station to see them go by. He's not allowed on the road bridge.'

A murmur rose from the crowd. This was the bridge I'd stood on with Percy as we'd tried to see into the garden of Mill Ponds. As Percy had pointed out, it wasn't a bridge to take at speed as the low walls on either side were all that stood between a pedestrian or motorist from falling onto the railway track below.

Could Luke have gone there on the day of the murder and seen something? But that didn't make sense. He'd been cycling home just before I'd encountered Archie by the jetty.

'The railway line has already been checked, and there's no sign of an accident,' Ben said, pre-empting the awful suggestion that Luke might have fallen. 'PC King is going to lead a group to search the area by the railway station and along the line of allotments. My group will go further afield and search all the way around to the south side of the lake to Heron Bay.'

'What about in the water?' Hugh Alvarez asked in a low voice.

'It's too late to search the water tonight. If he's not found, a diver will be called in tomorrow. What we can do is to keep an eye on the shallows and reedbeds for any sightings. When he was last seen, Luke was wearing his grey school uniform and black leather shoes.'

Sid began to organise the men into groups, and Millicent and I hurried over to Ben.

'What can we do?' I asked.

'Go and see Mrs Siddons and Mr Laffaye. If Luke has been at the lake at any time today, they or their staff might have seen him. If he's not found, Sid and I will go door-to-door to all the houses on roads leading from Waldenmere. But to start with, let's concentrate on the houses located around the lake.'

'Has Mill Ponds been searched?' I thought of Archie lying bleeding in the trench. Help had been close by, but no one except the person who'd fired the shot had known he was there.

'Thoroughly. House and gardens,' Ben said before turning away. Then he called over his shoulder, 'I've given out all the torches we could find, so go home before it gets too dark.'

Millicent and I set off down the driveway to the lake footpath.

'Which way? Left or right?' Millicent asked.

If we turned right, Horace Laffaye in Heron Bay Lodge would be the first house we came to. If we went left, we'd reach his close neighbour, Mrs Siddons at Grebe House. Both properties were situated on the southern side of the lake.

'It depends if we want to check on Sand Hills Hall too.' I glanced towards the door of Mill Ponds, where the Tolfrees were now standing, watching Ben and Sid assign each volunteer an area to search. 'Could Luke know about the summerhouse?'

Millicent considered this. 'It's possible, though now is probably not the time to ask the Tolfrees, especially if it was

Jennifer meeting Archie there. Let's go that way and take a look before we go to Grebe House.'

We turned left and followed the path around to Willow Marsh and the foot of Sand Hills before climbing the slope up to Sand Hills Hall.

'How did it go with Superintendent Cobbe?' Millicent asked, hitching her long skirt as she climbed the hill.

'He threatened to arrest me,' I replied, glad of my practical navy woollen trousers. 'I don't think he wants to, but I suppose he feels I haven't given him much choice.'

She shot me a sideways glance, confusion in her eyes. 'Why are you protecting this man?'

'Because he has nothing to do with this, and it wouldn't be fair to drag him into it. He's gone away to start a new life and deserves to be happy.'

'What about you? You're not happy.'

'I just want to find out who killed Archie so this will all go away.'

'And if it doesn't?'

There was no answer to that, so I changed the subject.

'You said Luke's not been himself recently. In what way?' I asked.

'He's been withdrawn. Normally he's an outgoing boy who likes to take part in discussions, particularly in natural history lessons. But recently he's been quiet, as though something's troubling him.'

'Did you speak to him about it?'

'I've tried a couple of times. He just gives a polite answer. I was going to mention it to Jennifer Tolfree when I saw her, but it's often Gertrude who picks the children up from school. I thought it best to address the issue with his mother rather than grandmother.'

'Could he have run away?'

'I hope so.' Millicent's brow creased with concern. 'Because the alternative is worse.'

We quickened our pace and walked the rest of the way in silence. When we reached the iron gate, we made our way around the perimeter stone wall until we came to the gap where the summerhouse lay.

Millicent grabbed my arm. 'The door's open. I remember we closed and locked it.'

'But we left the key in the lock. Hugh Alvarez might have gone back in.'

'If Luke's in there, he might not be on his own,' Millicent whispered. 'Someone could have brought him here.'

We stood motionless, listening for sounds from inside. All was quiet and that only added to our apprehension. I couldn't help thinking the iron doorstop would make a lethal weapon. Careful not to create a noise, I crouched down and picked up a branch lying in the undergrowth. The dank smell of rotting leaves heightened the sense of menace the summerhouse had taken on.

Slowly, we made our way over to the door, and I nudged it open a little wider with my foot. A cry from inside made me jump back in alarm.

27

Luke Tolfree was lying on the wicker sofa. And, to my relief, he was alone.

At the sight of me wielding a branch, he shrank back in fright. Millicent pushed past me, and he leapt up, rushing forward to bury himself in her long skirt.

'Miss Nightingale,' he sobbed.

'It's alright, Luke.' Millicent wrapped her arms around him. 'You're safe now.'

I went out and threw the branch into the undergrowth, standing by the oak tree until Millicent calmed him. When his sobs turned to hiccups, she took him by the hand and led him out of the summerhouse to where I was waiting.

'This is my friend, Miss Woodmore. We're going to take you home to your mummy and daddy.'

'I'll get in trouble,' he whispered.

'You're not in any trouble.' Millicent squeezed his hand. 'We just want to know why you didn't come into school today.'

'Because I decided to run away.' He sniffed. 'But I didn't

bring enough food. I ate all my sandwiches this morning, and I'm hungry.'

I smiled at him. 'Why did you want to run away?'

'Because Mummy and Daddy had a row, and it's all my fault.' He buried his head in Millicent's skirt again, and she shook her head at me to indicate that now wasn't the time to ask questions.

Gently, she prised him from her skirt. 'Let's go and find Mummy and Daddy. I promise they're not angry; they just want you to come home. Supper will be waiting.'

The mention of food seemed to entice him more than the thought of seeing his parents, and he let Millicent guide him away from the summerhouse. I glanced inside and saw his grey school cap lying on the wicker sofa. I picked it up and then strode ahead of them, leading the way around the stone wall and back to the iron gates of the hall. When I reached the top of the slope, I paused to allow Millicent and Luke to catch up.

I saw two figures on the footpath below, walking some distance apart. I assumed they must be members of the search party and was relieved to see one of them had a torch. The light was beginning to fade, and Millicent and Luke were walking slowly.

The figure with the torch was Hugh Alvarez. He was striding along the footpath, swinging the light from side to side, checking the undergrowth on the edges of the path.

Behind him was Gertrude Tolfree. She was walking more slowly, making no effort to catch up with Hugh. I realised she was carrying a torch as well, but it wasn't switched on. The cautiousness of her steps and the way she walked close to the tree line made it look like she was following Hugh and trying not to be seen.

When Luke spotted Gertrude, he let go of Millicent's hand and began running down the slope, yelling, 'Granny!'

He dashed through bracken, the smell of trampled vegetation filling the air. Millicent and I followed, taking the path and walking at a more sedate pace, and I was able to watch Hugh and Gertrude's reaction to Luke's appearance.

Hugh swung around in surprise at the noise. He looked up at Luke and then in the direction of where he was running. It was difficult to see his expression in the dusk, but the start of his body seemed to indicate he hadn't been aware of Gertrude's presence behind him.

By the time Millicent and I caught up with Luke, he was wrapped in Gertrude's arms.

'Thank God,' she muttered, kissing the top of his head.

Hugh walked over to join us, smiling. 'That's a relief. Where did you find him?'

'The summerhouse,' I replied.

'The summerhouse?' Gertrude held Luke close as if he were about to be snatched away. 'What summerhouse?'

'The one at Sand Hills Hall,' Millicent explained. 'Someone seems to have been using it recently.'

Hugh shot me a bemused glance, which made me suspect he knew who Archie had been meeting there. 'How did you know about the summerhouse, Luke?' he asked.

'I saw it when I went to look for dormice. Vincent told me there's a nest in the big oak tree up at Sand Hills Hall. I knew the one he meant because I've played in the garden before when Mummy used to visit Mrs Thackeray.'

At this, Hugh frowned. He looked as if he were about to say something when Vincent appeared. He'd been walking at speed and was breathing heavily.

'You've found the lad,' he panted, bending double with exertion. 'Where was he?'

'Perhaps we should discuss this when we get back to Mill Ponds?' Millicent said. We were making slow progress, and the temperature was dropping. After his dash down the slope, Luke seemed tired, and Gertrude was fussing over him.

'Why don't Vincent and I go ahead and let everyone at Mill Ponds know he's safe?' Hugh suggested. 'We need to get word out to those still searching.'

'That would be sensible,' Millicent agreed.

Hugh clamped his hand on Vincent's shoulder, leaving him no choice but to comply, and set off at a brisk pace. Vincent staggered, trying to keep up with the taller man's longer stride.

Gertrude was still holding Luke close. 'Why did you leave the school this morning? We've all been so worried. We didn't know where you'd gone.'

'I ran away. To stop everyone arguing.' Luke's bottom lip began to tremble. 'I knew the summerhouse would be safe now he's gone.'

'Now who's gone?' Gertrude frowned, perplexed by Luke's rambling explanation.

'Archie. The man who died.'

'Did you see Archie at the summerhouse?' I asked before I could stop myself, which earned me an elbow in the ribs from Millicent.

Luke nodded. 'That afternoon. Before he died. He was in the summerhouse with Mummy.'

'Mummy? Why would she be...' Gertrude's expression changed as realisation dawned.

'She was there with him,' Luke insisted. 'When I went to look at the oak tree I saw them in the summerhouse. He was holding on to Mummy's arm, and I told him to let go or I'd tell my daddy.'

Luke gazed expectantly up at Gertrude, clearly hoping his grandmother would reassure him he'd done the right thing. But she seemed unable to speak.

'That was very brave of you.' Millicent smiled encouragingly. 'Did he let go of Mummy's arm?'

He nodded. 'Mummy said there was no need to tell Daddy and we had to go straight home so that we'd be there when Daddy got back otherwise he'd be worried. I told her my bicycle was at the station and that I had to go and get it. Then Archie told her to go home and said he'd walk with me to the station to get my bicycle.' Luke's face became stubborn. 'I tried to run away from him as we were going down the slope, but I fell over.'

That seemed to rouse Gertrude from her stupor. 'Did he hurt you?'

Luke shook his head. 'He held my hand and said I was naughty to be out so late, but I wouldn't get into trouble as long as I didn't tell anyone where I'd been.' He raised his big blue eyes to look up at me. 'When we got near the station, he saw you getting off the train and let go of my hand. I told him I wouldn't say anything and ran to get my bicycle. I'm sorry I nearly rode into you; I just wanted to get home.'

I smiled at him, relieved to know Archie hadn't been lying in wait for me on the jetty that afternoon. It also explained why he'd left his bicycle behind. 'That's alright. I would have wanted to get home, too. When you got there, did you tell your daddy what you'd seen?' I ignored Millicent's reproving look. I needed to hear the rest of Luke's story. Had Gordon learnt of his wife's infidelity mere hours before Archie's murder?

Luke nodded, his lip trembling. 'Granny had said I was

allowed out, so I hadn't been naughty like Archie said. I told Daddy that I didn't like Archie and that I thought Mummy should keep away from him.' His eyes filled with tears. 'Perhaps I shouldn't have said that because they had a row. But I was allowed out, wasn't I, Granny?'

Gertrude rallied at this point and knelt down so she was face to face with her grandson. 'Yes, you were. I'd said you could go out, so you hadn't done anything wrong. Grown-ups sometimes argue for no reason. You mustn't think it has anything to do with you.'

Millicent motioned to me not to ask any more questions and took Luke's hand. 'I think it's time we got you home.'

I reached out and helped Gertrude to her feet. She stumbled, and I steadied her by linking my arm through hers.

'We need to get to Mill Ponds. It's getting dark.' I took the torch from her and switched it on, handing her Luke's school cap.

'Of course.' She didn't pull away and allowed me to escort her along the path.

She stared at the back of Luke's head as he walked hand in hand with Millicent, now happily chatting about the dormouse he'd seen.

'You never trusted him, did you?' Gertrude whispered. 'Archie, I mean.'

'I knew him too well.'

'I thought... I thought he was a good man. He helped Gordon to find his way. He helped me, too. He made us feel like we could be part of something again. Part of the community.'

'Archie did many good things. But there was a dark side. Especially when it came to women.'

'I can see that now. He and Jennifer—' Her voice caught. 'I should have realised.'

I understood what she was trying to say. Little exchanges between the pair of them probably made sense to her now.

'Archie could be persuasive. He had a strange charisma. I expect Jennifer regrets... regrets anything that happened.'

She pursed her lips and took a moment to consider this. Then said in a harder tone, 'Your discretion in this matter would be appreciated.'

I gave a slight nod, deciding not to commit myself with words. I wouldn't be writing any gossip for the newspaper. But I wouldn't keep this a secret from the police. Not when they suspected me of murder.

To distract her, I asked, 'Were you following Hugh Alvarez?'

She didn't answer immediately and made a show of navigating the tree roots protruding across the footpath. I guessed she was giving herself time to think.

Eventually, she said, 'Yes. I was. There's something about him I don't trust. I didn't really believe he'd taken Luke, but I had to be sure. Please don't say anything to Mr Alvarez. I've probably done him a great disservice.'

'I won't,' I replied, thinking that Hugh probably already knew. When he'd swung around at the sound of Luke's cries and seen her behind him, he must have wondered why her torch hadn't been switched on.

'Thank you.' Gertrude squeezed my arm. 'And thank you for finding Luke.'

We were now at Mill Ponds, and Gordon and Jennifer Tolfree were running down the driveway towards us. Gordon swept Luke up in his arms, and Jennifer wrapped herself around them both.

As much as I wished the family well, I wouldn't comply with Gertrude's request to keep quiet about what Luke had said. If Gordon was aware of his wife's affair, they would both have had good reason to want Archie dead.

28

Polly and Micky Swann laid on tea and sandwiches for everyone who'd helped in the search, and the lounge of Mill Ponds looked how I imagined it had during the war. The room was filled with men chatting and laughing, exuding a sense of elation at a mission having gone well.

Millicent and I glanced at the throng of men and clouds of smoke and decided to head home for some cocoa. We were about to leave when Superintendent Cobbe summoned us to the study.

He'd spent a short time with the Tolfrees before allowing them to take an exhausted Luke home to Sycamore Lodge. Fortunately, there was nothing wrong with the boy that supper, a bath and a good night's sleep wouldn't cure.

The superintendent sat down heavily in the captain's chair behind the desk. His usually immaculate uniform was rumpled, and the skin beneath his eyes sagged.

'What made you go to the summerhouse?'

'We knew someone had used it recently and thought it was a place no one else might think to look,' Millicent explained.

Normally she was the one in authority, asking the questions; however, she seemed unperturbed at being on the other side of the desk.

I was the one sinking into my chair, feeling like a nervous schoolgirl. Would Superintendent Cobbe make good on his earlier threat to arrest me?

'I'm glad you did. I wouldn't have liked him to have been out all night on his own. But what I meant was, what made you go to the summerhouse on the day you found Mr Powell's bicycle?'

When I told him I'd eavesdropped on a conversation between Hugh Alvarez and Vincent Owen, he rolled his eyes in a way that made him look scarily like Elijah.

'So Mr Alvarez and Mr Owen were aware the summer-house was being used?'

'Mr Owen used to work for the Thackerays and sometimes goes to Sand Hills Hall to keep an eye on the place. I think he must have spotted Archie there one day.'

'Why would Mr Powell want to visit a disused summerhouse?'

'I guessed he and Jennifer Tolfree had been meeting there in secret. Tonight, Luke confirmed it.' I repeated what the boy had told Gertrude.

Superintendent Cobbe regarded me through tired eyes, keeping his expression impassive. I'd expected him to be more enthusiastic about this new development, but he didn't react. Perhaps he thought I was trying to shift the focus of his investigation away from me. Or maybe he was just fed up with the whole case.

'I'll take a look at the place myself tomorrow.' He rose from his chair, stifling a yawn. 'I'm going to leave things here in the capable hands of Sergeant Gilbert and PC King and return to Winchester. I'll drop you home on the way.'

Millicent and I quickly got to our feet and followed him out into the hallway, eager to avoid the walk back to Victoria Lane. This showed a definite thawing in the superintendent's attitude towards me. Rather than being arrested, I was being offered a ride home. Things seemed to be looking up.

* * *

The following morning, I got to the office early to write an article on the previous day's events – leaving out a few unprintable details. Of course, I relished telling Elijah the whole story.

'So Gordon knew about the affair? It doesn't look good for him or Jennifer. In fact, I wouldn't even rule out Gertrude.' He waved his cigarette at me. 'She's a frequent visitor to Mill Ponds. If she found out what was going on, she'd be incensed on her son's behalf.'

'I don't think she did know what was going on.' I thought of Gertrude's expression when she realised the implications of what Luke had seen. 'And it's clear she suspects Hugh of being the killer.'

He nodded. 'I don't blame her for following him under the circumstances. Not when her grandson was missing. It's crossed my mind that Hugh Alvarez might not be quite what he seems.'

I agreed. 'He's pleasant enough, but I get the feeling there's something going on under the surface.'

'It could be just a case of lying in order to obtain a room at Mill Ponds. He might have left his last job under a cloud. I wonder how he's faring at the Tolfree & Timpson factory? It doesn't strike me as his usual type of work. And if anyone can sniff out his secrets, it will be his fellow workers. They'll be able to tell if he's one of them or not.' He stubbed out his cigarette. 'Perhaps it's time we followed up on how our first Mill Pond House residents are progressing.'

I grinned. 'I was thinking the same thing. Why don't I call in at the factory this afternoon and see how he's getting on?'

'Sounds like a good idea to me.'

* * *

At the biscuit factory, I decided to speak to Nora Fox before I went in search of Constance or Hugh. I found her standing by the window with her friend, Gwen. They'd removed their white muslin caps, which was a sure sign the boss wasn't on the factory floor – as was the hum of chatter that could be heard above the noise of machinery.

Nora smiled when she saw me. 'Don't tell me, you're checking up on our new boy.'

Gwen, a large woman with curly blonde hair and a red face, snorted. 'I'd hardly call him a boy.'

'We've been having bets over his age.' Nora took out a little notebook from the pocket of her apron. 'I reckon he's in his early thirties, but Gwen thinks he's nearly forty.'

'I wouldn't put him that old.' I gazed out of the window and saw Hugh directing a lorry that was backing into the yard. 'I thought you might have wheedled it out of him by now.'

'Plays his cards close to his chest, that one does.' Nora was watching Hugh, evidently liking what she saw.

'Has he said much about his previous job?' I wondered how Hugh was finding the cloying, sweet-smelling confines of the biscuit factory compared to his previous life on the road. 'Do you think he's done work like this before?'

'He's done his share of manual labour, I'd say,' she replied. 'He's good with his hands.'

Gwen giggled at this.

'As you can see, he's made quite an impression. On every-one,' Nora said with a wink. 'And I mean, everyone. If you're looking for Miss Timpson, she's outside with him.'

I stared out of the window and was surprised to see Constance standing to one side, waiting for the lorry to come to a standstill. In contrast to Nora and Gwen, she wasn't casting admiring glances in Hugh's direction. Instead, she had a look of deep irritation on her face as she waited for the driver to open up the back of his lorry. Her annoyance seemed to be directed at Hugh, who was now standing beside her.

'What's going on?' I asked.

'We're not sure – that's why we're being nosy.' Nora nudged me. 'Go and find out for us. You're always game for anything.'

I had a reputation amongst the factory workers of Tolfree & Timpson for reasons that were best left unsaid. Although I didn't want to be branded as someone who was 'game for anything', I was curious to know what was going on, so I hurried to the back doors of the factory.

I sauntered casually across the yard, aware of Nora and Gwen watching me.

'Something wrong?' I asked when I reached Constance.

'I'm about to find out,' she replied drily. 'Mr Alvarez insists that Kenwrights, the haulage company Timpson Foods has been using for some years without complaint, is, in fact, ripping me off. I've asked him to show me proof.'

Hugh beckoned Constance over, and I followed with interest.

She peered into the back of the lorry, which was stacked high with crates.

'Well?'

I smiled at her flashing eyes and imperious tone. Constance had been known to reduce men to quivering wrecks with a raise of one perfectly shaped eyebrow.

Hugh seemed unperturbed as he pulled down the ramp at the back of the lorry. 'This isn't a full load.'

'It looks full to me,' she replied through gritted teeth.

'I need to sort things out before I can begin unloading.' The burly lorry driver was glancing between Hugh and Constance. 'I could do without an audience.'

Hugh brushed him to one side and started to lift the crates from the lorry and carry them down the ramp.

'You can't do that—' the driver began, but one look from Constance silenced him.

Hugh obviously wasn't going to stop until he'd proved his point. Within minutes, he was sweating, and his linen shirt clung to his chest. I stood back, admiring his stamina and mentally deducted a few years from his estimated age. Inside the factory, Nora and Gwen were clearly enjoying the view. And a slight gleam in Constance's eyes told me she wasn't as immune to Hugh's charms as she pretended.

Hugh emptied the lorry faster than expected. Then I realised why. And so did Constance. It hadn't been full in the first place. All the crates had been placed towards the rear of the lorry, leaving a gap at the front.

Hugh gestured to the empty space. 'You could get double the amount in there. But I guess you're being charged for the number of journeys. Half the load, double the trips.'

Constance examined the empty lorry, then turned to the driver. 'Is that it? Where's the rest of my order?'

The burly man shrank back. 'I believe there's more being delivered tomorrow. We didn't want to overload the lorry.'

Hugh snorted. 'That was nowhere near overloaded.'

'I'm not a fool,' Constance snapped at the lorry driver. 'There was plainly enough room for the rest of the goods.'

The man held up his hands. 'I just do the deliveries. I'm not in charge.'

He made to go, but Constance held up a gloved hand and stopped him in his tracks. 'Make sure you tell Mr Kenwright what's happened here today. I expect him to telephone me with an explanation.'

Constance waved him away, and the man mumbled something unintelligible before scurrying to the front of the lorry and clambering into the driver's seat.

Hugh was watching Constance with what looked like amusement mingled with admiration.

'What will you do?' I asked her.

'Talk to Kenwright. However, he knows that not many haulage companies will deal with a woman. Which doesn't give me much leverage.' Her eyes narrowed. 'Perhaps I should buy my own fleet of lorries.'

'Not a bad idea,' Hugh agreed. 'Or you could try Skelton & Son. I used to work for them, and they seemed a decent enough outfit.'

'Thank you for bringing this to my attention, Mr Alvarez.' Constance's tone made it clear the conversation was over.

'My pleasure, miss.' Hugh gave an exaggerated tuck of his forelock and then wandered off.

I glanced at Constance. Her cheeks were pink and she was regarding him with an exasperated expression.

'How's he getting on here?' I asked tentatively.

'He's a good worker. It's just his attitude,' she mimicked the way he'd tugged his forelock, 'is extremely infuriating.'

I smiled. 'Elijah and I don't know what to make of him.'

'I'm glad I'm not the only one. I can't keep him on if he acts like that toward me.'

'Maybe you won't have to,' I said. 'When I first spoke to him, he seemed to think he'd soon get another job. I presume he meant as a lorry driver.'

'That would solve the problem.'

But I noted the wistfulness in her voice. Her eyes were still fixed on Hugh, and I got the feeling he was a problem she was enjoying having.

'Is that Paul Richardson?' I asked, noticing a single leg sticking out from underneath a van and a toolbox and elbow crutch lying on the ground beside it.

She nodded. 'I've given him a few odd jobs. He's useful to have around. He certainly knows how to fix anything mechanical. But there isn't really enough for him to do here. He'd be better off working in a garage.'

'I'll mention that in my article. Elijah wants us to follow Paul, Vincent and Hugh's progress, if they're agreeable. Could I quote you saying something like, "Paul would be an asset to any garage owner"? It might help him find a more suitable position.'

'By all means. I'd be happy to give him a reference. He's polite, hardworking and gets on with the rest of the staff.'

'And what of Mr Alvarez?' I said with a wink. 'What would you say about him?'

She gave a wicked grin. 'I'd say he's attractive to look at and infuriating to deal with.'

'What will you do with him?'

'Either sack him or let him run the company.'

I laughed – something I hadn't done for a while.

Constance adjusted her fitted suit jacket with a gloved

hand. 'I'd like to trust him. I'm just not sure if that would be wise.'

I shrugged. 'I wish I could offer some advice. But I have no idea either.'

'I feel wiser heads than ours may be needed. I'm planning to have another meeting at the hall – this time it will be a more social occasion. Mr Laffaye, Mr Whittle, Mrs Siddons and the redoubtable Ursula Nightingale should have enough combined wisdom to offer some guidance.'

My smile faded. 'Good idea. But Daniel may not want me to be there.' I felt a stab of pain as I remembered his suggestion that I go to live with my father rather than drag Millicent into a scandal.

Constance linked her arm through mine. 'What he said hurt you, didn't it?'

I gulped, feeling tearful.

'You know Daniel would never intentionally be cruel. He only said it because he worries about Millicent. I think he's sorry for upsetting you.'

'It stung because he was right. Perhaps I should move away. I couldn't bear to hurt any of my friends.' It wasn't just Millicent and Daniel I was thinking of.

As if reading my mind, she said, 'I'm going to invite Percy, too. I'll send a car over to collect you and Mr Whittle, and Millicent and Ursula. The nine of us are going to eat lobster, drink champagne and sort this bloody mess out.'

29

My second picnic of the year was nothing like the first.

While Percy, Millicent and I had eaten chicken and ham pie and drunk beer on a blanket by the lake, the Timpsons' idea of dining al fresco was to serve champagne and lobster on crisp white tablecloths. Silver cutlery, wine glasses and a centrepiece of pink roses adorned the long table erected on the lawn.

Millicent and I had dug out our glad rags, which in her case consisted of a demure white blouse and long blue skirt. I was more daring in a calf-length green crepe dress my stepmother had bought me and my precious silver swan brooch pinned to my chest. Ursula outshone both of us in a silk turquoise creation, complete with matching turban.

Constance had sent the Daimler to pick us up, and we'd collected Elijah on the way. His only sartorial concession to the occasion was to swap the jacket of his work suit for a navy blazer.

We arrived at Crookham Hall to find Daniel and Percy playing croquet on the lawn, both looking fetching in casual flannel trousers and open-necked shirts. Mrs Siddons and

Horace Laffaye sat in brightly coloured deckchairs nearby, an open bottle of champagne in an ice bucket on a stand between them.

Percy called us over, declaring that he and I would compete against Millicent and Daniel.

He handed me a mallet, saying, 'Cobbe didn't arrest you, then?'

'No. Although I'm not in the clear yet. Let's not talk about that this afternoon.' I glanced meaningfully towards Daniel and Millicent. 'I think Daniel's still concerned I'm going to ruin Millicent's good name, and I don't want them to have another row.'

'Good point. Let's avoid all talk of your secret liaisons for the time being.' With that, he bounded over to kiss Ursula, leaving me in no doubt that I was far from forgiven and that he'd be raising the subject at a later date.

Despite what had happened, I still cherished every moment I'd spent with Marc. And I missed him. Had he gone away and my life returned to normal, I might have been able to move on more easily and accept our relationship was in the past. Instead, I found myself thinking about him constantly. I missed having him to confide in, especially with all that had happened.

I tried to put all thoughts of Marc out of my head. But when I saw Daniel coming toward me, I sensed the subject of my 'secret liaisons' was going to be broached once more. To my surprise, I was wrong.

'I wanted to apologise for what I said. About you lodging with Millicent and Ursula. I could see I'd upset you, and I... I'm sorry I hurt your feelings.' Daniel's dark blue eyes were genuinely sad.

'You were concerned for Millicent. I understand that. I'd

hate it if I were to cause any damage to her reputation. I hope the situation will resolve itself when they find out who killed Archie. But if it doesn't, I'll move out. And I'll make it clear to Millicent that it has nothing to do with anything you've said. It will be my decision.'

When he started to protest, I held up a hand to stop him.

'I've made up my mind. If my family and friends continue to suffer because of me, I'll move away from Walden.' I smiled. 'Of course, Superintendent Cobbe may have his own solution to the problem, and I could end up in prison.' Sadly, I was only half joking.

'I don't believe you had anything to do with Archie's death. And I'd be highly surprised if the superintendent did either. But if it were to come to that, I'm sure we could rustle up a pretty good defence team between us. I've never forgotten what you did to help my mother.'

I was touched by his words. As I looked at the steps of Crookham Hall, a vision of the late Lady Timpson came into my head.

'You must miss her.'

'I miss them both.'

I nodded, understanding the complicated relationship he'd had with his parents.

'But I've put the past behind me and intend to focus on the future.' He stared at Millicent as he said this.

'Good. I hope one day...'

'So do I.'

The subject of marriage was a tricky one. As much as she loved Daniel, Millicent was reluctant to give up her profession as a teacher. I also knew acquiring the title of Lady Timpson was not something that appealed to her.

As we joined the others, I contemplated what Daniel had

said about rustling up a good defence team. When I looked around at the gathering, I realised what he meant.

Mrs Siddons was holding court, dressed in the bright green frock she'd worn for the open day. She held a champagne flute in one hand and the yellow parasol in the other. Horace, wearing a natty cream linen suit topped with a Panama hat, puffed on a cigar as he refilled her glass. The pair had many things in common, the most obvious being wealth and an enviable number of influential contacts. Horace had built a network of powerful acquaintances during his years as an international banker, and Mrs Siddons had done the same through her work as a politician.

Ursula and Elijah were rich in experience rather than money. They were seated close together, chatting in low voices, and I had a horrible suspicion the subject of their conversation was me.

I knew I could also count on the support of the younger members of the party – Daniel, Constance, Millicent and Percy. But I didn't want to drag any of them into my mess. For everyone's sake, we needed to discover the truth about Archie's death and clear my name of at least one of the things I'd been accused of. Other rumours might be a little harder to quash.

After we'd eaten and drunk our fill, we reclined in deckchairs on the lawn to discuss Archie's murder.

'The Tolfrees have the strongest motive after what Luke saw in the summerhouse.' Elijah paused to draw on the cigar Horace was lighting for him.

'I'm surprised Gordon hadn't guessed. Jennifer didn't exactly hide her feelings for Archie. We noticed it at the carol concert last year, didn't we?' I said to Millicent.

She nodded. 'When Luke told him what he'd seen, Gordon must have known immediately what was going on.'

'If he can prove an adulterous relationship with Archie, Jennifer faces losing her children,' Mrs Siddons commented. 'In a divorce court, a judge will give Gordon custody. She won't have a say in the matter.'

'But can Gordon prove it? That's the question,' Horace said, not without relish. 'We're only surmising what Jennifer and Archie got up to. They could have been playing cribbage together for all we know.'

For some reason, this made me blush. I thought of my protestations that Marc and I were just friends and all we did was talk. Although this was true, it was undeniable we'd both wanted more – which meant our relationship wasn't as innocent as I maintained.

'The pocket diary.' Percy jogged my arm, causing me to spill my champagne. 'Didn't Ben say Archie's pocket diary was missing?'

Involuntarily, I shuddered as I remembered Archie flicking through its pages, pretending to search for Marc's details.

'What is it? Oh, you're worried that...' Percy must have guessed my train of thought because he stopped abruptly. He whipped a handkerchief from his pocket and handed it to me.

I dabbed at the spillage on my dress, giving me time to regain my composure. Then I shuddered again as something else occurred to me.

'If the diary was on Archie's person when he was shot, and the murderer took it, they must have realised he was still alive when they left him. Jennifer is the person most likely to have known about the diary – and to want to destroy it.'

Mrs Siddons grimaced. 'If it contained details of their illicit meetings, Gordon could use it against her in the divorce courts.'

'I don't think we can rule out Gordon or Gertrude, as they

might have seen Archie with the diary and realised its implications. And all the Tolfrees are familiar with hunting rifles.' Elijah looked at me. 'Are you sure Gertrude didn't know about the affair between Jennifer and Archie?'

'From her expression when Luke told her what he'd seen, I'd say it came as a complete shock.'

Millicent agreed. 'I'd swear she didn't know.'

'But she was suspicious of Hugh Alvarez. Enough to follow him.' Daniel glanced at his sister. 'I'm not sure it was a good idea to give him Micky's job at the factory. He could be dangerous.'

Had Daniel noticed the chemistry between Constance and Hugh? There was definitely a spark between them, even if it was a combative one. The Honourable Constance Timpson and a homeless, unemployed ex-serviceman. It was an unlikely match.

'I don't believe he's dangerous. Although I think there's much we don't know about him.' Constance reclined lazily in her deckchair, looking the epitome of modern elegance in a short blue chiffon summer dress that I was sure would have Hugh swooning.

'Perhaps it would be prudent to find out a little more about Mr Alvarez,' Mrs Siddons said to Horace.

'I've already tried,' he replied. 'Given that Alvarez isn't a common name, I didn't expect it to be particularly difficult. However, I was proved wrong. My contacts can't find any information on him.'

Mrs Siddons peered at him through her lorgnette spectacles. 'What does that mean?'

'Either Hugh Alvarez isn't his real name. Or he's led an uneventful life and shows up in few public records. My contact says he needs more information to know where to search.'

Elijah turned to me. 'What have you found out about him so far?'

I thought back to all the conversations I'd had with Hugh. 'When I first met him, I asked if the name Alvarez was Spanish. He said it was and that his grandfather was a wine merchant. I think he said he had a business in Winchester, although that was some years ago. Oh, and his mother died earlier this year. He ended up at the hostel after losing his job as a lorry driver but expects to find work soon.'

'He mentioned once working for a company called Skelton & Son,' Constance added. 'I've heard of them. They're a reputable haulage business.'

Horace puffed on his cigar. 'I'll make enquiries with the owners, though they may not keep detailed records of their drivers. It would help to know a little more about his background, such as his parents' names or where he was living. I think I'll start with his war records. See if that gives any clues to his parentage.'

'Constance,' I said suddenly.

She looked at me in surprise.

'That was Hugh's mother's name. He was asking me about you and said that was his mother's name.'

Constance flushed a little at this.

'Constance Alvarez,' Horace repeated, taking a tiny pocket-book from his jacket and making a note of this.

'If the grandfather lived in Winchester, would your friend at the *Hampshire Chronicle* be able to help?' Percy swung his long legs out of the deckchair and reached for the champagne.

I nodded. 'Kevin owes me a favour. I'll get him to ask around to see if anyone remembers a family by the name of Alvarez living in Winchester.'

'What about the other occupants of Mill House?' Ursula

held out her glass for Percy to top up. 'Surely they're as much under suspicion as this Hugh fellow.'

'Paul Richardson seems to be rekindling his relationship with Teresa Powell. We saw them together at Mill Ponds on the night Luke was missing, and it's obvious they still care for each other. Could Archie have been standing in their way?' Millicent suggested. 'Otherwise, I can't see what motive Paul would have. Archie helped him by giving him a room at the hostel. What about Vincent Owen? It was odd how he came running up after we found Luke.'

'It was strange, wasn't it?' I thought back to the scene on the footpath. 'He seemed very agitated. On the other occasions I've spoken to him, his demeanour was completely different. He showed little emotion when he told me about his life at Blackthorn Park. He used to work for Jennifer Tolfree's father, Lord Darrington, and lived in a tied cottage on the estate. His favourite part of the job was tending the horses. It occurred to me he might have been involved in the shoots held at the park and could be familiar with firing a rifle.'

'He's an ex-serviceman, like the others. He'd have handled firearms during the war.' Elijah tapped the end of his cigar. 'If he is involved, it might be because of Jennifer Tolfree. Would he do her bidding?'

'I'd say that's a distinct possibility,' Mrs Siddons replied, then let out a long sigh. 'The opening month of Mill Ponds hasn't been a resounding success. The manager shot dead and the residents under suspicion. I'd hoped for a more harmonious bedding-in period to give locals the chance to get used to having a hostel in town.'

'It evidently hasn't put someone off living in Walden.' Horace paused for effect, which meant he was about to divulge the latest gossip. 'I've heard on the grapevine that someone has put in an offer for Sand Hills Hall.'

He was rewarded with murmurs of surprise. At a time of austerity, few could afford to purchase such a sizeable property, especially when it was in need of modernisation.

I felt a wave of sadness at the news, and when Percy went to top up my glass, I found my hand shaking. It was silly. The place couldn't stay empty forever. But the thought of someone else, perhaps a family, occupying Alice's home gave me a desolate feeling – as if more of her was disappearing into the past.

Was this another sign that it was time for me to leave Walden and start a new life in London?

30

I'd heard from Kevin Noakes at the *Hampshire Chronicle* that a Señor Alvarez had once owned a wine shop on Hyde Street in Winchester. He mentioned the shop's current owner, Mr Harrison, had been a friend of Señor Alvarez.

When I told Elijah this, he said he thought Horace sometimes purchased vintage port from Mr Harrison. As a result, Horace invited me to accompany him on a trip to Winchester to replenish his cellar.

It was strange to be seated in the back of the Daimler without Elijah. I didn't think I'd ever travelled alone with Horace before, if you could call being in a chauffeur driven car alone. I soon found out why Elijah hadn't joined us.

'Mr Whittle is concerned about you,' Horace began as soon as I'd settled myself on the expensive leather upholstery. 'He's worried you're going to take off like you did before.'

'I'm not planning on "taking off". If I leave, it will be because I don't want to cause any more upset to my family and friends in Walden. It's not fair on Millicent to sully her good name. If I go, I'll tell you when and where I'm going. That's if Superintendent Cobbe lets me leave Walden.'

'He won't arrest you,' Horace said with a glint in his eye. 'I'll see to that.'

I was grateful and touched by his words. But if the superintendent believed I was responsible for Archie's death, even Horace wouldn't be able to stop me from being charged. Although, as Daniel had said, I could be assured a good defence.

'Cobbe doesn't have any evidence against you,' Horace continued. 'Unfortunately, he doesn't have sufficient evidence against anyone else either. The problem is, Archie's killing was opportunistic. Someone saw their chance and took it. Unless an eyewitness suddenly comes forward, which is unlikely at this stage, there's no physical proof to determine who killed him.'

He was right. We'd speculated about motives, but even if Superintendent Cobbe could demonstrate someone had a solid reason to kill Archie, it wasn't enough to convict them of carrying out the deed.

'What are we hoping to find out today?' I asked.

'Anything that might give us an insight into the background of Mr Hugh Alvarez. Or the man who's calling himself Hugh Alvarez.'

'You don't think that's his real name?'

Horace shook his head. 'I didn't like to say too much in front of Constance. Or Daniel. It's clear he's concerned about his sister employing this man. But I got someone at the agency I use to look for the name in war records, and there was no one in the services called Hugh Alvarez.'

'So he's lying?'

'One way or another, yes. He either served under a different name.' Horace paused. 'Or it occurred to me that he could be a conscientious objector. Not something he'd want to admit when seeking accommodation in a hostel for ex-servicemen.'

'It's possible,' I replied, although I wasn't convinced of this. I thought of Hugh's camaraderie with Paul and Vincent. And of the old army jumper he'd worn. I didn't think a conscientious objector would risk staying in a hostel full of ex-servicemen. He'd be sniffed out too easily. 'I wondered if he might have used a false name in case Archie recognised his real name. Say Archie once trifled with a woman Hugh was close to? A relative or girlfriend perhaps, and Hugh wanted to get back at him.'

Horace nodded approvingly. 'An excellent theory. However, Skelton & Son, the company Hugh claims he once worked for, have confirmed he was in their employ. So, he was using the name before he came to Mill Ponds. We need to establish his connection to Señor Alvarez, the wine merchant. Is he really his grandson? He must be related somehow, as I doubt he'd choose such an unusual surname at random.'

I nodded. If you wanted to remain anonymous, you'd choose a surname like Brown or Smith. Alvarez was a bold choice.

When we reached Hyde Street and pulled up outside L. Harrison Esq, Wine Merchant, Mr Harrison came hurrying out of the shop. Horace's Daimler was far from inconspicuous.

'Mr Laffaye. What a pleasure to see you again. Please do come in.'

Judging by his obsequious manner, Horace was a good customer.

We stepped into the old-fashioned shop, which smelt satisfyingly of brandy-soaked wood. Along one wall was a row of wooden barrels, with taps protruding from each one and buckets below to catch the drips.

Horace sniffed appreciatively. 'This is Miss Woodmore, she works for me at *The Walden Herald*. She's acquired a taste for sherry, though her usual variety comes from Fellowes Emporium on Walden high street. I'm sure you can provide something a little more refined.'

'Please, take a seat.' Mr Harrison motioned to the row of high wooden stools by the counter. 'How about my latest import from Andalucía? It's wonderfully smooth with a rich nutty aroma.'

'It sounds delightful.' Horace nimbly hopped onto one of the stools and removed his gloves.

I followed suit and watched Mr Harrison pour two glasses from a dark brown bottle.

Horace held his glass up to the light, admiring the clarity of the glowing amber liquid. Then he closed his eyes and brought the glass to his nose, inhaling deeply. Feeling self-conscious, I copied, swirling the sherry in the glass and then sniffing its sweet aroma before taking a gulp. To my inexpert palate, it tasted divine, and I said so. Horace savoured his for rather longer before nodding his approval.

Mr Harrison smiled and dived behind the counter to retrieve a bottle of port.

'You must try this while you're here. It has an unusual flavour, and I'd welcome your opinion.'

I declined the offer of port and enjoyed the rest of my sherry while the two men discussed the merits of grapes from different regions of Portugal.

'You have an exceptional palate.' Horace raised his glass to Mr Harrison. 'I seem to remember your predecessor, Señor José Alvarez, was also a most knowledgeable gentleman. Of course, I was very young when I met him.'

'That was a long time ago. I took over the premises from

Señor Alvarez in 1887. He had an extensive knowledge of wines, and we corresponded regularly. We'd occasionally meet when I was in London and kept in touch until his death.'

'Oh dear. I hadn't heard Señor Alvarez has passed away. When was that?'

'Shortly after the war. He was in his eighties. He was married to an English lady, Bertha. She died a year before, and I don't think Señor Alvarez got over her death. I wasn't surprised when a mutual acquaintance wrote to tell me that he'd passed away.'

'How sad. I'm trying to track down one of his relatives by the name of Hugh. Do you know him?'

Mr Harrison shook his head. 'We mainly discussed trade matters and exchanged recommendations. I only know the names of his immediate family.'

'You wouldn't happen to have an address for any of his children?'

'I'm afraid not. I used to correspond with Señor Alvarez at his shop's address on Gray's Inn Road. It's changed hands now. He and his wife had a house in Holborn, and his daughter lived nearby, but I don't have her address.'

Horace put a finger to his lips as if struggling to remember. 'I was sure Señor Alvarez had a son. Perhaps I'm mistaken.'

'He had two daughters. Harriet and Constance.'

Constance. At last, a connection. Did this mean Constance Alvarez was unmarried when she'd had Hugh or had he simply chosen to go by his mother's maiden name?

Horace appeared perplexed. 'Perhaps it's his grandson I'm thinking of? Constance's son?'

'No. Constance died not long after the Alvarezes moved to London. Early in 1888, I think. The boy was Harriet's. I don't recall if his name was Hugh.'

'Ah, of course. I remember.' Horace smiled. 'Now, back to business. A case of the port, and I believe Miss Woodmore has given the sherry her seal of approval.'

I drifted in and out of the conversation as they discussed the merits of various vintages. Why did Hugh say Constance was his mother's name when it was his aunt's? It seemed unlikely Constance could be his mother if she died in 1888, but it was possible.

'Where does that leave us?' I asked Horace when we were in the Daimler and heading back to Walden with two cases of booze in the boot.

'We have names we didn't know before. And we have the area where Harriet Alvarez is living. I use an agency that's extremely adept at following up leads. A trip to Somerset House should provide more information.'

Somerset House, a magnificent Georgian building by Waterloo Bridge in London, was where the Registrar General of Births, Marriages, and Deaths was kept.

'They'll need to search the records for a birth, marriage and death. How did Constance die? She could only have been in her twenties. And who did Harriet marry? That should provide us with Hugh's real surname. Then perhaps we can find out when he was born.'

'The plot certainly thickens,' Horace observed, sounding almost gleeful. 'Plenty there to keep my investigators busy.'

31

Curiosity drove me to Mill Ponds House the following morning. Unfortunately, I encountered Teresa Powell on the way in.

Micky Swann opened the front door, and I stepped into the hallway as Teresa came out of the lounge with Paul.

Her nostrils flared when she saw me approach. 'Returning to the scene of your crime?'

Paul reached for her hand. 'Don't, Teresa,' he said gently, causing tears to form in her eyes.

Before I spoke, I took a deep breath, telling myself that she was speaking out of grief. 'I had nothing to do with what happened to your brother. No matter what our differences, I would never have wished that upon him.'

'You put him in prison,' she retorted.

'A judge and jury put him in prison. It's true I went to the police with what I knew, and I don't regret it. If he'd been allowed to carry on, he might have killed someone.'

'He was suffering from shellshock and was sorry for what happened. He didn't deserve to go to prison.' Her green eyes flashed with anger, reminding me horribly of the way Archie had once looked at me. 'He thought you cared for him. He cared for you and was devastated when you betrayed him.'

I felt queasy at the thought of Archie mentioning me to his family. I'd certainly never mentioned him to mine. I was at a loss to know how to defend myself. I had no desire to argue with Teresa, though I was certain Archie hadn't been sorry for what he'd done, and nor had he been suffering from shell-shock. But it was what Teresa had chosen to believe, and I hadn't the heart to dissuade her from that.

To my surprise, Micky came to my defence.

'Your brother helped a lot of men,' he told Teresa. 'I'll always be grateful to him for what he did for my family. But he was no good when it came to women. I warned Iris not to get involved with him. I knew it would only end in tears.'

'His tears,' Teresa spat back. 'She led him on. And now it seems she's been carrying on with a married man.'

'I haven't been carrying on with anyone. Unlike your brother.' I regretted the words as soon as they left my mouth. However, I was getting fed up with the hypocrisy of the Powells.

'What do you mean?' Teresa snarled. 'My brother was planning to get married.'

Micky decided to break up the spat. 'Hugh and Vincent are in the garden if you want to speak to them.' He jerked his thumb towards the open study door.

I didn't need telling twice and darted into the room and out again through the patio doors to the rose garden where I'd witnessed Archie clutching Jennifer Tolfree's hands. I walked around the side of the house and into the walled kitchen garden, where Vincent was kneeling on the ground, sowing seeds into furrows.

He glanced up, and his face broke into a smile when he saw me. 'Thank you.'

'For what?' I wondered if he was thanking me for finding Luke. He'd seemed unusually upset about the boy.

'Lord Timpson invited me to Crookham Hall to look at the stables. He said you'd told him I enjoyed working with horses. He's going to see if he can find a part-time job for me there.'

'How wonderful. I didn't know he was going to do that.' I blessed Daniel for his kindness. 'I'm so pleased for you.'

I found Hugh in the extended garden, a large drawing pad resting on a wooden easel in front of him. He was sketching the newly erected greenhouse with the arched bridge in the distance.

I strolled over to him and asked, 'How old are you?'

Hugh started, having been unaware of my presence, but recovered quickly enough to laugh at the question. I'd pondered the best way to find out his age and decided to take the extremely obvious and undiplomatic approach of asking him outright.

'What business is it of yours?'

'I'm wondering if you're too old to be smitten with Constance Timpson.'

He grinned. 'I'm sure there's more than just my age against me.'

'True,' I replied.

'Though I've noticed a lack of social pretention in Miss Timpson. Given her titled background, I'd have expected her to steer clear of friends with somewhat dubious reputations.'

I smiled at the insult. 'You would have thought so, wouldn't you? She seems to hold loyalty in higher regard to such considerations.'

'She's certainly an unusual young woman. And so are her

friends. Mrs Siddons. Horace Laffaye. You and your boss, Mr Whittle. And then there's Ursula and Millicent Nightingale. Daniel Timpson appears particularly taken with the latter. Yet he's a lord, and she's a humble schoolteacher, so perhaps I'm not so far out of Miss Timpson's social standing.'

'Miss Nightingale is a respected member of the community.' I retorted. His bark of laughter told me my jibe wasn't lost on him.

'I'm a thirty-six-year-old man with little to offer except a nose for sniffing out dodgy business deals.'

A quick calculation told me he must have been born in 1888. He could be Constance's son. It was the year after the Alvarez family had moved to London. That couldn't be a coincidence.

'What about murderers? Are you any good at sniffing them out?' I was curious to hear if he had any theories regarding Archie's death. After all, he was in an ideal position to see what was going on, and he seemed to make a habit of spying on people.

He shook his head. 'I won't deny I've done some snooping, like you. But I still don't know who killed Archie.'

'What about Paul?' I suggested, more to get a reaction than anything else. Paul was my least favourite suspect.

He shook his head. 'No. I've ruled him out. He would have struggled to hold the rifle. Besides, he doesn't have a motive.'

'Perhaps Archie didn't want him to marry his sister.'

He bent to take a different pencil from a leather roll lying on the ground. 'I think the opposite. I get the impression that's exactly what Archie wanted, and it's why he brought Paul here. To somehow get them back together. He knew they both still cared for each other.'

I had to admit, I thought he was right.

'What about Vincent? Would he let his loyalty to Jennifer Tolfree cloud his judgement and perhaps help her to get revenge?'

To my surprise, he laughed.

'Again, I believe the opposite.'

'What do you mean?'

Hugh looked amused. 'You think Vincent is loyal to her?'

I took a moment to digest this, then realised how stupid I'd been. The casual mention of Jennifer's prowess with a rifle. The comment that had led us to the summerhouse to discover where she was meeting Archie. Telling Luke about the dormice nesting there. I'd misread the situation completely.

'He's got it in for Jennifer?'

'Vincent's wife died towards the end of the war of influenza, just before he was discharged from the army. He thinks Jennifer's family didn't do enough to care for her. He and his wife lived in a tied cottage at Blackthorn Park, the Darrington estate. The cottage was in a poor state, and the roof leaked. Lord Darrington was on his uppers and had neglected properties that were his responsibility and did little to look after his tenants. Vincent blames the Darringtons for his wife's death.'

'It must have been devastating for him. I'm not surprised he resents the family.' It was a tragic situation, and I couldn't help wondering if this gave Vincent a motive of sorts. 'How far do you think he'd go to get revenge for what happened to his wife?'

'If you're asking if he'd go so far as to shoot Jennifer Tolfree's lover and try to pin the blame on her, then, no, I don't think he'd go that far. You saw the state he was in when you found Luke. He blames himself for the boy running away and wishes he'd never told him about the dormice by the summerhouse. That's where he was going that night, only you and Miss Nightingale got there first.'

'The killing was impulsive. Vincent might have seen the opportunity and decided to take it. After all, he was a soldier. He must know how to fire a rifle.' It was hardly compelling evidence, though it wouldn't hurt to look again at the alibis of the three men who'd been close by when the murder took place.

'We were all soldiers. It doesn't mean we shot Archie. I know we're the most likely suspects, but we were together all evening until we went to bed.'

'You must have left the room at some point to go to the bathroom or into the kitchen. It wouldn't have taken long for one of you to have walked into the garden.'

He shrugged. 'I suppose it's possible. I can't pretend we were together for every second. However, I don't believe either Paul or Vincent were involved.'

And where did that leave Hugh? Were his two comrades as certain of his innocence? They'd all told the same story. After returning from their walk just before half past eight, they'd gone up to Hugh's room to drink whisky. Paul and Vincent had noticed someone going past the window when they were getting glasses from the kitchen and had assumed it was Archie. They'd come downstairs at around nine o'clock and gone into the kitchen to make coffee and sandwiches to take into the lounge. Could one of them have slipped out at that point?

'What made you come here?' I asked. 'Vincent is a local man and got a room through his connection with Jennifer. Paul was helped by Archie. How did you come to hear about Mill Ponds House?'

'I told you. I read about it in one of the London newspapers.

I'd met Archie a few times during the war when he was an army chaplain and thought I'd come here.'

So he had come across Archie before. However, his story didn't quite add up. 'Archie's name wasn't mentioned in any newspaper. The vicar and Mrs Siddons made sure of that because of his criminal record. And I don't believe any London newspapers have written stories about the opening of Mill Ponds House – only local ones have covered the event.'

'The article I read wasn't about Mill Ponds. It was about the Christmas Close murder. It described Gordon's charity work, including the foundation of a hostel. I'd heard from one of my old army pals that Archie was involved. As I found myself in need of temporary accommodation, I came here and asked the vicar and Archie if I could have a room.'

It was true Mill Ponds had been mentioned in one of the newspapers in that context. But I still wasn't convinced by Hugh's story.

'How well did you know Archie before you came here?'

'Not well at all. As I said, our paths crossed a few times during the war. I remember once I saw him painting in a field in northern France, and we talked about art. I paint a little myself.'

'What regiment were you in?'

'A plain old infantry unit.'

It was apparent he wasn't going to offer more than that, so I decided to get his views on Archie instead. How had he really felt about the man?

'What was Archie like when you first met him?' I asked.

'He wasn't afraid to go into battle. I admired him for that. He certainly wasn't like any other army chaplain I'd encountered in the trenches.'

'I know what you mean. He was unlike any vicar I'd ever

come across before.' I smiled, recalling the first time I'd seen Archie. I'd been captivated by his green eyes and brazen sexuality – then bewildered when I'd seen the dog collar around his neck. My smile faded when I thought of his body lying only feet away from where I was now standing.

Hugh followed my gaze. 'You said you were once close. Before he took aim at your friends.'

'I was intrigued by him. By his contradictions. He was a brave man. Daniel Timpson told me Archie had saved his life during a battle – that made it even harder for Daniel to come to terms with what Archie did.' I stopped, aware of Hugh's rapt expression. For some reason, Teresa's words made me want to reminisce about a man I still couldn't fathom.

'Go on,' Hugh urged. 'Archie fascinated me too, and I'm curious to know more about him.'

'I suppose I found it inspiring that despite what he'd witnessed on the frontline, he never lost his faith. I remember once asking him about his paintings – their serenity surprised me. He told me they celebrated the healing powers of nature and helped him to see the world as God meant it to be seen.'

Hugh nodded. 'His pictures were beautiful. It was a shame he'd stopped painting.'

'Had he?' I felt a strange sadness at this. 'I didn't know.'

'He told me he hadn't painted in over a year. He never said why, though I could tell his demons had got the better of him. I came to realise you were one of those demons. He never got over what you did to him.'

Hugh's words echoed Teresa's and left me feeling a bewildering mix of emotions: part guilt, part resentment.

'I'm sorry things turned out the way they did. But I don't regret going to the police,' I said, trying not to sound defensive.

'Nor should you. I would have done the same.' Hugh bit the

end of his pencil as if perplexed. 'I found it inexplicable that Archie thought the church was his calling. Anyone who knew him would question that. He loved being a holy man – he just didn't seem to understand that it wasn't compatible with his actions. Or his physical desires.'

I flushed as I remembered the heat of the kisses I'd once shared with Archie. There had been nothing holy about them.

I nodded. 'I question now why I was so drawn to him. I should have known better.'

'A lot of people were drawn to Archie and taken in by him. Men and women. There was something dangerous about him, yet he was a priest. That contradiction is quite compelling. I suppose all of us can be good and bad, but he was an extreme example.' Hugh's eyes narrowed. 'And that type of person makes enemies.'

32

Conversations with Hugh Alvarez always left me with more questions than answers. I was certain he was hiding something. At the same time, I had to admit I was growing to like him, and I could understand the attraction I was sure Constance was feeling.

Hugh's comments had somehow helped me to come to terms with the bizarre relationship I'd found myself in with Archie. When he'd said Archie had taken in many people – men and women – had he counted himself as one of them? I couldn't help wondering if Hugh's insights were derived from the fact that he had a similar personality. And I didn't want Constance to fall prey in the same way I had.

Although she wasn't as impulsive as me, I knew she was lonely. As a young businesswoman running a successful company, she had few suitors. Men were put off by her power. It made me think that someone older and with Hugh's confidence might not be a bad match. Perhaps the ten years between them could work to their advantage. But... what was his story?

While I waited for Horace's contacts to carry out their searches, I decided to go back to Winchester and call on Kevin Noakes at the *Hampshire Chronicle* to see if I could find out more about the Alvarez family. Kevin made it his business to know everything that went on in the city and had plenty of local contacts who might be able to provide some historical information.

The previous year, I'd witnessed Kevin's tenacity first-hand when we'd reported on the Christmas Close murder. The crime had occurred on the day of the Prince of Wales's visit to Winchester, and we'd switched from covering the royal event to investigating the murder of a young actress.

I'd enjoyed spending time with Kevin, who had a quick brain and mischievous sense of humour. It didn't hurt that he was good-looking, with laughing blue eyes and neatly cropped blond hair. However, he was a compulsive flirt and had a tendency to overdo the pomade and cologne in a bid to impress the fairer sex.

I waited outside the *Hampshire Chronicle's* offices on Winchester High Street until Kevin appeared, snappily dressed in a smart grey gaberdine suit.

To my surprise, we walked past the Old Rectory Café – our usual lunchtime haunt. I was about to ask why when Kevin stopped to examine the billboard outside the cinema. A rather lurid poster advertised the evening screening of *Prodigal Daughters* with Gloria Swanson.

I waited for the inevitable question.

'Looks racy. Do you fancy seeing it with me tonight?'

'I have to get back. I thought you were courting Florrie from the café?'

'It didn't last.'

'That's a shame.' I guessed that's why we weren't eating at the Old Rectory Café.

'It is.' He sighed. 'She made the best sandwiches in town. I can't show my face in there now.'

I shot him an accusatory glance.

He held up his hands in a defensive gesture. 'It was just a misunderstanding.'

I didn't need to enquire what sort of misunderstanding. I suspected Florrie hadn't been the only girl he'd been courting.

'What about you?' he countered. 'I thought you and Percy Baverstock were an item. Then I heard rumours you were seeing a married man.'

'Whatever you've heard, it isn't true. I'm not seeing anyone, and I intend to keep it that way.'

'If you change your mind...' he said with a wink. 'Are you still trying to find out about José Alvarez? Did you speak to Mr Harrison?'

I nodded. 'Apparently, Señor Alvarez had two daughters, Harriet and Constance. I guess they would have been living here until 1887. That's when Señor Alvarez sold the shop and moved to London. Constance died shortly afterwards. And if Hugh is to be believed, and I'm not sure that he is, his mother, who could be Harriet, died earlier this year.'

'What sort of age are we talking about?' he asked.

'Hugh Alvarez is thirty-six. I'm guessing his mother would have been in her late fifties, early sixties when she died. I'm looking for someone of a similar age who might have known her? A local who knows everyone else's business?'

He considered this for a moment, then laughed and gave me a lascivious wink. 'Why don't we go back to my lodgings and find out.'

'What?' I spluttered, then realised what he meant. 'Mrs Durling?'

'If you want local gossip, she's your woman. She seems to know the hidden secrets of every family in Winchester. I've only got to mention a name, and she comes up with some juicy little titbit for me.'

The perfect landlady for a reporter, I thought.

'If she's in a good mood, she might even make us a sandwich.'

I'd made Mrs Durling's acquaintance the previous year when she'd played the fairy godmother in a charity pantomime of *Cinderella*. It was a performance never to be forgotten, and I could still picture her prancing across the stage in her silvery tutu.

She seemed delighted to see me and treated us to more than just sandwiches, producing a large home-made gala pie and a bottle of ginger beer.

Her boarding house on Lower Brook Street was colourfully decorated in shades of pink and blue. Mrs Durling herself was dressed in a bright pink housecoat, wisps of her greying blonde hair poking out of a matching pink scarf wrapped around her head.

'I remember Constance and Harriet Alvarez. I didn't know them well, I was five years younger, but my mother was friends with Bertha, their mother. Harriet took after Bertha, with the same pink cheeks and pretty blonde hair. Constance was completely different. She was a real beauty, with long dark hair and big brown eyes. Very exotic. I suppose that came from her father. He was Spanish, I seem to recall.'

'Do you know why the family moved to London?' I wondered if it had something to do with Hugh's birth – both events occurred within a year of each other.

Mrs Durling shook her head. 'I can't remember. I'm not sure my mother kept in touch with Bertha after that.'

'Were Harriet or Constance married?'

'I have a feeling Harriet was.' Mrs Durling topped up Kevin's beer. He was working his way through a huge slice of pie, half listening to the conversation as he scanned a newspaper.

'Do you remember her husband's name?' I asked, more interested in finding out information than eating, delicious as the pie was.

She shook her head.

'What about Constance? You said she was a beauty.'

'She wasn't short of admirers.'

'Anyone in particular?'

'The most famous one would have been Redvers Tolfree. He was Gordon's father. That's when everyone ate Tolfree Biscuits. Even Queen Victoria.'

At this, Kevin started taking a bit more notice. He was well aware of the Redvers Tolfree scandal.

'What happened?' Knowing what I did of Redvers, his romance with Constance probably hadn't ended well.

'I'm not sure. I expect Isaac Tolfree put a stop to it. Even though the family was trade, Isaac mixed with some fancy folk. It didn't surprise me when I heard Redvers was engaged to Gertrude Enderby, Lord Enderby's daughter.'

Could Constance have been pregnant when Redvers ended the relationship? Hence the family move to London, away from prying neighbours. Hopefully Horace's contacts would discover the truth in the records at Somerset House.

Mrs Durling couldn't tell us much more, and Kevin had to return to work, so we thanked her for lunch and strolled back into the city centre.

'Our old friend, Redvers Tolfree.' Kevin dug his hands into his pockets. 'Did you get what you came for?'

I shook my head. 'I'm even more mystified than before. I was looking for a connection between Hugh Alvarez and Archie Powell, not the Tolfrees.'

'What's Gertrude Tolfree like?'

'Not what I expected. She wasn't seen out much after Redvers' fall from grace, and I had her pegged as the subservient wife. But since she's become involved with Mill Ponds House, I've realised what a formidable woman she is.'

'It doesn't surprise me that Constance Alvarez was the one to get the old heave-ho, despite her exotic looks. A wine merchant's daughter wouldn't be able to compete financially or socially with the daughter of a lord. So where does Archie Powell fit into all of this?'

I shrugged, unwilling to reveal the affair between Jennifer Tolfree and Archie. At present, that seemed the most likely motive for the killing. However, I was still curious to know why Hugh Alvarez was lying about his past. And what did it have to do with Archie?

When I arrived back in Walden, I debated whether to risk calling in at the station house to see if there had been any developments. However, I didn't fancy running into Superintendent Cobbe and decided it would probably be safer to go first thing in the morning before he'd have the chance to drive over from Winchester.

Unfortunately, I didn't have to wait that long. The decision was taken out of my hands when Ben caught up with me as I was walking along the high street.

'Can you come to the station house with me now?'

'Why?' Dread crept over me. It had to be about Marc.

'Superintendent Cobbe will explain. Some new information has come to light concerning your...' Ben hesitated. 'This man you were seen with on the jetty.'

'His car,' I mumbled. The witness to the kiss must have remembered seeing the red Austin Seven.

Ben looked puzzled. 'The stationmaster didn't mention a car.'

The stationmaster? I cursed myself for being such an idiot. I'd somehow got it into my head that Hugh had been spying on me, even though it was unlikely he'd have been able to leave Mill Ponds at that time without Paul or Vincent noticing. And I wished I hadn't just mentioned the bloody car.

I sighed, falling into step with Ben. 'Come on. Let's get this over with.'

'The thing is,' he said in an undertone, 'Archie Powell's diary has been found.'

I wanted to scream. Whenever I thought Marc was safe, something else happened to put him in danger of discovery.

'Where was it?' I asked.

Ben shot me a wry smile. 'Inside the Bible by his bed.'

'Inside?' I spluttered. 'I don't understand. How could it have been hidden inside?'

'Because he'd cut a hole into the pages so that it fitted into a gap. From the outside, it looked like a normal Bible.'

'Good grief.' Words failed me.

'Teresa Powell found it when she was sorting through Archie's belongings.'

'Doesn't that give her some inkling that her brother might not have been as sincere as she supposed?' I made no attempt to hide my sarcasm.

'I think she's more concerned with the indiscretions of those featured in the diary than the man who wrote it,' Ben replied. 'She's saying it gives you a motive for murdering Archie.'

Yet again, I suppressed the urge to scream, emitting a low groan of frustration instead. The fact that I was now being escorted to the station house to be interviewed by Superintendent Cobbe did not bode well.

I'd been lucky to avoid arrest last time. I had a feeling my luck had just run out.

33

'This is Archibald Powell's diary.'

Superintendent Cobbe held the small black book between two fingers. He was seated once again behind Ben's desk at the station house.

To my surprise, he'd asked if I wanted Ben to be present during our interview. I'd refused, preferring to face this one alone.

'The entries in it are brief but revealing. It's interesting that Mr Powell always calls you by your first name. Entries such as "Iris meets with M.J.". He refers to most people by their initials.'

My fingers tightened around the satchel on my lap. Is that all he had? Marc's initials.

'In an earlier entry, Mr Powell notes he followed a man you met in St James's Park back to his office in Holborn and discovered he was a solicitor by the name of Marc Jansen working at Tyler & Simcock, Chancery Lane.'

I relaxed my grip. It was over. There wasn't much left I

could do to protect Marc. Or the ending that I'd wanted for our relationship.

'Perhaps you could tell me how you know Mr Jansen?'

I thought back to the first time I'd seen Marc and smiled, remembering the curiosity in his brown eyes as he walked purposefully towards me.

'During the war, I was part of a VAD unit in Park Fever Hospital in Lewisham. The hospital had been given over to housing refugees. Marc arrived in 1917. He was looking for his wife and parents, who'd left Belgium at the beginning of the war. He'd stayed behind to fight in the Resistance.'

'You became close?'

I nodded, trying not to betray the emotion I felt at relating these events to someone who was bound to judge me.

'We did become close. I helped him to track down his family. They'd been housed in Devon, and through my grandparents in Exeter, I was able to find out where they were living. Marc left the hospital to travel to Devon to see his family before he joined the Belgian army.'

'And you kept in touch with him all these years?'

'I never expected to see him again after he left the hospital. I didn't even know if he'd survived the war.' My voice shook. 'Then last year, when I was in Devon for my father's wedding, we met. He and his wife had settled in Exeter. It was a shock to see him again.'

'And you rekindled your relationship?'

In truth, that's exactly what we'd done. Although we'd tried to avoid physical intimacy, our feelings had become intense.

'Marc started a new job in London, and when I was in town, we'd meet.'

'Where is Mr Jansen now?'

'He and his wife have moved back to Belgium.'

'Whereabouts in Belgium?'

'I don't know. Somewhere in Bruges. It's where he spent his childhood and where his parents still live. His wife, Annette, lost her family before the war, and she's very close to Marc's parents.'

Superintendent Cobbe was staring at me with a curious expression. I thought I could detect sympathy in his grey eyes, although that might have been wishful thinking on my part.

'You've chosen to protect this man, even though you're under suspicion of murder.'

It seemed to be a statement rather than a question, so I stayed silent.

'Presumably, because you don't want his wife to find out about your affair?'

This time it was a question.

'There was no affair. You must see that from Archie's observations. He saw us walking and talking in a park. I won't deny that Marc and I were close, but we did nothing more than you'll find documented in those pages.'

Superintendent Cobbe turned the pocket diary between his fingertips as if it were an incendiary device.

I pointed at it. 'Does Archie mention his meetings with Jennifer Tolfree in the summerhouse? Does he acknowledge his hypocrisy in accusing me of seeing a married man when he was engaged in an adulterous relationship?' I was sure the initials J.T. must feature in those pages, though maybe initials weren't considered solid evidence.

His lips twitched, but he didn't reply. He didn't have to. It was obvious some of the entries had related to Jennifer. Why had Archie bothered to conceal the diary in such an elaborate hiding place unless it was to protect his own secrets?

I decided to press home my point. 'I'm guessing it was

Archie who ended their relationship. Did Jennifer know he hoped to persuade Victoria Hobbs to marry him? Surely Jennifer or Gordon has the strongest motive for wanting Archie dead.'

A glint in the superintendent's eyes told me he was well aware of this.

'I have no physical evidence to place either of them at the scene,' was all he said.

'You don't have any evidence to place me at the scene.'

'How do you know?' he asked.

'Because I didn't kill Archie. I didn't go anywhere near Mill Ponds that night.'

'That's not true. You were on the jetty nearby. I'm guessing it was Mr Jansen you were seen kissing?'

'We were saying goodbye. I went straight home after that. And so did he.'

'How can you be certain? He could have gone to Mill Ponds and shot Mr Powell.'

'I saw him get into his car and drive away. He wasn't even aware of Archie's existence.'

'I only have your word for that.'

'I can promise you it's true. Marc knew nothing about Archie or Mill Ponds. He'd never set foot in Walden before that night. Do you seriously think he would have found his way into the garden, picked up the rifle, and shot someone in the back?'

'That's exactly what someone did. Why not Mr Jansen? Why not you? This diary proves you both had a motive for killing Archie Powell.'

'Please.' I wasn't beyond begging. 'There's no need to drag Marc into this. He's starting a new life with his family in Belgium.'

'You're very loyal to him, aren't you?' The superintendent was staring at me with that curious expression again.

I wanted to say it was because I loved Marc. But I wasn't about to tell Superintendent Cobbe this when I'd never been able to say those words to Marc.

'I'll be frank with you, Miss Woodmore. I'm no nearer to finding out who killed Mr Powell, so I have no choice other than to continue investigating every lead, which includes tracking down Mr Jansen and interviewing him. Perhaps he did know who Archie Powell was. And perhaps he saw him that evening by the lake and followed him into the garden of Mill Ponds and shot him.'

It was possible but implausible, and the superintendent knew it.

'How could he have seen him? Victoria Hobbs was with Archie at a quarter to eight. What did Archie do after that?'

'He went into the house to change his clothes. He took the bag Mrs Hobbs had given him up to his room. He appears to have put on one of the jumpers belonging to Mrs Hobbs's late husband. An old khaki army jumper. Mrs Swann hadn't seen him wear the garment before, but when Mrs Hobbs told us about her donation, it explained where it had come from.'

Was this telling? An indication that Archie couldn't wait to step into Victoria's husband's shoes? Or simply that the evening had become chilly, and it was the first jumper he had to hand?

'Polly Swann told me the last time Archie went out digging in the garden was on Easter Sunday. That was when he'd first asked Victoria Hobbs to marry him, and she'd refused. She rejected him again on the evening of his death, which caused him to go outside to vent his annoyance through manual work.'

'I had surmised that much from what Mrs Hobbs told us,' the superintendent said drily.

'Polly also mentioned that on Easter Sunday, Jennifer Tolfree had gone into the garden to talk to Archie. In Polly's words, Jennifer had received short shrift. Isn't it likely that anyone approaching Archie on the evening of the eleventh would have been on the receiving end of his temper? Perhaps he upset them so much they lost their own temper and picked up the rifle?'

It was clear Jennifer was the most likely candidate, particularly if she'd witnessed the scene between Archie and Victoria.

Superintendent Cobbe stood up. 'I think we'll leave it there for this evening. I'm sure you want to go home as much as I do. Once I've had a chance to make a few enquiries as to Mr Jansen's whereabouts, we'll speak again.'

I wanted to argue with him, to plead with him not to involve Marc in this, but I knew it would be futile.

I left the station house weighed down with despair. It seemed all my relationships were destined to have unhappy endings.

34

'Horace has news.' Elijah replaced the mouthpiece of the telephone in its cradle.

'What about?' I'd been staring at a blank piece of paper in my typewriter for some time now. Abandoning my attempts to write something worth reading, I got up and wandered into Elijah's den.

'Hugh Alvarez. Remember your trip to Mr Harrison's in Winchester? Has all that sherry addled your brain?'

'Hugh, yes, of course. I was miles away.' In another country, in fact. I was fretting over what would happen if Superintendent Cobbe contacted the Belgian police and got them to track down Marc. Would he ever forgive me? I tried to drag myself away from these thoughts and focus on what Elijah was saying.

'Put your coat on then.'

'Sorry? What?'

'Horace is on his way.'

'Here?' It was unusual for Horace to visit the office. He usually summoned us to go to him at Heron Bay Lodge.

'He's coming to pick us up. He's been talking to Daniel Timpson, and we're going to Crookham Hall.'

This got my attention. Horace must have found out something interesting if he wanted an audience. Were we close to finding out who killed Archie? Close enough to prevent Superintendent Cobbe from pursuing his investigation into Marc?

'What's he discovered? Did Hugh do it?'

'He wouldn't tell me over the telephone.' Elijah rose from his chair and stretched his back. 'Come on, let's wait outside.'

He buttoned his tweed jacket, plucked his homburg hat from the hatstand and made his way slowly down the stairs while I locked up the office.

Outside, he lit a cigarette before asking, 'What are you keeping from me now?'

I wasn't surprised by the question. 'Superintendent Cobbe interviewed me again last night.'

'Why?'

I shrugged, relieved to see the Daimler appear at the end of the road. Once we were seated in the back, I looked expectantly at Horace.

But he merely raised a finger and said, 'Patience, my dear. I'm not going to tell this tale twice.'

To avoid answering Elijah's questions about my meeting with Superintendent Cobbe, I told them what Mrs Durling had remembered about the Alvarez family.

'Our old friend, Redvers Tolfree. That doesn't bode well,' Elijah remarked.

'Indeed,' Horace said with an infuriating smirk.

He refused to say more, and the short drive to Crookham Hall seemed interminable. When we arrived, Daniel came out to greet us and showed us into the reception room, where Constance and Mrs Siddons were waiting.

To his credit, Horace didn't keep us in suspense. He produced a single sheet of notepaper from his briefcase and proceeded to read.

'Redvers Tolfree married Constance Alvarez on 8 March 1887.'

'They married,' I gasped. 'Mrs Durling told me Redvers had been in love with Constance, but she thought he'd jilted her in favour of Gertrude.'

Horace shook his head. 'Not so. Sadly, Constance Tolfree died in childbirth in January 1888.'

Constance sank back into the green velvet sofa. 'Hugh Alvarez is Constance and Redvers' child?'

Horace nodded. 'There's a birth certificate for Hugh Tolfree. His father's name is given as Redvers Tolfree, and his mother is Constance Tolfree.'

'Gosh,' I breathed. This was not what I'd been expecting.

Constance sighed. 'So his mother's name *was* Constance.'

'So what is Mr Alvarez, Tolfree or whatever his name is, doing in Walden?' Elijah asked.

'Hoping for some Tolfree money,' Daniel suggested.

Horace leaned forward in his chair, a smile hovering on his lips. Elijah and I exchanged a glance, knowing this signalled more was to come.

'Mr Skelton has no need of Tolfree money.'

'Mr Skelton?' Constance queried.

'Hugh Tolfree was adopted by Harriet and Nicholas Skelton. Harriet was Constance's sister.'

'Skelton?' Constance's brow furrowed, then her face relaxed, and she began to laugh.

I frowned, trying to remember where I'd heard the name recently.

'What's so funny?' Daniel asked.

'Hugh Skelton's wealth far outstrips that of his half-brother, Gordon Tolfree,' Horace explained.

'Skelton & Son.' It suddenly came to me. Hugh had said he'd once worked for Skelton & Son and had suggested Constance stop using Kenwrights' lorries and switch to them. 'Presumably, they're some sort of haulage company?'

'The biggest in the country,' Constance replied. 'They've amassed a fortune since the war. Nicholas Skelton had a fairly modest business. Then his son took over the company and purchased up old army stock. There was a huge surplus of lorries when the war ended.'

Daniel shook his head in disbelief. 'So what is Hugh Skelton doing at Mill Ponds House, pretending to be homeless and unemployed?'

'That is the question.' Horace sat back, looking gratified by our reaction to his revelations. 'And one that only Mr Skelton can answer.'

Constance rang a bell, and Miss Grange appeared. 'Could you bring us tea and cakes? Also, can you find Pritchard? I'd like to speak to him.'

'Of course, Miss Timpson.'

Miss Grange returned soon after with the tea tray and Pritchard, the Timpsons' chauffeur, in tow.

'Pritchard. I'd like you to drive to the factory and bring back Mr Hugh Alvarez.'

'What? Now?'

'Yes, now,' Constance said with a smile.

If Pritchard was curious about his task, the look on Constance's face told him not to ask any questions. He gave a brief nod and departed.

During the three-quarters of an hour it took for him to return, Elijah, Horace and Daniel consumed whisky and sodas while Constance, Mrs Siddons and I contented ourselves with tea and cake. We spent the time speculating on the reason behind Hugh's subterfuge.

'It must have something to do with Archie's death,' Daniel said with conviction.

Elijah disagreed. 'He may feel some animosity towards the Tolfrees. But none of this gives him a motive for wanting Archie dead.'

'Unless Archie found out about Hugh and tried to black-mail him.' I knew from experience Archie wasn't above threat-ening to expose people's secrets.

We stopped talking when the door opened, and Hugh strode into the room, leaving Miss Grange trailing in his wake. He showed no nerves or surprise at the audience that awaited him.

'Thank you, Miss Grange.' Once the housekeeper had left, Constance turned her attention to Hugh. 'Thank you for coming so promptly, Mr Alvarez.'

He gave a slight smile. 'Your chauffeur made it sound like a request I couldn't refuse.'

Constance didn't return the smile. 'Please take a seat. We wish to ask you a few questions.'

Daniel stood by the mantelpiece, whisky and soda in hand, watching him with suspicion. Mrs Siddons, Horace, Elijah and I sat back, preparing to enjoy the spectacle. Constance was queen of this house, and she would direct proceedings.

Hugh sat down, his eyes travelling to each of us in turn. 'Quite a gathering of minds.'

Constance ignored this. 'I want you to tell me truthfully what your name is.'

'Hugh Skelton,' he replied without hesitation.

'Then why do you call yourself Alvarez?'

'Because it was my mother's maiden name. I would have given myself a less conspicuous name had I known the attention I was going to receive.'

'Who were your parents?' Constance asked.

'Nicholas and Harriet Skelton. My mother, Constance, died in childbirth, and I was brought up by her sister, Harriet, and her husband, Nicholas. They legally adopted me, and I became Hugh Skelton.'

'And your real father?' Constance's tone was polite but insistent.

'I think you already know who that is.' Hugh shifted his gaze from her to me. 'I'm afraid your investigations have led you down a blind alley. You've done a good job of discovering my identity. However, my reasons for calling myself Alvarez have nothing to do with Archie's murder.'

'With all due respect, Mr... Mr Skelton,' Constance interjected, drawing his attention back to her. 'We only have your word for that.'

'True.' Hugh inclined his head in acknowledgement. 'And I concede that you have every right to be suspicious of me under the circumstances. But you don't have the right to question me. That prerogative belongs to the police, and I've already arranged to discuss the matter with Superintendent Cobbe.'

No one could argue with this, and the room fell silent.

'If that's all.' Hugh rose from his seat, but Constance held up an elegant hand to stop him.

'Please sit down, Mr Skelton.'

It was said in the politest of tones with just a hint of authority. Nevertheless, there was a collective intake of breath as we waited to see if Hugh would obey. He didn't. However, he made no move to leave either.

35

'I apologise for bringing you here and asking such personal questions,' Constance continued in her silvery voice. 'In different circumstances, I wouldn't dream of subjecting you to such a public interrogation. However, both my brother and my friend have been questioned by the police over Archie's murder, so you'll understand our anxiety to find out the truth.'

Hugh inclined his head but stayed standing.

Constance's jaw tightened a fraction. 'You also accepted a job in my factory under false pretences. Given your true circumstances, I'm struggling to comprehend why you did that.'

'How else could I get to know you?' he replied with a grin, leisurely returning to his seat.

It was a statement intended to charm, and by Horace and Mrs Siddons' smiles, it had worked on them. Elijah was a tougher nut to crack and looked on in cynical appreciation at Hugh's handling of the situation. Daniel's uncertain expression indicated he wasn't entirely won over, although he did offer Hugh a whisky and soda, which was accepted.

I was torn. I wanted to be on Hugh's side but without knowing why he'd come to Mill Ponds, I couldn't allow myself to trust him. I caught Constance's eye and knew she felt the same way. If his flattery had wrong-footed her, she wasn't letting it show.

I was just relieved that the tension had finally been broken, and the atmosphere was now more cordial. Unfortunately, this state of harmony didn't last long.

'Look around the room, Mr Skelton. I surround myself with people I can trust. The way to get to know someone is through honesty. And as I only found out your real name a short time ago, you'll appreciate my reluctance to have further dealings with you until you tell me why you came to Walden.' Constance reached for the bell to summon Miss Grange. 'I'll ask Pritchard to take you to Mill Ponds where I expect you to pack your bags. Please don't set foot in my factory again.'

It was a tactic I'd seen Constance use before in business. Her terms were clear. You either gave her what she wanted, or she walked away from the deal. And I knew she never bluffed. If she walked away, she didn't come back. However, in this case, it was Hugh who would be doing the walking.

Hugh gave her that look of amusement and admiration I'd seen before. I had a feeling Constance would get what she wanted.

He took a sip of his whisky and soda and then began his story. 'As I think you already know, my real father was Redvers Tolfree. But as far as I'm concerned, Nicholas Skelton is my father. I've never known any other.'

'Why didn't Redvers Tolfree bring you up?' Constance's expression was softer now, and I guessed she was relieved Hugh hadn't walked away.

'He showed no interest in me, perhaps due to the circumstances of my birth. By all accounts, Redvers was heartbroken when Constance died. However, his father, Isaac Tolfree, was not. He'd never approved of the marriage and had hoped for a more profitable match for his son than the daughter of a Spanish wine merchant.'

'Gertrude Enderby?' Horace's hands were clasped together as though he'd had to stop himself from clapping in glee at finally getting to hear Hugh's tale.

Hugh nodded. 'She'd been in love with Redvers and was the daughter of a lord. Isaac saw his chance. Constance and Redvers had run away to London together and married in secret. As far as Isaac was concerned, no one need know that his son was a widower.'

'Apart from the inconvenient fact he had a son,' Horace commented.

'Harriet had cared for me from birth, and Redvers never came near me. When it was clear this wasn't going to change, she and Nicholas asked if they could adopt me. Harriet was unable to conceive and was desperate for a baby. Gertrude Enderby had no desire to take me on, no doubt anticipating she and Redvers would have children of their own. My grandfather, José, saw a way to give his daughter, Harriet, what she wanted and to make some money at the same time. I believe it was José who approached Isaac with a proposition.'

'So Isaac paid your grandfather to...' Horace paused diplomatically.

Hugh grinned. 'To get rid of the problem. Me. Redvers was free to start a new life with Gertrude, and Harriet and Nicholas could adopt the child they'd longed for. It worked out well for all parties. My mother and father, and I mean Harriet and Nicholas when I say that, told me the truth years ago. It was a shock, but it didn't affect me too much. I was loved and never wanted for anything.'

'What made you come here now?' Constance's tone was casual, as if she was asking why he'd chosen a particular holiday resort, but I knew how crucial Hugh's answer was to her. Would it clear him of Archie's murder? Or incriminate him?

'I was curious to meet my half-brother.' Hugh shrugged as if he knew his response was somewhat underwhelming. 'That's all there is to it. I would never have come looking while my mother or grandfather and grandmother were alive. They would have hated that. We were a close-knit family. We had each other and didn't need anyone else.'

'Was it your adoptive mother, Harriet, who died earlier this year?' I asked.

Hugh nodded. 'Not long after she died, I saw Gordon's name in the newspapers. It was an article on the Christmas Close murder he was involved in. It piqued my curiosity. I talked about it with my father, who suggested I should engineer a meeting with Gordon to see what he was like for myself. At first, I was going to visit Tolfree Motors and pretend to be a customer. But what would that reveal about the man?'

'Why couldn't you just tell Gordon who you were?' Daniel's tone was curious rather than accusatory, and I had a feeling he was beginning to thaw.

'Because I didn't know if he'd been told about his father's first marriage. Or about me. I didn't want to upset him or his family. I just wanted to see for myself what sort of man he was. Then I read another report on the murder trial, which mentioned Gordon's charity work and his involvement with Mill Ponds House. I thought that would be the ideal way to get to know him. From what I've seen, I don't think he has any idea he has a half-brother.'

'Do you intend to tell him who you are?' I wasn't sure Gordon would welcome yet more revelations so soon after discovering his wife's affair.

Hugh hesitated. 'Archie's murder has complicated everything. I was only just starting to get to know Gordon when the shooting happened. I'm reluctant to reveal who I am until Archie's killer is caught.'

Horace nodded. 'I can understand that. However, I'm afraid Superintendent Cobbe is making little headway with the case.'

'I plan to tell the superintendent my sorry tale – not that it's likely to help his investigation.' Hugh sank the remainder of his drink. 'What a mess this turned into. I'd only intended to stay at the hostel for a week or two at most, then say I had a job and move on. Shortly afterwards, Skelton & Son would make a donation to Mill Ponds House that would more than cover my bed and board, and no one would be any the wiser – unless I'd decided during the course of my stay to confide in Gordon. But then Archie was killed and... well, you know the rest.' Hugh looked across at Constance and smiled. 'Despite everything, I'm still glad that I came.'

This time, she returned his smile. 'Thank you for your honesty, Mr Skelton. I appreciate the difficulty you found yourself in and why it was necessary to continue your deception. I'll call Pritchard and get him to drive you to Mill Ponds. Or wherever you wish to go.'

'Before I leave, I'd love to take a look at this magnificent estate.' Hugh turned to Daniel. 'Would it be presumptuous of me to ask you to give me a tour?'

All eyes were on Daniel, and there was an awkward moment while he seemed to consider the request. I suspected he hadn't entirely made up his mind about Hugh and was still feeling protective of Constance.

However, he stood up and replied curtly, 'It would be a pleasure.'

We all sank back into our chairs with a collective sigh of relief after they'd left the room.

'Well.' This time, Horace did clap his hands together. 'That solves the mystery of Hugh Alvarez.'

'But not the mystery of Archie Powell,' Elijah reminded him, reaching for the silver cigarette box.

'True,' Horace replied. 'I'd say the Tolfrees are still the main suspects.'

'No wonder Alvarez, Skelton or whatever the damn man's name is, doesn't want to reveal who he is,' Mrs Siddons commented. 'I'm not sure it's an association to be proud of.'

'The Tolfree name has taken rather a battering over the years, and this could be the final nail in the coffin,' Horace agreed.

'So what do we all make of Mr Hugh Skelton?' I asked the room in general. Before I moved on to the Tolfrees, I wanted to hear what everyone had made of Hugh's story. If we were dismissing him as a potential suspect, it at least narrowed down the field.

Horace steepled his hands beneath his chin and gave the matter some consideration before announcing, 'I thought he seemed like a decent chap.'

Elijah nodded his agreement.

'Very easy on the eye.' Mrs Siddons winked at Constance. 'I like him.'

I smiled. 'Me too.'

We waited for Constance's judgement. I thought Hugh had done enough to win her over. However, I was wrong.

'I believe he was telling us the truth. But I'm afraid I won't be able to trust him completely until I know who killed Archie.'

Horace gave a slight nod. 'Very wise.'

'The problem is, we may never find out who fired that rifle.' Elijah looked troubled as he drew on his cigarette.

Constance sighed and rubbed her eyes. 'That's very much what I'm afraid of.'

'One of the Tolfrees did it,' Elijah said with a certainty that surprised me. 'But with no physical evidence, it will be impossible to prove.'

'There might be a way.' I'd been going over the previous evening's conversation with Superintendent Cobbe, and a thought had struck me. 'Although it would be risky.'

Elijah scrutinised me warily, clearly not liking the sound of this. 'What is it?'

'To entice the killer to strike again.'

Horace tutted. 'Why would they kill again? Haven't they got what they wanted?'

I shook my head. 'If what I suspect is correct, I don't think they have.'

36

'Bravo.' Mrs Siddons clapped her hands together at the sight of the finished greenhouse. 'You've done a splendid job.'

'You have indeed.' Gordon Tolfree beamed at Hugh, Paul and Vincent, who smiled and tried not to look embarrassed.

'Mrs Tolfree was a great help.' Vincent bowed in Gertrude's direction.

'You three did all the hard work,' she replied graciously.

Jennifer's smile was painfully forced, her expression indicating she'd rather be anywhere but in the garden of Mill Ponds. Her shoulders were slumped and her eyes red. I was beginning to realise how strong her feelings for Archie had been. And to bring her here, to where he'd taken his last breath, was perhaps cruel.

However, the need to discover who murdered Archie had overridden the concerns Mrs Siddons, Horace and Elijah had raised to my plan to see if we could induce his killer to reveal themselves.

Finally agreeing, Mrs Siddons had set the scene by inviting the Tolfrees and the vicar to attend Mill Ponds House at eleven o'clock for the opening of the newly built greenhouse. She'd insisted their presence was necessary if they were to show the world that the hostel was proving a success.

It had been a relief to wake up that morning to warm June sunshine, and Mrs Siddons had dressed for the occasion in an eye-catching purple silk dress topped with a matching wide-brimmed purple hat. She could have been launching an ocean liner rather than cutting the length of yellow ribbon Polly had tied across the door of the greenhouse.

I was gratified to see Reverend Childs, who knew nothing of our plan, taking the event seriously and solemnly presenting Mrs Siddons with a pair of scissors.

'I declare this greenhouse open.' Mrs Siddons cut the ribbon to a smattering of applause and the click of a camera. 'I won't keep you long, but after all your efforts, I thought it only fitting we should celebrate your achievement with tea and cake.'

Robbie, *The Walden Herald's* photographer, snapped a few more pictures before departing, saying he was going to get a shot of the greenhouse from the bridge over the railway line. The rest of us stayed in the garden chatting while Polly handed out cups of tea and plates of home-made fruit cake. Jennifer stood silently beside her husband, the stiffness between them introducing the only note of tension to what was otherwise a relaxed gathering.

'Is our greenhouse really going to make it into the newspaper?' Paul asked.

'It certainly is,' I replied. 'Hopefully Robbie was able to get a picture of it from the bridge so it can be seen in all its glory.'

'Clever idea to photograph it from up there.' Hugh gazed up at the arched bridge, which could be seen in the distance. 'I think I'll go and make a sketch of it from that viewpoint.'

When Polly began to gather up the tea things, it was a cue for the party to disperse, and Hugh helped her carry the cups and plates back to the kitchen. Vincent and Paul stayed in the garden to sow seeds in the newly dug vegetable beds while Mrs Siddons, the vicar and I walked around to the front of the house with the Tolfrees.

'I'm going into town if you'd like me to drop you at the church,' Mrs Siddons said to the vicar.

'Thank you, but I have my bicycle.' Reverend Childs hastily began wheeling it down the driveway. Most people in town were familiar with Mrs Siddons' style of driving and were reluctant to accept a lift.

She turned to me. 'In that case, I can drop you back at the office.'

I nodded, making my way over to her two-seater sports car. I'd known the vicar would refuse her offer and dart off before she could insist on strapping his bicycle to the rack on the rear of her car.

At that moment, Hugh emerged from the house carrying a sketch pad in one hand and a shooting stick in the other.

'Be careful if you're going up to the bridge,' Mrs Siddons warned. 'The walls are very low. I've been talking to the council about making them higher.'

Gordon nodded in agreement. 'We don't allow Luke or Daisy to go near that bridge. It's about time the council did something to make it safer.'

He was holding open the front passenger door of his red Sunbeam Tourer for his wife, but she ignored it.

'I'm going to walk into town,' Jennifer murmured. The animosity between the couple was palpable.

'As you wish,' Gordon replied curtly. 'Mother?'

Gertrude shook her head, putting on her gloves. 'It's such a lovely morning, I think I'll stroll by the lake for a while. I'll see you at home for lunch.'

'In that case.' Gordon turned to Hugh. 'Hop in, and I'll drive you up to the bridge. I bet you've never been in one of these before. It's the latest model. It only came into the showroom this week.'

I cringed at the patronising way Gordon addressed his half-brother – not that he was aware of the relationship – I was fairly certain of that. From what we now knew of Hugh, he could afford a far more expensive car than the Sunbeam.

'Thank you.' Hugh smiled. 'It's a beautiful motor.'

I exchanged a glance with him before jumping in the passenger seat of Mrs Siddons' sports car. I'd barely even closed the door before she sped off down the driveway.

I looked back to see Gordon still standing next to the Sunbeam, pointing out its various features to Hugh.

'It's a sharp bend,' I said pointlessly as Mrs Siddons accelerated too fast towards the left-hand turn at the end of the driveway.

We passed Jennifer and Gertrude, who were walking some distance apart. Evidently that relationship was as strained as Jennifer and Gordon's marriage. I watched as Jennifer turned right in the direction of the train station and Gertrude went left and took the lake path in the direction of Willow Marsh.

I gripped the sides of my seat as Mrs Siddons practically launched the car over the steeply arched bridge. I winced at the closeness of the low brick walls on either side. A slight swerve off course could see us veering into a wall and plummeting onto the railway track below.

Safely across the bridge, she turned left and pulled over into a lay-by.

'Be careful. If anything were to happen to Hugh...' she called as I jumped out.

On that ominous note, she sped off, and I dived into the bushes at the foot of the bridge where Ben was waiting.

'What's all this about?' He didn't look pleased at having to subject his uniform to the combined effects of mud and damp greenery.

'It might not work...' I began.

'What might not work?'

'Shush and stay back.' I knew Ben wouldn't approve of what we were doing. And I was starting to have doubts myself. I was pretty sure the murderer wouldn't attempt to strike again with a rifle. And Hugh was an imposing figure to try to confront with any other weapon. If the killer were to succeed, they'd need to catch him unawares.

And it was this that had led me to consider the idea of a trap. If presented with an opportunity to make the death look like an accident, would the murderer be tempted to try again?

However, Walden was hardly a teeming metropolis with danger around every corner. The riskiest place I could think of was the high bridge over the railway line.

At that moment, Gordon's Sunbeam came into view, and, unlike Mrs Siddons, he drove sedately onto the bridge. When he reached the centre, he came to a sharp stop at the highest point. Hugh emerged from the passenger seat and opened the rear door to remove his shooting stick and drawing pad from the back seat.

I'd expected Gordon to drive on, but he got out of the car too and walked around to where Hugh was driving the point of the shooting stick into the ground. He unfolded its leather seat and perched on it – precariously close to the low brick wall. Below him was a long drop down onto the railway track.

Ben and I watched as Gordon and Hugh exchanged a few words. They were examining the garden of Mill Ponds and pointing towards the greenhouse. I held my breath as Gordon moved closer to Hugh, but it seemed he was only saying goodbye, as he then made his way back to the car.

Gordon started the Sunbeam and Ben and I ducked into the bushes as he drove over the bridge and turned left towards the town. He kept his eyes on the road ahead, not looking back at the bridge nor to the left in our direction.

From our hiding place, we watched Hugh pull out his leather pencil roll from his jacket pocket. He placed it on the low brick wall, uncurled it, and took out a pencil. Glancing over to the garden of Mill Ponds, he began to sketch, seeming oblivious to the eyes that he knew were upon him.

'What are we waiting for?' Ben whispered.

'For a Tolfree to make a move,' I whispered back, an uneasy feeling in the pit of my stomach. When we'd discussed the plan at Crookham Hall, it had sounded straightforward enough. But now, seeing Hugh in place, seated unsteadily on the shooting stick close to the low brick wall, it seemed far too risky. Was he doing this to prove himself to Constance, I wondered?

I was tempted to rush out and tell Hugh to abandon the scheme. I didn't think Gordon would return – I'd never been convinced of his guilt – which left Jennifer or Gertrude. Would one of the Tolfree women make their way to the bridge to see if they could finish what they'd started? I knew which one my money was on.

It was a long time before anything happened. By a long time, I mean around ten minutes, but that feels an age when you're waiting to see if someone will attempt to murder a man.

I was about to give up when a figure appeared on the other side of the bridge. It made its way towards Hugh, who was gazing in the direction of Mill Ponds, seemingly oblivious to the danger approaching.

As the person got closer, I saw it was Gertrude Tolfree. She walked slowly towards Hugh and when he turned, she raised her hand in greeting. He smiled, and she stopped to look at his sketch.

I held my breath. It was unlikely she would choose to return to town this way as it would mean walking alongside the main road. It was much pleasanter and faster to go via the lake path. But if Gertrude were the killer, she didn't seem in a hurry to act. Then I realised why.

I heard the twelve o'clock train pulling out of the station. The guard's whistle blew, doors were slammed, and steam was released through the stack. The locomotive started to roll along the track, smoke billowing, as it approached the bridge.

Was this what she'd done before? Had she waited for the noise of the train before raising the rifle and firing it into Archie's body? Gertrude chose her moment to perfection – and in that second, I knew that was exactly what she'd done.

She nodded goodbye to Hugh and began to walk away. He turned his attention back to his sketch, pausing to watch the oncoming train.

Gertrude looked from one side of the bridge to the other, presumably checking that no one was nearby. Suddenly, she spun around, moving with remarkable speed for a woman her age. My heart lurched as I saw her reach out her hands to push Hugh over the wall and into the path of the oncoming train.

She acted with such force and determination that she would have succeeded if Hugh hadn't been prepared for the attack.

'What the hell...' Ben leapt out of the undergrowth and began to run.

At the same moment, Constance appeared from the bushes on the other side of the bridge and sprinted towards Hugh. Daniel wasn't far behind.

Instead of standing, Hugh was attempting to catch Gertrude's hands in his. It was a risky tactic as she could still unbalance him, perhaps plunging them both over the edge.

Ben and Daniel were fast, but Constance beat them to it. Grabbing Gertrude by the waist, she dragged her away from Hugh, and the two women stumbled.

Ben managed to grip Gertrude's arms and steady her before she fell. Hugh caught hold of Constance, and the pair clung to each other as the train gathered speed and hurtled along the track beneath them.

37

'What the hell went on here this morning?'

I'd never heard Superintendent Cobbe swear before, and it rather threw me. I was already uncertain how to explain the clues that had led me to suspect Gertrude, and now I was completely tongue-tied.

But the superintendent wasn't the only one watching me expectantly. Hugh, Constance and Daniel had waited in the lounge of Mill Ponds for me to explain why I'd put them through this morning's ordeal.

It was wretched to have to describe the tragedy of Archie's death surrounded by his spiritual paintings. I couldn't help contemplating them before I turned to address Superintendent Cobbe, who was standing by the mantelpiece.

'Ben didn't know what I had planned. I asked him to hide on the other side of the bridge so he could make an arrest if anything did happen.'

'You don't need to tell me that,' the superintendent snapped. 'Sergeant Gilbert would never have acted in such a foolhardy manner.'

'But Gertrude acted exactly as you thought she would.' Daniel's voice was filled with an admiration I didn't think I deserved.

Although Hugh had assured me that he would be able to restrain Gertrude if she did attempt to push him off the bridge, it had still been a risky strategy. I'd asked Ben and Daniel to be nearby as a precaution. And, of course, Constance had insisted on being there too.

'I still can't believe she did it. If she'd succeeded.' Constance shuddered.

'If she'd succeeded, I'd be tempted to arrest every one of you in this room.'

I felt like pointing out that Hugh would likely be dead if Gertrude had pushed him, so he wouldn't have been able to arrest him. However, this wasn't the time to antagonise Superintendent Cobbe any further.

I watched as he picked up a chair from the side of the room and placed it opposite me, then sat down heavily.

'Sergeant Gilbert has taken Mrs Tolfree to Winchester police station. I'll be interviewing her myself later this afternoon. Before I do, I'd like to know what led to this fiasco. From the beginning, if you please.'

It was disconcerting to be on the receiving end of Superintendent Cobbe's accusatory glare. I knew I had to convince him my reasoning had been sound, but in truth, I was still untangling the clues that had pointed me in that direction. I had to think back to when I'd first started to consider if Archie's murder could be a case of mistaken identity.

'When I was up at the summerhouse at Sand Hills Hall a couple of weeks ago, it was dusk when I saw Hugh walking across the lawn towards me. For a brief second, I'd imagined he was Archie.'

Superintendent Cobbe scrutinised Hugh, then nodded slowly, seeming to acknowledge the resemblance.

'When you described the jumper Archie was wearing when he was killed, I began to think about his physical similarities to Hugh, his stature and hair colour,' I continued. 'It was getting dark when Archie was shot. And it was unusual for him to be digging in the garden. Polly had only seen him do it once before, whereas it was normal to find Hugh, Vincent and Paul out there.'

'True,' Hugh agreed.

I turned to him. 'I noticed that you often wear a khaki woollen jumper when you work. Is it an old army jumper?'

Hugh nodded. 'I dug out my army kit before I came here. I didn't have any other old clothes.' He had the grace to appear sheepish at this.

Superintendent Cobbe cast him a withering look. He hadn't been impressed by Hugh's deception.

'Archie had just put on a khaki army jumper he'd taken from the bag of clothes Victoria Hobbs had given him.' I turned back to the superintendent. 'When you said the other evening that Polly had told you it wasn't a garment she'd seen him wear before, it made me wonder if the murderer had shot the wrong man. If that was the case, the intended victim must have been Hugh as it was an item of clothing he often wore.'

Superintendent Cobbe pursed his lip. 'Are you suggesting Gertrude Tolfree went to Mill Ponds with the intention of shooting at Mr Alvarez... I mean, Mr Skelton?' he corrected, with a sideways glance of irritation at Hugh.

I shook my head. 'I think it was an impulsive act, as we've always suspected. She left Sycamore Lodge at half past seven to go in search of Luke, knowing he was probably playing at the lake or watching trains. He'd left the house at six o'clock under strict instructions to be home within an hour, but he was much longer than that as he'd gone all the way to the summerhouse. She probably looked for him at Heron Bay, one of his favourite spots, before going to the railway station, where the station-master told her he'd seen Luke heading home on his bicycle.'

Daniel scratched his head. 'But why did she go to Mill Ponds?'

'Because she's been bringing over cuttings and seeds to help get the garden established. I think she brought some with her that evening, knowing she'd be passing close to Mill Ponds. I'm guessing she walked around the side of the house and through the gardens, planning to leave them in the shed. That's when she saw the rifle leaning against the wall. Perhaps she'd noticed it before – she'd spent a lot of time in the garden with Hugh, Paul and Vincent. The light was fading and in the distance, digging the foundations for the greenhouse, was a figure she took to be Hugh – someone who'd been causing her anguish ever since his arrival at the hostel.'

'I had no idea,' Hugh said under his breath, his face ashen.

'A train was pulling in or out of the station. I believe it was the eight-thirty from London, and...' My breath caught as I imagined the scene. 'She picked up the rifle, loaded a cartridge and fired.'

Constance closed her eyes. 'Poor Archie,' she whispered.

Daniel shook his head in disbelief. 'It was a crazy thing to do. Anyone could have seen her.'

'It was a quiet Sunday evening. Archie's bicycle wasn't outside, and she probably assumed he was at the church with the vicar. She knew Polly wouldn't be returning that day. And she'd just seen Vincent and Paul in the kitchen getting glasses from the cupboard, which meant they weren't about to go out into the garden. They saw the shadow of someone walking past, but as they had their backs to the window, they didn't see who it was. She took a calculated risk, and it nearly paid off. There were no eyewitnesses and no clues. She would have been wearing gloves, so there was nothing to indicate who'd picked up the rifle.'

'Why?' Superintendent Cobbe shot the question at me. 'I'm with you so far, but why was Mr Skelton causing her anguish, as you put it?'

'Because Redvers Tolfree married Constance Alvarez. Hugh is his first-born son. His legal heir.'

Constance's brow creased. 'Redvers Tolfree was in debt when he died. I was under the impression there was nothing left to inherit.'

'Just one thing. The family home. Sycamore Lodge is bequeathed to the eldest son. Isaac Tolfree made it a stipulation when he built the place. Redvers couldn't sell it because of the caveats in his father's will. Legally, it belongs to Hugh.'

'Ahhh.' Superintendent Cobbe leant back to consider this. 'That does provide a motive for the Tolfrees to want Mr Skelton out of the way.'

'But why did you think it was Gertrude?' Constance asked. 'To me, she seemed the least likely out of all three of them.'

'I don't believe Gordon has any idea he has a half-brother. I doubt he was ever told about his father's first marriage and first-born son. And it's unlikely Jennifer has any inkling.'

Constance nodded. 'So that left Gertrude.'

'When Hugh arrived here calling himself Alvarez, she suspected who he was. She was also in earshot when he told me his mother's name was Constance. That confirmed her suspicions. Gertrude knew very well that Constance Alvarez was Redvers' first wife. And that they'd had a son together.'

'She can't imagine I'd have kicked the family out of their

home.' Hugh ran a hand through his already dishevelled hair. 'I don't need money. I only came here to see what my half-brother was like.'

'Gertrude has no idea of your wealth. When you turned up, apparently unemployed and homeless, she imagined you'd come to claim your inheritance. Redvers had already squandered away the family business and any remaining money. Sycamore Lodge was the only thing left to pass to his son. Gertrude wasn't about to let you take away Gordon's precious family home. I suspect she was also keen to avoid people knowing your identity. I don't think she could bear to go through yet another scandal.'

'But after getting it wrong the first time, why did you think she would try again?' Daniel was clearly still reeling from having witnessed Gertrude's second attempt on Hugh's life.

'During the search for Luke Tolfree, Gertrude followed Hugh around the lake. At the time, she said she didn't trust him and was concerned he might have had something to do with Luke's disappearance.'

'You didn't believe her?' the superintendent queried.

'I did at the time. It was only later, when I was considering whether Hugh had been the intended victim, that I thought back to it. It made me wonder if she was perhaps hoping an opportunity to have another go would present itself. Something that she might be able to make look like an accident.'

'So you decided to pull this morning's trick.' Superintendent Cobbe's scowl told me I wasn't forgiven, despite my explanation.

'It was the only way to be certain. With no physical evidence or eyewitnesses to say she pulled the trigger, it was going to be impossible to prove she was the murderer.'

The superintendent wasn't about to admit this was true,

and the room fell silent. We all knew how damaging it would have been to have lived with the uncertainty.

I saw Hugh's eyes drift to Archie's paintings and heard him murmur, 'May he rest in peace.'

'God knows we had our differences.' Daniel rubbed his eyes. 'But, yes, rest in peace, Reverend Powell.'

Constance reached out to squeeze his hand. She knew he was remembering the army chaplain who'd saved his life. Not the Archie who'd so callously taken aim at her and Mrs Siddons.

Our reverie was broken by the clanging of the front door-bell, and the superintendent got to his feet, moving his chair back against the wall.

'I sent a message to Miss Powell asking her to call here before she returned to London. Please excuse me.'

He left the room, and I hurried after him, desperate for a quick word before Polly admitted Teresa.

'Have you contacted the Belgian police about Marc?'

I thought he was going to brush me aside, but then he seemed to relent. 'I was due to speak to a commissioner in Belgium this afternoon. I've asked my secretary to inform him I no longer require his assistance.'

My knees went weak with relief, and I mumbled my thanks.

38

I stood for a moment by the greenhouse, the acrid scent of smouldering vegetation filling my nostrils. Vincent had built a bonfire to burn piles of garden waste, and its billowing smoke stung my eyes.

I wiped away tears with a handkerchief, but as I did, I let out a sob. For the first time since his death, I cried for Archie. I remembered his arrogance, his kindness, his violence and his compassion. And I still remembered the taste of his kisses.

'Did you care for my brother?'

The question made me jump, and I turned to find Teresa watching me.

I tried to think of a truthful answer to this. 'We had a complicated relationship. One that changed over time.'

'I could tell that from his diary. He was wrong to follow you the way he did. I believe he was jealous.'

I shook my head. 'Archie didn't care for me any more. He was in love with Victoria Hobbs.'

'I know. But from what he wrote, he was still possessive of you. He wasn't able to control you, and he didn't like that.' She pulled her cardigan tighter around her, even though the day was warm. 'Archie could be manipulative, particularly with women. I sometimes think it was our fault. My mother and my sisters, I mean. We made him the head of our household and elevated him too much. You were the first woman to defy him.'

'He told me how fond he was of you all.'

'He was a good man, but he had his failings. Paul has helped me to see that.' She reached into the pocket of her cardigan and took out Archie's diary. 'Superintendent Cobbe returned this to me. He said it's no longer needed as evidence.'

I felt a tremor of apprehension as I thought of Marc's name on those pages. From what Ben had said about her accusations, Teresa had obviously read the diary. She must also have seen the entries detailing Archie's meetings with Jennifer Tolfree.

With a flick of the wrist, she tossed the book onto the smouldering bonfire.

'I think that's the best place for it.'

I let out a slow breath.

'Paul and I are leaving now.'

'Together?' I asked, hopefully.

She smiled. 'I've persuaded him to come with me. We're planning to get married. This time, I think it will happen. Now Paul's been offered a job as a mechanic at Skelton & Son, he feels he's in a position to provide for me. Not that I ever asked him to.'

'I'm so happy for you both. I think it was what Archie had hoped for all along.'

Teresa nodded. 'So do I.'

I followed her back into the house where Paul was waiting. Hugh helped him to carry his bags out to the taxi.

'You gave Paul a job,' I said as we waved them off.

'I'd be a fool not to. We're always looking for good mechanics, and Paul knows his way around an engine.'

We returned to the lounge, Hugh sinking his hands into the pockets of a jacket I noticed was much smarter than the one I'd previously seen him wearing.

I wasn't surprised to find Mrs Siddons deep in conversation with Constance. She wasn't the only one desperate to know what had happened. I was under strict instructions from Horace to go straight from Mill Ponds to Heron Bay Lodge, where he and Elijah were waiting for news.

'I guess I should pack my bags too.' Hugh gazed around the room as if he'd miss the place. 'Would you like me to work my notice at the factory?' It sounded as if he was also reluctant to leave Tolfree & Timpson Biscuits.

Constance shook her head with a smile. 'Consider yourself sacked for impertinent behaviour. However, I will be requiring your services again in the near future. Once I've terminated my contract with Kenwrights, I'll be visiting your London office to discuss Skelton & Son taking over from them. I trust we can agree favourable terms?'

Hugh grinned. 'I'm sure we can come to some sort of agreement. And there's no need for you to travel to London. I'll be staying in Walden while I complete renovations on my new home.'

'New home?' Constance enquired.

'Yes. I've purchased Sand Hills Hall.'

This was met with a stunned silence.

Mrs Siddons was the first to recover. 'I'm glad. The hall can't stay empty forever. It's not a mausoleum.'

As she said these words, I realised that was exactly what Sand Hills Hall had become to me. I'd started to think of it as some sort of shrine to Alice.

Hugh turned to me. 'I've been made aware of its history. I know it might take you a while to get used to the idea.'

'I'm pleased you're staying in Walden.' This much was true. However, I'd need time to reconcile myself to his presence in a place that held so many memories of Alice.

'I look forward to seeing more of you.' Constance glanced up at him from under her lashes. 'Daniel's recently had some renovations done at Crookham Hall and would be happy to recommend local craftsmen. Come over for dinner one evening, and you can talk to him about it.'

'Thank you. I'd like that,' Hugh replied, his eyes twinkling.

I couldn't help thinking Daniel was going to have his work cut out playing gooseberry in the coming months.

'As I plan to live in Walden, I'd like to become more involved with the hostel. I wonder if you might consider me becoming a patron at some stage?' Hugh addressed this last remark to Mrs Siddons.

She nodded. 'Let's wait for an appropriate time before we announce any changes. But, yes, I believe Mill Ponds House will have a more secure future with your involvement and that of the Swanns. However, at present, I think we need to give the Tolfrees time to come to terms with everything that's happened.'

'Of course. I intend to go and see Gordon to offer my support. I'm not sure if I'll be welcome, but I plan to extend a hand of friendship and see where it leads.' Hugh's eyes drifted to Constance. 'I'm hoping good things will come from this tragedy.'

39

Millicent lifted her long skirt as she waded through the overgrown grass. 'Will Hugh Alvarez mind us trespassing?'

'It's Hugh Skelton, not Alvarez,' I corrected. 'And we're not trespassing. Hugh said I could come here while he's in London with his father. He even offered to give me a key to the hall, but I don't want to go inside.'

'Why did you want to come here again?' Percy was holding up his wide-legged trousers in much the same way as Millicent was gripping her skirt.

'Just to take one last look at the place before it all changes.' I gazed up at Sand Hills Hall, where my beloved Alice had once lived. 'Hugh's planning to renovate the place.'

Millicent let go of her skirt to take my hand. 'How do you feel about that?'

'I think it's the right thing to do. Alice would have, too. She always wanted her father to modernise the hall.'

I was glad of Millicent and Percy's company as we strolled around the neglected grounds. In the walled kitchen garden, blossom had fallen and fruit was beginning to form on the trees. I knelt by the strawberry patch, which had run wild and now covered the adjoining beds.

'Alice and I used to come here when we wanted to keep out of the way of her father. We'd pick berries and eat them while we gossiped about the latest goings-on in town.'

We each gathered a handful of strawberries and went over to the old wooden bench where I'd once used to sit with Alice.

'The first time I saw Alice was after that meeting at the town hall when Mrs Siddons and Lady Timpson were standing against each other in the election.' Percy smiled at the memory. 'Do you remember we walked around the lake afterwards? Alice was painting at Heron Bay, and Ben was sitting on a log watching her. She was one of the prettiest girls I'd ever seen.'

I nodded. 'You admired her painting and then told her all about the nesting habits of grey herons.'

'I was showing off. Then I saw the way Ben was looking at her. I thought to myself, they'll be wed before the year's out.' He hastily wiped his eyes, then popped a strawberry in his mouth.

'She had such a sweet soul,' Millicent murmured. 'People in town often talk about her kindness. She helped so many of them, especially during the war.'

I joined Percy in wiping tears from my eyes. 'I still think about her every day. She'll always be with me, and Hugh moving into Sand Hills Hall won't change that. The same as Katherine marrying my father didn't change my memories of my mother, as I'd once feared.' I gave an unladylike sniff. 'Mother's death, followed so soon by the war and all those years of uncertainty, makes me want to cling on to things.'

Percy nodded. 'The war changed all of us. I remember all the pals I lost and wonder why I'm still here and they're not. There's no sense to it all.'

'We all hold on to things that help us to feel safe,' Millicent observed. 'It's a natural reaction.'

'Yes, but sometimes it's not the right thing to do. You have to recognise when it's time to move on.'

'Move on from Walden?' Millicent asked tentatively.

I shook my head. 'What's happened has made me grateful for the people I have around me.' I squeezed her hand. 'I haven't treated them as well as I should, and I want to make it up to them.'

'You don't have to do that. We all act...' She paused. Even Millicent's diplomatic skills were tested when it came to describing my recent actions. 'Unwisely on occasion.'

I smiled at her loyalty. 'I kept secrets and I shouldn't have.'

'Which reminds me. What did happen to Archie's diary?' Percy asked. 'Was it ever found?'

I told them about Archie's unusual hiding place. 'Superintendent Cobbe has since returned it to Teresa Powell. And she threw it onto a bonfire in the garden of Mill Ponds.'

'A sensible move,' Millicent remarked. 'I hope she and Paul will be happy together.'

'So that's an end to it. We'll never know the identity of your mystery man.' Percy's attempt at nonchalance failed miserably.

'If Iris has put it in the past, then so will we,' Millicent declared. 'It makes no difference to us.'

This might have been true for her, but I didn't think it was for Percy.

'My past is part of who I am. That's why I want to tell you about Marc. Although I've made mistakes in my life, he wasn't one of them. I don't regret a single moment I spent with him.'

I expected Percy to pounce on the name and start interrogating me. Instead, he nodded slowly as if he'd been right about something. 'Marc Jansen?'

I gazed at him in astonishment.

Millicent screwed up her face as if trying to remember. 'I know the name, but I can't quite place it.'

'You met him last summer,' I told her. 'At Smugglers Haunt.'

For a few moments, Millicent looked confused; then her expression changed to shock.

'Marc from Devon? The solicitor who worked with Katherine's brother at Damerell & Tate?'

I nodded, staring at Percy. 'How did you know?'

'When I was wondering who it could be, he came into my mind. And then the more I thought about it, the more the pieces fitted.'

'Why did he come into your mind?' I demanded.

'What pieces?' Millicent seemed peeved that he'd guessed and she hadn't.

'I remembered the way he looked at you when we were in Devon. And after your father's wedding, I saw him slip a note into your purse. I didn't think anything of it at the time. I thought it might have been a message for you to give to your father. But later, much later, when you came back to my flat and told me he'd gone abroad, I began to go over things in my head. Did you see him that last night in Devon when you sneaked off?'

I nodded. 'That's when he asked if we could meet once he was settled in London.'

Percy nodded. 'I remember last year, during the Christmas Close business, you mentioned a solicitor a few times. The only time I could recall you having any dealings with solicitors was when we were in Devon and visited Damerell & Tate. There had been that leaving dinner for Marc and his wife to wish them well for their new life in London.'

Millicent had been listening to this in silence. Now she asked. 'Why?'

'Why what?'

'Why Marc? I don't understand. It never occurred to me he was your London boyfriend. He seemed so devoted to Annette.'

'He is devoted to her. That's why he's gone back to live in Belgium. To make her and his parents happy.'

'I thought they were happy here?'

'Marc is. Annette, less so. They married in haste at the outbreak of war. Both have come to realise that perhaps, had things been different, their childhood romance may not have stood the test of time.'

'So Marc turned to you?' Millicent seemed to be taking this worse than Percy.

'It wasn't like that. It's hard to explain. When we first met, we became close.'

'You had a wartime romance?' she exclaimed.

'Yes, sort of.' I suppose that's what it had been, although I'd never thought of it as such. 'It wasn't an affair. We just had some sort of connection, and now we've broken that connection.' I decided I'd had enough of explaining and changed the subject. 'I had a letter from my father and Katherine this morning,' I told Percy. 'They're coming back soon, and Katherine says we can have Smugglers Haunt for the summer.'

But he wasn't so easily distracted. 'If Marc hadn't been married, do you think you and he—'

'I don't know,' I cut in, wishing I'd never started this confessional. Perhaps sharing secrets with friends was something that took practice. 'Do you want to come on holiday with me or not?'

'A romantic break for two?' he replied sarcastically.

Millicent smiled. 'She's already invited me and Ursula.'

He made a harrumphing noise. 'Just the four of us, then.'

'I'm not sure Ursula will come, but Daniel plans to motor down and stay somewhere nearby.' Millicent began to eat the strawberries lying in her lap.

Percy gave an exasperated sigh. 'He might as well join me at the Jewel of the Sea boarding house then.'

I took this as confirmation that Percy would be coming with us.

Millicent pulled a face. 'I think he might find Emerald Dubois rather overwhelming. I bet Freddie would adore her, though. You said he could do with a break from his studies.'

'Daniel could stay at the Rougemont Hotel in Exeter,' I suggested. 'Horace and Elijah are planning on joining us and booking suites there again. It's going to be Horace's sixtieth birthday.'

Percy threw up his hands. 'Just the six of us, then. In that case, I may as well bring Freddie along and introduce him to the delights of Emerald Dubois and that lethal French brandy she keeps in her smugglers' cave.'

Millicent grimaced. 'I'm not going near any smugglers' caves again. Not after last time.'

I agreed. 'No dead bodies on this holiday. We've had enough of those. I want us to have fun. We haven't had much of that recently.'

'Speak for yourself.' Percy pushed his floppy hair back over his brow. 'You two just don't know how to have fun. You're far too serious.'

I couldn't help thinking there was some truth in this. 'When we're on holiday, we'll paddle in the sea each morning, go dancing at night, and spend every day generally being silly and carefree.'

Millicent looked doubtful. 'I've never been a particularly silly person.'

'I'm sure Percy can teach you.'

In response, Percy threw a strawberry into the air and caught it in his mouth.

* * *

MORE FROM MICHELLE SALTER

Another book from Michelle Salter, *Murder at Merewood Hospital*, is available to order now here:

www.mybook.to/MerewoodHospitalBackAd

ACKNOWLEDGEMENTS

Thanks to the following people for their continued support: my parents, Ken and Barbara Salter – particular thanks for my dad's help with historical research; Jeanette Quay for 'numpty days'; and Barbara Daniel for advice and encouragement.

Thanks as always to the whole Boldwood team, in particular my brilliant editor, Emily Yau, and special thanks to Rachel Lawston for her fabulous cover designs.

As ever, I'm indebted to the numerous people, books, libraries, museums, and archives that contributed to my knowledge of this period. A special mention to local history groups and fellow history enthusiasts for always being happy to share their knowledge.

ABOUT THE AUTHOR

Michelle Salter writes historical cosy crime set in Hampshire, where she lives, and inspired by real-life events in 1920s Britain. Her Iris Woodmore series draws on an interest in the aftermath of the Great War and the suffragette movement.

Sign up to Michelle Salter's mailing list for news, competitions and updates on future books.

Visit Michelle's Website: www.michellesalter.com

Follow Michelle on social media:

 x.com/MichelleASalter

 facebook.com/MichelleSalterWriter

 instagram.com/michellesalter_writer

 bookbub.com/authors/michelle-salter

ALSO BY MICHELLE SALTER

Poison
& Pens

POISON & PENS IS THE HOME OF
COZY MYSTERIES SO POUR YOURSELF
A CUP OF TEA & GET SLEUTHING!

DISCOVER PAGE-TURNING NOVELS FROM
YOUR FAVOURITE AUTHORS &
MEET NEW FRIENDS

JOIN OUR
FACEBOOK GROUP

BIT.LYPOISONANDPENSFB

SIGN UP TO OUR
NEWSLETTER

BIT.LY/POISONANDPENSNEWS

Boldwood

Boldwood Books is an award-winning fiction publishing company seeking out the best stories from around the world.

Find out more at www.boldwoodbooks.com

Join our reader community for brilliant books, competitions and offers!

Follow us
@BoldwoodBooks
@TheBoldBookClub

Sign up to our weekly deals newsletter

https://bit.ly/BoldwoodBNewsletter

Printed in Great Britain
by Amazon

60528196R00167